"You're going to transcribe your notes, I hope, before you forget what they mean," Greenfield said drily.

"I *never* forget," I replied.

"Debatable. Include everything. Not only the conversation, not only what was said about the girl. I want everything you learned."

"About Lucas and Moss and . . . ? Why do you want that? I mean, it's interesting, if you're planning an ethnographic study of Sloan's Ford, but it's not going to tell you anything more about . . ."

"Just leave it on my desk when you're finished."

"That's going to be a lot of typing!"

"Not all of life is pleasant."

"You know, Mr. Greenfield, *The Times*, the *Post* and the *News* have all offered me big money . . ."

"You wouldn't be happy with them." He hung up.

C.B. GREENFIELD:
NO LADY
IN THE HOUSE

LUCILLE KALLEN

BALLANTINE BOOKS • NEW YORK

Copyright © 1982 by Lucille Kallen

All rights reserved including the right of reproduction in whole or in part in any form. Published in the United States by Ballantine Books, a division of Random House, Inc., New York, and simultaneously in Canada by Random House of Canada, Limited, Toronto, Canada.

Library of Congress Catalog Card Number: 81-21839

ISBN 0-345-30870-0

This edition published by arrangement with Wyndham Books

Manufactured in the United States of America

First Ballantine Books Edition: February 1983

ACKNOWLEDGMENTS

My thanks to Maxwell Lillienstein,
Muriel Forrest, Rudy Wirth,
and Jeanne Thelwell,
for information they provided.

this one is for
Max Liebman
who was a university where
so many of those now acclaimed
once learned craftsmanship

1

THE VILLAGE HALL in Sloan's Ford stood on one edge of a pocket village green, a square, two-story building, vintage 1880, white stucco, peaked roof, long, narrow, mullioned windows, spare and functional. A modest affair, but still a monument of sorts to the cultural aspirations of a pre-turn-of-the-century community that had yearned for an auditorium in which to present "musical evenings" and the inspirational dramas of the traveling Chautauqua troupes.

Now, of course, the place served a number of less exalted purposes. There was a large, sparsely furnished ground-floor room used for municipal court hearings and, with removable curtained booths, for the democratic process of choosing the lesser of two evils. To one side a ground-floor wing was occupied by police headquarters. A small wing: crime might grow like bindweed, but the Sloan's Ford police force grew like a pine tree, one millimeter a year. The upper story was given over to the meeting room where the Village Board held sway, and to the municipal offices where the village manager managed the village, the clerks typed and filed, and the small elderly woman who loved opera made out my annual dog license.

It was a symbol of order in an orderly village of tidy houses sitting in the shade of hundred-year-old elms and oaks and maples that were beginning to turn color in the cobalt-blue darkness of a clear October evening.

Not a place, one would think, where fear could inhabit the dark streets and death come from unnatural causes.

I pulled into the parking lot adjacent to the hall, resigned to the tedium of the coming Village Board meeting. All the parking spaces but one had been taken and I had to maneuver into it gingerly, inasmuch as the parrot-green Alfa on the left had parked at an angle, the rear right wheel standing a good two inches into the empty slot. I knew the car, but even if I hadn't, it would have been an easy guess that it belonged to Dina Franklin. It *looked* like her: extroverted, self-congratulatory, eager to pass every vehicle on the road, and cheerfully taking more than its share of space as its natural privilege.

I squeezed into the reduced space, locked the car, and started across the lot, when there was a sneeze from several yards to my left and I saw Sidney Michaels coming toward me. A good-natured, middle-aged family man, an orthopedic surgeon, he lived several houses south of me on Putney Lane. Reaching my side, he sneezed again.

"Allergies," he explained.

"What we should really do at this meeting tonight," I said, "is perform a rain dance, wash some of the pollution out of the air."

"Somebody doesn't like us, Maggie," he said stuffily as we walked on. "A drought and a crime wave. You heard about the Davises and the Robatos? This week there were three more. Barber, Spector, and Simms."

I stopped and stared at him.

"All of them? In one week?"

"Cleaned out, they say." He sneezed again. "And apparently on the other side of Hawthorne they've been having break-ins regularly. Seems to be a gang of kids. Eighteen or nineteen years old. Or so they *think*."

"How you gonna keep them down on the farm," I murmured, "after they've seen TV." We opened the door onto the faintly musty, wainscoted hallway redolent of that long-gone era when the wild adrenaline of adolescence had spent itself on nothing more sinister than sledding down Poplar Avenue, defying the heady danger of collision with the one-a-day automobile that might appear and might, possibly, be exceeding the eight-mile-an-hour speed limit. Fairy-tale days, more inconceivable now than any prehistoric age.

The stairway smelled of wax and stale smoke, the meeting room, as usual, was packed, airless, and buzzing with talk. On a raised dais at one end of the room, the mayor and the trustees of the Village Board. To one side, the village attorney representing the zoning board. In the first row of folding chairs, the deputy clerk, fidgeting with her shorthand pad.

And a small sea of my cotaxpayers, divesting themselves of jackets or sweaters.

I knew a good many by name, some to say hello to, but the only one there I could call a friend was Gordon Oliver, in whose study, sitting with his cello behind a music stand, I had met Charles Benjamin Greenfield, monarch of the Sloan's Ford *Reporter,* and the man responsible for my being in that room with my notebook and my Bic, to spend three stupefying hours sitting on a folding chair taking notes.

As I made my way to an empty seat in the second row, Gordon, slender and elegant, like a Giacometti sculpture in walnut wood, looked up from his chair in the middle of the room.

"Charlie?" he asked.

"Someone had an extra ticket to the Rostropovich concert."

Gordon made a face to indicate he was impressed. I was not so much impressed as envious and resentful. How infinitely preferable, to be sitting in Carnegie Hall. And equally, had there been no concert, Greenfield would have been here, and I would have been home rereading *The Comedians*. Greenfield did not always cover the Village Board meetings, but he had a personal interest in the outcome of this one, and only the chance to see and hear a master cellist could have kept him away. I, on the other hand, had an antipathy to Village Board meetings, and this one was no particular exception. But then, I worked for Greenfield, not he for me.

I continued down the aisle, noting familiar faces: Jessie Lucas, in bulky sweater and jeans, with her clever brown eyes and cloud of roan-colored hair liberally highlighted with gray. Jordan Moss, endocrinologist, with his sunlamp tan and his tennis-taut abdominal muscles, thinking about his malpractice insurance. His wife Roberta, large-eyed, quivering with intensity, and thin to the point of attenuation. The Messinas, who lived at the end of my block and drove Lincoln Continentals and ate Big Macs. Naomi Gardner, in a dark purple blazer, smiling and looking restless and out of place, like a racehorse in a stable full of drays. Fred Bryce, of Bryce Realty, and his good lady Agnes, two upright, buttoned-down, good-of-the-community workers. The tired-looking Gillises who ran the luncheonette in the shopping center. . . .

And up on the dais, Naomi's husband Leonard Gardner, attorney, six-foot-something, with his arrogant nose, tinted eyeglasses, and humorless handsomeness, holding forth to the only woman on the board of five: Dina Franklin of the parrot-green Alfa.

A cashmere-sweatered dynamo, Dina; her face lit up with the inner neon of blazing self-esteem, her geese each and every one a swan. With seemingly innocent self-congratulation she would tell the merest acquaintance about her perfect marriage, made even more perfect for not being complicated by children, her brilliant successes as an architect, her ability to point at the ground and say "grow" and the earth in her garden would abound with dahlias, her lavish parties attended only by social lions, for which she could whip up *poulet farci parisienne* and *tonille aux fraises* in twenty minutes with no sweat while simultaneously designing a neo–I. M. Pei building for the County Cultural Arts Center. She was thirty-six. For the average woman on the wrong side of forty-five, to watch Dina Franklin perform was to know precisely how Salieri felt about Mozart.

I sat down. The mayor stood and cleared his throat. I dug into my bag for my notebook and Bic.

"This issue . . . which has been before us several times in the past . . ."

The mayor, James K. Sprague, pink-cheeked and silver-haired, looked as though he should have been standing before the Adams fireplace of his country seat holding a goblet of port with a hunter at his feet; actually he had only recently sold his plumbing concern.

". . . address the question of . . . comprehensive plan . . . zoning map . . . productive use of the building . . . beneficial in terms of tax dollars . . . planning board's position . . ."

I scribbled.

The "question we were addressing" was the disposition of a large, old, empty school building, originally built to house the entire student population of Sloan's Ford from kindergarten through high school, and adequate for the purpose in those days before World War One. Subsequently, of course, both a new elementary and high school had been built, and then, more recently, a junior high school. No sooner had the new school been cornerstoned and dedicated than the birthrate whimsically plummeted, the flood of young families from the city slowed to a trickle, and the old school became superfluous. The big, graceful old building was boarded up, leaving, on three acres in the valley off Glenbrook Place, a thirty-thousand-square-foot, ivy-covered fire hazard.

The school board was dying to sell it. The village was dying to get it on the tax rolls. But the area was zoned for single-family houses and no developer in his right mind was going to commit financial suicide by building any of *those* at the moment. Over the years a variety of entrepreneurs had displayed interest in acquiring the property for things like shopping malls and co-op apartments, but at each suggestion the screams of the neighboring homeowners echoed in the land, and a small army of citizens waging war against increased traffic congestion, unfair competition to small-business owners, and above all the lowering of real-estate values, defeated each proposition in turn.

Then along came the Brant Institute, proposing to use the property with no exterior changes for "nonindustrial research," no test tubes, no noxious gases, just desks and telephones and computers, and it seemed like a better idea than most. The referendum was passed and now the board was holding a hearing preparatory to voting on the proposal.

As the meeting droned on, various people got to their feet to voice an opinion, or a protest, or just to hear the sounds of their own voices.

A man with a paunch and a mustache wanted to ensure there would be a clause in the contract stating that in the event of the institute's going broke and trying to sell out to a bowling alley or some other pernicious enterprise, the zoning would automatically revert to one-family housing. A member of the fire department issued a warning about the dangers of antique building code regulations and the necessity for sprinkler systems. Jessie wanted the village offices moved into the school and the remaining space used for a new library and cultural center. A nervous woman who obviously watched a good deal of daytime television wanted the building sold immediately before some tragedy occurred, such as a gang of rowdies breaking in one of the windows and some innocent child crawling through and getting trapped inside and dying of starvation. Naomi Gardner reminded everyone that at a previous meeting it had been the consensus of the board that the property must be used for the benefit of the community as a whole and the use of the property for a community center was the community's most urgent need. Carl Spector, introducing a note from a completely different song, demanded an immediate subsequent meeting to form a Watch Group to deal with burglaries in the area. Roberta Moss felt we were losing an opportunity to do something socially constructive with the property in terms of senior citizens. Bill Curry urged us all to show a little common sense and give the board the go-ahead so that we could start collecting those much-needed tax dollars. And so on.

A letter, addressed to the Village Board and delivered by Greenfield's hand earlier in the day, was read aloud by one of the trustees. It was designed to give Greenfield a voice in absentia, and set forth his stand on the matter which, divested of its superior vocabulary and syntax, was simply that he was all for the sale. He gave a number of persuasive reasons but not the one that really concerned him: that due to a conditional clause in the school budget, if the sale went through, a portion of the money thus received by the school board would be allotted to the high-school orchestra so that its members could avail themselves of an invitation to participate in a music festival in Vienna.

I sat there recording the salient points and stifling yawns, my quotes peppered with standard phrases. "Let there be a record—" "Responsive to the community—" "The intent of the board—" and finally, just about five minutes before the hard seat under me would have left a lifelong impression on the backs of my thighs, the meeting drew to a disgruntled close.

Chairs scraped, people stood up, the room hummed with comment. I looked around for Gordon Oliver, saw him being talked at by an officious-looking man and waited, watching, meanwhile, the postmeeting activities.

Carl Spector, still soliciting support for the idea of our guarding each other's houses, had collared a young Swedish couple I recognized from seeing them jogging every weekend, with their pale hair, high color, invincible physiques, wearing shorts even in January, and looking as though they ate raw whale for breakfast.

"But who is going to do the guarding?" the Scandinavian goddess asked. "Everybody works, men and women. There is no one home."

Naomi Gardner, Jessie Lucas and Roberta Moss had converged at the dais and were speaking simultaneously to Dina Franklin.

"Are you joking?" Dina chirped, in her high clear voice that carried above the general chatter. "I haven't got a free *minute* in the next few days!" she announced happily, alerting half the room that Dina Franklin was in demand. "I couldn't *possibly* schedule anything else. I *know* what you want to talk about, Naomi, but I can't spare the *time*. Howard's in London for a week and I have to fly down to St. Louis on Wednesday to take care of our business down *there*, and I won't be back until *Sunday*. No, impossible, tomorrow night I won't be back from the city until after *ten*, I have meetings all *day*—"

On my right Fred Bryce, also at the dais, was nodding importantly at something the mayor was saying, while Agnes Bryce sat on a chair nearby in her outfit of neat Chesterfield coat and gloved hands, copied from news photos of First Ladies. She looked anonymous, as though deprived of identity by the temporary absence of her husband. When a tubby little man approached to engage her in conversation she twitched her cupid's bow lips in a brief, uncertain smile: the protocol for this eventuality had not been clearly defined.

"Miss that boy of yours," the tubby man said heartily. "Can't get any of these kids today to do a good job on my lawn."

Agnes looked down modestly and brushed a speck from her coat with her gloved hand. "Billy will be graduating from West Point next year." Her voice managed to encompass both self-effacement and a smirk of satisfaction. "He's doing very well, and so is Phyllis."

Tubby nodded, beaming. "Nice to hear that kind of thing for a change, all the messed up kids these days. You've got something to be proud of. Just saying, Fred—" he leaned back on his heels to look up at Fred Bryce who had turned away from the dais to join them "—if we had more decent, hard-working kids around like yours—"

Fred Bryce grinned. He'd been told he had an engaging grin and so he grinned whenever possible. Clean-cut, broad-shouldered, navy pinstriped, Fred was the moving force behind the Little League and could be seen every spring on the small diamond in Brower Park, in short-sleeved shirt outlining muscular torso, exemplifying the fitness born of wholesome outdoor sports.

"Well, we tried to do a good job," he grinned, speaking quietly, affecting the slight drawl that worked so well in committee meetings, suggesting authority. "Just tried to instill the old-fashioned virtues. There's a difference between right and wrong: they had to know it. Respect for parents, for property, for authority. All those things—" he raised a humorous eyebrow "—nobody seems to have use for anymore." He gave Agnes' lap a casual glance and she quickly tugged at the hem of her coat, making sure it covered her knees.

Tubby sighed. "You can say that again. Crime all over the place—"

Fred Bryce sucked in his cheeks, eloquently: crime was a natural consequence of a society of non-Bryces. "No standards. No discipline." He mouthed his final words as though they tasted of alum. "Permissive parents."

"Lazy, dirty boys all over that high school," Agnes put in mutedly. "Billy would *never* let his hair grow." She pushed her gloves down carefully, finger by finger, as though they were little decorations for blameless living.

For a moment I wondered what it must be like to be Agnes Bryce, having your husband check your lap for a lapse, living in eternal pursuit of merit badges.

I saw Gordon detach himself from the man who had button-holed him, and I moved to meet him.

"Where's Shirley?" I asked. "She usually gets a charge out of attending these meetings, God knows why."

"She didn't want to leave the children alone in the house tonight. Our next-door neighbors, the Smalls—" he sighed, frowning "—their house was broken into this afternoon."

2

"WHAT DO YOU think," I asked, "about a piece on the burglaries? I can't think of a topic more pertinent—that's your word, pertinent, you're always telling me we have to be pertinent, well, every living soul in Sloan's Ford is talking about burglaries. At the meeting last night, in the supermarket this morning—even first graders waiting for the school bus are talking about it. *Dogs* are talking about it. *Squirrels*."

Greenfield rotated gently in his whining swivel chair. Behind him the huge, cluttered oak desk was pushed up against the second-floor windows of the old mansard-roofed house, and beyond the windows the branches of the ancient maple showed an anemic blush of autumn in the last rays of the sun. He might have been posing for the portrait of a genial, bemused professor in some dappled grove of academe.

He turned the page of a booklet he had picked up at Superior Sound when he'd purchased the new arm for the complicated stereo system he kept in his living quarters on the floor above; a system of components designed and assembled for Greenfield's discriminating use by a young genius whose grasp of technical intricacies and imaginative fusing of exquisitely sensitive elements had, according to Greenfield, created a listening apparatus that was the Mount Parnassus of hi-fidom. Just before leaving to take up residence, for some reason, in Belgium, the genius had advised Greenfield that if he wanted some frosting on his audio cake, this new arm was a thing to be desired. No sooner said than bought, and now that he had the power to command the most esoteric tone-control of his choice library of recordings, Greenfield could really ask little more of life.

He wore his customary expression of benign melancholy, a kind of facial habit not to be accepted at surface value, as many a hack politician and fast-talking salesman had learned to his detriment. But there was a patina of contentment over his features that I'd never seen before; what with the arm installed and the memory of the Rostropovich concert lingering like the taste of good wine ("The man barely needs an instrument"), he was, if not actually happy, at least imperturbable. He'd even passed up the opportunity for a cutting remark when he discovered I hadn't arrived with the typed report of the board meeting. "Tomorrow's Wednesday," he'd reminded me mildly. I'd said I would have it in first thing in the morning, and went on to more interesting matters.

"Charlie? What do you think? You can hardly dismiss it as trivial. Someone's been breaking into houses all over the village. Even the Olivers' next-door neighbor—"

He put down his booklet, stretched his long, slope-shouldered frame adorned in shapeless brown corduroy pants and a beige sweater I had admired years earlier before it began to pill, and regarded me from under the hedge of toothbrush bristles he called his eyebrows.

"You wouldn't suggest, I'm sure," he said tranquilly, "doing two hundred words on a new wonder drug called penicillin? Or ripping out the front page to report the crash of the Hindenburg?"

"I speak only English. A few words of French. What are you saying?"

"If every Sloan's Ford resident already knows about the burglaries, what conceivable function would we be performing?" He got up and went to the filing cabinet. "A newspaper can be bland and survive, or sensational and thrive, or conscientious and scrape by, but one thing it can't be is redundant." He dropped the booklet in among assorted items in the A file. (For audio?)

"I wasn't going to *announce* the burglaries. I was thinking of some kind of survey. What time of day does it usually happen? What kind of things do they take? Is there a common denominator? Suggestions from the police on what steps to take to protect—"

Feet thumped up the stairway leading from the floor below to Greenfield's office. Not the staccato clatter of Calli Dohanis' ankle-strapped sandals, nor the sturdy clomp of Helen Deutsch's L. L. Bean's, either of which would not be surprising as they were working in the *Reporter* office below. This was the labored tread of someone who was well past a quick climb. I waited, saving the rest of my argument for after the interruption, and in the doorless opening, Mrs. Lacey's face appeared, with an expression that was both tentative and determined.

"Mr. Greenfill?" she said, "could I talk to you a minute?"

Greenfield looked at her cautiously. "Is everything all right?"

"Everything's fine, Mr. Greenfill. I just only want to talk to you a minute."

He nodded. "Sit down."

She trotted into the room and perched on the edge of one of the slowly decomposing armchairs, depositing a gaudy beach bag containing her working clothes on the floor at her feet and holding her navy blue plastic handbag in her lap with both hands. She sat on the edge partly because she was not accustomed to sitting in his presence and partly because the seat of the armchair, like all other horizontal surfaces in the floor-through room, was piled high with much-handled newspapers, magazines, folders, pamphlets, leaflets, brochures, and books.

Mrs. Lacey had left her sixtieth birthday behind her, grizzled hair escaped from under the beige felt hat on her head, and there was a vague and slightly mad smile on her wrinkled acorn of a face. She had been vacuuming the rugs, dusting the furniture, and scouring the sinks in Greenfield's living quarters on the floor above for the past fifteen years, to his reasonably complete satisfaction.

Greenfield went back to the swivel chair, and sat facing her. "I'm listening," he said pleasantly.

"Mr. Greenfill," she said, not looking at him, "I have to leave."

Greenfield glanced at his watch. "Well? It's time. You've been here for seven hours."

"No," she said, "I mean leave. For good."

Greenfield stared at her. "I don't understand."

"For *good*. You know. I won't be here next week. Or after that." She paused. "Or after that." She opened her plastic handbag, removed a house key, and gave it to him.

Greenfield looked at me as though possibly I had the explanation for such an unheard-of decision, then looked at the key, and then at Mrs. Lacey.

"It's not you, Mr. Greenfill," she said. "You're a good man. It's not you. It's my back. This back is gone. It's just gone. The Lord told me. He told me it's time to stop working and I got to retire now. Time to go. No use arguing with a back, when the back gets tired it just lets you know it's through working. So I have to say good-bye, Mr. Greenfill, and I hope the Lord is good to you, you're a good man."

The good man regarded his defecting former chattel with an expression that suggested he was watching the last rooftop of civilization disappear in the rising waters of a global flood. Mrs. Lacey kept her eyes on the floor.

"It's a matter of medical fact," he said, finally, throwing accuracy to the winds, "that retirement plays havoc with the body. Your back will only get worse if you don't use it. I'll have a very good doctor look at—"

"Oh, Mr. Greenfill, I had enough doctors look at me to last me the rest of my life. The Lord knows what He's up to, you can believe that, and if He says it's time, it's time. The Holy Book says there's a time to work and a time to retire, it's right there for anybody to see, in the Holy Book."

"I know you're a religious woman," Greenfield persisted desperately. "You may have heard the saying, '*Laborare* . . .'" He caught himself. "Work is prayer."

"I pray enough for ten people, Mr. Greenfill. Don't have to worry about my prayers, no sir." She stood up, with a small stop on the way to unkink her back. "My son called me from Detroit and he says it's time for me to come stay with him. I got five grandchildren in Detroit and three in St. Louis and two in Baltimore and I pray for all of them, and the Lord told me to go to Detroit."

There was a tone of finality about this last speech that even Greenfield could not ignore. He accepted defeat with the resignation of a man who is no stranger to perfidy.

"You have some money coming to you," he muttered, and swiveled around to the desk.

"You left the money in the same place, Mr. Greenfill," she said, with honesty if not enthusiasm, "under the begonia."

"I know about that." Greenfield found his trusty Parker 51 among the debris on the desk top and scribbled on a blank check.

"We'll miss you, Mrs. Lacey," I said, thinking of the much-trafficked area below, where the assembling of the weekly Sloan's Ford *Reporter* left grime and grit gathering everywhere until Mrs. Lacey's occasional moonlighting from the domestic quarters revealed once again the pattern on the linoleum and the actual porcelain of the lavatory sink.

"Going to miss you too, Mrs. Rome. Miss you all. You're all good people."

"Do you know anyone who might want this job?"

"Well, I asked my niece, but she says she wants to take up to be a computer." She accepted the check from Greenfield, holding it up to her eyes to confirm the unexpected figure written there, her little acorn face growing a shade rosier. "You're a good man, Mr. Greenfill, the Lord sees everything and He's got a place in heaven waiting for you."

Greenfield, who did not seem anxious to avail himself of the reservation, said, "Anyone who does a responsible and conscientious job is entitled to severance pay. It's not conscience money."

Mrs. Lacey had no idea what he was blabbing about, nor did she particularly care. Money was money. She picked up the beach bag, told Greenfield to take care of himself, never to let anyone put wax on the stair treads, said she would ask the Lord to look out for us all, and went trotting out through the doorless opening, down the unwaxed stairs and out of our lives, leaving Greenfield char-less. And, had we known it, vulnerable to much worse than that.

He stared morosely at a hole in the carpet, confirmed once again in his conviction that life was a minefield honeycombed with barbed wire. The mellow mood had been well and truly demolished.

"It's possible," I offered hopefully, "that after a month's vacation she'll have a change of heart."

"She hasn't had a change of heart," he said with great, dirgelike precision, "in fifteen years. She decided fifteen years ago that the soap dish belonged on the left-hand side of the sink. Every Tuesday night for fifteen years I've moved it back to the right, and every following Tuesday morning she has moved it to the left. A woman like that is not given to reconsideration." He swiveled furiously back and forth, setting the chair screeching in agony.

"Well, don't get overwrought. We'll find another Mrs. Lacey somewhere." I wasn't quite as sanguine as I tried to sound.

He gave me a look that clearly rated my grasp of reality at minus zero, unwound himself from the chair, and went to the cabinet where his second-best stereo and a collection of tapes stood mute and waiting. I made a mental wager on Mahler. He was going to sit here, submerged in mordant music and brood about the dear dead days beyond recall, the days before widowerhood, when he had no need to concern himself with the squalid domestic details of life, and the days after his wife was gone, when another female took over the grubby concerns, and all he had to do was remember once a week to put the money under the begonia.

It was clearly going to be a long time before he got over the loss of Mrs. Lacey. Even assuming this was not the dead end of domestic help, he was a man who had great difficulty believing in the reliability of any person or man-made object until he, she, or it had been tested in the crucible of time. After which, substitutions were unthinkable.

He inserted a tape into the machine, dropped back into the protesting swivel chair, and stared with gloomy thoughtfulness out the window at the turning leaves of the huge ancient maple. Is there life after the departure of a cleaning woman? Not bloody likely. Music issued from the speaker. Mahler. I sighed for all the mental money I'd made over the years.

"Don't despair," I said. "I know a couple of people I can call who are sure to be able to recommend someone. And there are agencies. And for that matter you could run an ad in the *Reporter*."

"Maggie. Go home."

"Nicely put. Do you still want me to finish the board meeting report? Or is our paper about to cease publication?"

No reply. I moved toward the stairs.

"Anything else I can do for you? A cup of tea? A teaspoon of cyanide?"

No reply. I reached the stairs and *still* no reply. This was momentous. Since the night Greenfield acknowledged our introduction in Gordon Oliver's study by nodding to me across his cello and asking me to give him an A, I had never, ever, succeeded in having the last word.

I went down the stairs and turned into the room where Helen and Calli were working.

"Trouble," I announced. "We've got trouble. Right here in River City."

But Helen Deutsch had troubles of her own. A short, stolid figure, rushing the season in one of her nursery-governess outfits of brown wool, looking anxious, she was straining forward to reach the dial on the Varityper.

She turned to me, her lips pursed with worry. "The wheel's stuck. The handle won't catch. It doesn't cut the tape."

Calli Dohanis came clattering in on her three-inch heels, holding a screwdriver like a lance above her head. "Maggie! How many times I told him this old machine is going to break down! *You* talk to him!"

"Not today, thank you. Maybe not for quite a while."

"Sometimes he listens to you," she went on, ignoring me and attacking the dial connection with the screwdriver. "A *donkey* would listen to me before he would! What's the *matter* with this lousy—Oh, my God, the screw is *stripped*!" She cursed in Greek, the flame-colored sleeves of her blouse cleaving the air.

"I think the thing went inside," Helen said with authority.

"Thing? What thing?" Calli spun the dial furiously, making an empty, clicking sound.

"We'd better call the repair people," Helen said, making for the wall telephone.

There was a crunching sound and Calli lurched back from the Varityper with the dial in her hand. "Okay," she said, "I ripped it off. Now what?"

I went into the layout room as Helen began to dial, and deposited a photograph of the old empty school building in an envelope taped to the wall. Calli came in pushing her black hair back into its bun.

"I tell you honestly, Maggie, this job will give me a nervous breakdown." She said this about once a month. "If Charlie wants me to be a mechanic along with everything else, I want more money. I mean it." With great relish, she slapped the wax coater over a typed article and pasted it on the master page grid.

"This is the *good* part," I said, giving her an evil smile. "We'll all be mopping the stairs and scrubbing the john if we don't find another Mrs. Lacey."

I left her with a look of horror on her face and went through the outer office where Helen was still on the phone, busily smoothing out the typed sheet of advertising rates tacked to the wall beside her. I scrawled a note, "V. B. meeting report at dawn tomorrow," waved it at her, and put it down on the table amid a scatter of pencils, four pairs of scissors, and a plastic pot containing a few late-blooming flowers.

She nodded at me and said into the phone, "But this *is* an emergency!"

Twenty minutes later I emerged from the village supermarket, richer by a bag full of milk, yogurt, eggs, brown bread, and assorted household necessities, thinking about Mrs. Lacey and realizing that thanks to the brainwashing I had received upon being born female, I was, unlike Greenfield, hardened to the need for occasional vacuum drudgery. Thanks too to my job on the *Reporter*, which let me stay within reasonable distance of home so that I had time for it. Having once, for a year, subjected myself to a slavish dependence on household help, I felt profound pity for anyone in bondage to the whims of a cleaning woman.

Grocery bag on the seat behind me, I started the car and began to back out of my parking space, when three teenage girls on bicycles, screaming giddily, tore into the lot and up the aisle into which I was backing, missing the Honda by inches. A few choice words left my mouth, but I was luckier than a woman approaching her car in the next aisle, holding the twin of my grocery bag. The girls swooped around a corner and down the next aisle, and one of them, wobbling out of control, stretched out an arm as though to steady herself, the arm hit the woman's elbow, she dropped the bag, and girl and bike careened into the back of a neighboring car. The woman, squatting, grabbed at apples and rolls of paper towels, shouting at the girl who, unhurt, was biting her lip, looking half-ashamed and half-cocky, in her skintight jeans, high heels, and fringed jacket adorned with a large, orange, initialed plastic pin. While the girl's companions circled, hooting, the woman stood, pushed the girl in the direction of the spilled groceries, and the girl, shrugging, got down and began to gather them into the paper bag, the woman impatiently helping.

As I drove by I saw that the woman was Roberta Moss, and thought that if I'd seen her in the supermarket I'd probably have stopped her to ask if she knew of a cleaning woman for Greenfield, delaying her by a minute or so, and the whole silly episode would have been avoided. Now, though, was hardly the time to ask her. I drove on, deciding I would make some calls that evening. Surely one of the women I knew would have the name of a good cleaning woman.

3

IN THE BIG-CITY suburbs there had been a collision between two major social changes. One of the changes created a work force, the other decimated one. Because the one that was created depended for its continued existence on the survival of the one that had been virtually extinguished, the result was an interesting, not to say anxiety-ridden state of affairs.

Specifically, the upper-middle-class woman who, twenty-odd years earlier, had found it socially acceptable and even commendable to spend herself on the care and cleaning of her new house and its inhabitants, now found it socially imperative to leave that house daily and devote her energy to some paid employment. At the same time, a generation of black women who, twenty-odd years earlier, would have been forced to earn their living by doing housework, now, finally, had been allowed to seek less stigmatized sources of income, and—witness Mrs. Lacey's niece—they were damn well doing it.

The problem, of course, was that house. By its nature, it would not clean itself. I had no personal knowledge of those halcyon days of the Upstairs-Downstairs setup, but I could remember, not so very long ago, when for a modest weekly sum, you could avail yourself of everything from a strong matron of Middle-European descent whose idea of a clean house was one in which you could safely perform surgery on any surface, to an eager if unskilled young woman working off her transatlantic fare. They all seemed to have died off or gone on to better things, together with the once-available black houseworker. Help, now, came largely—the classic ethnic turnover—from the ranks of the new Spanish-speaking population, and seemed, judging from the phone calls I made that evening, to be less than the perfect answer.

My first call was to Gordon Oliver's wife. Shirley was a woman the neighboring ladies for a long time refrained from inviting to their parties, not because she was coffee-colored, but because she made every other female in the room look like a mattress that had been left out in the rain for a year. Not only was she gorgeous to look upon, she was also a mine of arcane information: where to find waterproof cushions for outdoor furniture, how to keep dried flower arrangements from shedding, what to do with well-preserved clothes that you couldn't bear to look at any longer.

"*Cleaning* help?" she asked, with the low growl she affected when discussing subjects that aroused her wrath. "*I'm* the only cleaning help around here. I *tried* having help. Why not, I can afford it, everybody else has cleaning help, what am I, an orphan? I used to call those agencies. Once they sent me a black girl who took one look at me and put on a face like she'd just swallowed a rancid avocado. She told Kibby and Gordon, Junior, they were Oreos."

"*Oreos*?"

"Cookies. Black on the outside, white in the middle. I kicked her out. The others they sent me were all Mexicans or Colombians or places like that. They had some pretty crazy ideas about this country, thought I should give them money to buy cars and teach them how to cheat the Internal Revenue. Anybody calls me prejudiced, watch out, I swear three out of seven did that. The others were always sick. Forget it, Mag, it's do-it-yourself time."

"This isn't for me, it's for Charlie. Mrs. Lacey retired."

"Oh my God, that's serious. Well, I'll ask around. Some of my neighbors have what they choose to call help. Oh, by the way, I had the piano tuned."

"That wasn't *my* idea, you know. It was Charlie who said

it made the Mozart sound as though Poulenc had written it. If you want my opinion it was his E string that was off."

"What the hell, it was probably due for a tuning anyway."

"I'll treat it gently from now on."

"Never knew you to beat up a piano, Mag. I'll let you know if I hear of somebody in the cleaning line."

"See you Friday night." I said it with carefree certainty, like a naval officer on Hawaii making a casual appointment for December 7, 1941, and broke the connection and dialed again.

The voice that answered was the voice of someone who has wandered the Siberian wastelands for months, lost and solitary, and has forgotten there are such things as fellow creatures: my divorced friend Barbara Wexler, mother of four, now in the third year of law school, and suffering every inch of the way.

"Cleaning woman?" There was a pause while she made the mental journey back from equity, jurisprudence, and products liability to the land of such incredibly luxurious concerns as cleaning women. "Well," she said finally, "I only know Josephine and you know what she's like."

I did indeed. I had once shared her with Barbara, and after several months of finding the piano half-dusted, the rugs half-vacuumed, the kitchen floor half-washed and the rest of the house ignored, all at an hourly rate close to that of a surgeon's, I had developed a rash, the cause of which was ultimately traced to burning resentment. After Josephine, I'd reclaimed my domestic burdens and my unblemished skin.

"Not Josephine, thank you. Nowhere in the Bill of Rights does it say anything about an inalienable right to receive an exorbitant sum for standing around looking at a mop."

"I know." Barbara's voice was faint, as though she had no energy to spare for this problem. "Try Vera. She's had some girl for about six years—"

I tried Vera.

"My cleaning woman? You wouldn't want her. I wouldn't recommend her to anyone. She's practically useless."

"Is this a new one? Barbara said you'd had one for six years—"

"It's the same one."

"And she's useless? Why do you keep her?"

"She shows up."

This was undoubtedly a virtue. So many of them had difficulty distinguishing between "once a week" and "once in a while."

Vera suggested I call Sandy Weller. Sandy Weller said she would not wish her girl on her worst enemy. "When she leaves I have to do it all over again."

She suggested I call someone else, who suggested I call someone else, and so on. All reports were negative, and all the women sounded either depressed or exhausted. What price liberation?

"Do you realize," I said at dinner to Elliot, father of my two sons, who was not above wielding a can of Ajax or a bottle of Windex a few times a year, "that roughly ninety percent of the upper-middle-class women in Sloan's Ford are out every day making their way in the world, contributing to the family coffers, also to the education of children and the well-being of senior citizens, and the arts and the sciences, and medicine, and law and government—and they all live in dirty houses?"

"Dirty? I doubt that," Elliot said comfortably, enjoying his red snapper with lemon pepper sauce.

"Or else they come home from a day's work to an evening of scrubbing and dusting. There's no such thing anymore as a reasonably efficient houseworker. The species is extinct. You don't know how lucky you are that I'm strong and a good worker."

"Listen, I checked you out, teeth and all, before I bought you. By the way, I have to go to Richmond on Thursday for a couple of days."

What was he implying? That he had his own troubles? More likely he was implying nothing, had simply lost interest in the subject. It was not a problem that had ever kindled any significant compassion in the male breast (except for Greenfield, and that was only hours old). The upper-middle-class female was fair game; few had any kind words to say about her when she was merely spending her time spending her husband's money, and now that she was out earning her own, disparagement had only been replaced with annoyance.

Well, God knew there were graver problems in the world than the fact that dust balls gathered under the sofas, mold grew apace under the kitchen sinks, and the suburbs echoed with the cracking of good wood drying out from lack of polish. Or alternatively, with the thud of liberated women as they collapsed on the floor beside the mop and pail at midnight. Still, I was not talking about heiresses, and the pain is real when you lose something you've struggled to acquire.

The phone rang as I was pouring the coffee.

"I hear," Shirley Oliver said, "that Dina Franklin has a new girl and I can't imagine Dina putting up with just anyone."

I called Dina Franklin, and her machine answered me.

"This is the Franklin residence," her voice, jaunty as ever. "We'll be happy to call you back if you'll just leave your—"

I left name, number, and message, left Elliot to clear away the dishes, and took out the typewriter. Elliot was reading in bed by the time I finished the board meeting report, and by more or less the crack of dawn the following morning, I delivered it to the old white mansard-roofed house on Poplar Avenue.

On Wednesday the *Reporter* goes to press, Calli Dohanis goes to pieces, and Greenfield goes without music, a negligible sacrifice considering that the din occasioned by the inevitable eleventh-hour crises would in any case drown it out. Helen Deutsch, the only solid rock in that heaving sea of an office, sat at her Justowriter, typing away, patience on a monument, while Calli clattered in and out of the layout room moaning that she'd lost her good scissors, and Stewart Klein gobbled chocolate-covered doughnuts—testimony to the sturdiness of a twenty-seven-year-old stomach—checked copy, thirteen characters to a column, and indicated type face (it was Stewart's great frustration that he had yet to need type for a banner headline). Large and confident, with a mass of wiry brown hair and a Hemingway mustache, he had graduated from NYU school of journalism, alienated the entire masthead of *The Village Voice* in just six weeks with his grandiose schemes for improving the paper, and was spending a few years with the *Reporter* while waiting for a position to open up at a foreign desk of *Time* magazine.

On Wednesdays I confined myself to essentials. While a telephone rang unanswered, I dropped my manila envelope on Helen's desk and retraced my steps to the front door, but with my hand on the knob I heard myself summoned.

Greenfield stood at the top of the narrow stairway, his gray hair on end, a sheaf of blue-penciled pages in one hand. "The phone. For you." He disappeared into the office.

I ran up the stairs. For me? Here? At this hour? It could only be disaster. Matt? Alan? Elliot? I picked the receiver out of the flotsam and jetsam on the desk. "Yes?"

"I tried you at home." Dina Franklin sounded spirited, but there was a hard note to her voice. "There was no answer. Sorry I didn't get back to you last night, I had a small problem here when I got home. Somebody broke into the house."

"*Your* house?!" The invulnerable Dina?

"They don't seem to have taken anything, the alarm must have frightened them off. Anyway—"

"Do the police have any idea—"

"The police haven't been here. What I—"

"But you said the alarm went off—"

"It's not connected to the police. The kids would have been gone anyway by the time they got here—"

"Kids?"

"Well—I have an idea who it might be. That's not for publication."

"If the police know, it's no secret."

"The police? Absolutely not. Make an accusation before I confirm it? I don't want that kind of trouble. Look, I don't have much time, I have to take care of a couple of things before I catch a plane this afternoon. About this message you left—if Charlie needs a cleaning woman I can let him have Mathilda this Friday—she comes to me on Fridays, but I won't be here this week. She's booked all the other days, but you never know, she might drop one of the others—"

"Well thanks, Dina. How do I get—"

"I gave her your number, you can make your own arrangements. And by the way, tell Charlie not to worry, it's going to be all right."

"What is?"

"He'll know."

I found the phone under a drift of paper and replaced the receiver. Greenfield had been leaning back in the swivel chair, eyes on the floor, and, with measured beat, tapping his pen on the desk to emphasize my interruption of his work. "I realize you're a dedicated nonconformist," he hunched importantly over the desk and rattled papers, "but in the interests of efficiency—mine—you might consider joining the rest of the world and having one of those message-taking machines attached to your telephone."

I looked around pointedly.

"I don't need one," he countered. "I have two message-taking machines downstairs, one of them Greek. Unfortunately they're out of service on Wednesdays due to temporary insanity."

"I will not get a machine. All they do is inform every would-be burglar you're not at home. If there's no answer, at least they can assume you're in the yard or the shower. That machine was probably responsible for the break-in at Dina's house last night. I suppose you heard that. They broke into her house. What's more, she has an idea who did it, but she hasn't told the police. Oh yes, and she had a special message for you. 'Tell Charlie not to worry, it's going to be all right.' She said you'd know what it meant. I had no idea you were on such familiar terms with—"

"Maggie. If you're not expecting any more calls—"

"The call," I said sweetly, "was for you." He looked up from under his bristly brows. "At least, on your behalf. I've found you an interim solution to the cleaning problem."

Gratitude was strangely absent from his expression.

"Certain adjectives," he informed me, "cannot justifiably be applied to certain nouns. Nuclear and safety, for instance. Military and intelligence. Interim and solution." He went to the landing and sent the word "Deutsch" down the stairs in that quiet voice that somehow could penetrate even a clash of armored warriors.

Adjectives. Thus are the virtuous rewarded. "She'll be here Friday morning," I said shortly, following him to the landing and starting down the stairs.

His voice came after me. "On Friday morning I'll be at the special session of the County Legislature."

I stopped halfway down, faced with a choice. Tell this girl to forget it, and suffer the consequences of Greenfield having to live in an unclean house, or resign myself to the job of receiving and instructing her.

"I'll be here," I told him grudgingly, as Helen Deutsch

came up the stairs hurriedly, her face flushed.

"That's only reasonable," he said. "You were the one who arranged it."

Oh well, it was something; if his humor hadn't improved, at least he was back to having the last word.

Before I reached the front door I heard him reading to Helen from an article she'd typed. " 'Spokesman for the Chamber of Commerce estimated there would be one thousand by 1983.' One thousand. Highways? Head of cattle? Gypsy moths?"

I went out into the cool sunny morning, looked up at the sky. Not a cloud in sight, and the air was dry, dry, dust-dry. The weather bureau optimistically suggested we might have a sprinkle on Thursday, but that never came to pass, and Friday morning dawned as clear and dry as every day had for a month and more.

I had made my arrangements, not with Mathilda herself, whose English was marginal—and that made my heart dance— but with the woman who apparently drove her to her various jobs. By nine twenty-five I was standing beside the Honda in the driveway that ran alongside the old white house, and ten minutes later she arrived, in a dusty cream-colored van driven by a large, baby-faced woman who pulled up to the curb and spoke to her rapidly in Spanish as Mathilda climbed out and stood on the sidewalk.

Mathilda was a pretty, delicately made girl in her mid-twenties with dark curling hair, big dark eyes, pointed chin. She had come to do housework in a pair of tight new jeans, sandals with two-inch heels, and an embroidered blouse under a leather jacket. Her manner was shy, even timid, certainly out of keeping with the clothes, which she wore awkwardly, as though she were taking part in some pageant. The Americanization of Mathilda.

I entertained no high hopes for the quality of the scouring and scrubbing, as she accompanied me down the driveway to the back of the house, mincing along on her heels. Her employment by a woman like Dina was proof positive of the desperate condition of the household-help market.

The driveway led straight to a white-painted frame garage where Greenfield kept his Plymouth, and beside this a neat rectangle of grass was surrounded on three sides by massive forsythia bushes and huge shrubs of yew and ilex forming a high, dense barrier between Greenfield's property and its surroundings: a neighbor on one side, a road on the other, and at the back a disused lane that straggled down a high embankment full of rocks and tangled trees to a tiny stream—a shortcut to a cross street several hundred feet away. The barrier of foliage was there, I assumed, mostly to allow Greenfield to stroll or sit out there in good weather, protected from the view, if not the sound, of his sole neighbor mowing the lawn. It also added to the illusion that home and office were two separate places; that, and the fact that there was no connecting inner stairway from his third-floor living quarters to the two lower floors where the business of the *Reporter* was conducted.

I unlocked the back door with the key Greenfield had given me, we went up two flights of stairs to the top floor, I showed Mathilda where the cleaning equipment was stored, gave her a quick tour of the Spartan kitchen, bedroom and bath and the big, brandy-colored living room with its walls of books and lithographs, its deep, warm armchairs, long, dark refectory table between the windows, nineteenth-century music stand, and huge carved French armoire behind whose doors the sacred components of his unique stereo system lived in the company of several hundred jacketed recordings. I explained, with gestures, the need for extreme caution in handling anything and everything in this room, added a few other specific suggestions and prohibitions, and told her I'd be back in a few hours to see how she was doing.

She said yes, yes, and yes, to everything, and as I went down the stairs I heard her singing to herself some strange, colorless melody from somewhere south of Chiapas. I hoped she would do even half of what needed doing, but I was far from optimistic. Mathilda looked like no domestic ball of fire to me.

I drove off down Poplar Avenue, heading for the Gorham road on an assignment concerning nothing less than the new Gorham Hospital Emergency Room Volunteer Squad. Far be it from this reporter to fly back and forth to the Middle East, or to waste time uncovering scandal and corruption in the federal government. I recorded, as someone said, not history, but life.

The squad of volunteers being trained for emergency assistance proved to be a group whose collective eagerness, nervousness, and uncertainty did little to inspire confidence. Even as I took notes, I decided that a report on their training program might be less useful than simply publishing a picture of the six of them as a warning to one and all to avoid any reckless behavior or dangerous activity that might incur their services.

It was past one o'clock by the time I got back to Sloan's Ford, and I was thinking longingly of poached eggs and buttered toast and coffee, but I wanted to check on Mathilda before Greenfield returned, to make certain she hadn't been (a) sitting around entertaining herself with wavering melodies, (b) just sitting around because she'd been too timid to touch things, or (c) touching things and breaking them.

Too late. Greenfield's new Plymouth (virtually indistinguishable from the old Plymouth, which had recently died of old age) already stood in the driveway. Whatever she'd done or hadn't done, Greenfield, by now, had seen. I hesitated, then decided it was, really, my responsibility, and parked at the curb, went around to the back, and ascended to Olympus.

When I reached the second landing I saw Greenfield's back, in his tan corduroy version of a loden coat, framed in the open doorway above. He stood motionless as I mounted the last flight.

"It's all right," I called, "you can go in. She's tame."

He turned slowly and stared at me without seeing me at all.

"Tame?" he said, in a strange, clipped voice. "She's dead."

I stopped on the second last stair tread, rooted, a pulse hammering in my throat.

"She's dead," he repeated. "Bludgeoned. She's lying on the floor beside the vacuum cleaner." There was a long pause. "And my turntable and speakers are gone."

4

THE BIG GRAY man in the gray overcoat with the gray face and the gray soul, sat on the edge of Greenfield's plum-colored wingback chair, his forearms on his knees, staring down at the dark stain in the bronze nap of the rug. Greenfield slumped in one of a pair of claret-colored armchairs, resenting Detective Pratt's appropriation of the wingback. I cowered in the other armchair, my fingers icy, my esophagus raw from throwing up. Sergeant Walchek, stolid and handsome and blank, stood by the open armoire staring at the empty spaces where the turntable and speakers had been, and Officer Mapes, bearlike and moon-faced, stood in the doorway, feet apart, hands clasped behind his back, like a minor character in a British movie.

The three policemen constituted one fifth of the entire Sloan's Ford police force, others having gone after completing the posthomicide rigmarole of searching the rooms and dusting various surfaces with powder. Mathilda, wearing her American clothes and a few deep American depressions in her head, had been removed. Statements had been taken, Calli and Helen on the ground floor in the *Reporter* offices had been questioned, had sworn they'd seen and heard nothing, had developed, respectively, a migraine and stomach cramps, and had gone home.

"The door was unlocked when you got back?" Detective Pratt repeated for the third time, in his gray voice, "and you two are the only persons with a key to that back door?"

"Detective Pratt," Greenfield said, his expression no longer merely one of habitual melancholy, but that of a man sitting on thorns, "I've sworn to it. In writing. We have both sworn to a list of things that would stretch from here to the county courthouse. Mrs. Rome has explained where she was from ten thirty this morning to five past one this afternoon. You only have to check it. I've given you an account of my whereabouts and you only have to check *that*. I saw this girl for the first time probably two hours—according to your ME—after she'd been hit on the head. Mrs. Rome saw her for the first time at nine thirty this morning and for the second time about three minutes after I found her. Neither of us knows anything about her except that she worked for Mrs. Franklin who, unfortunately, is unreachable somewhere in St. Louis."

"That's all you know?"

"That's all I know with regard to the girl. My entire store of knowledge isn't quite that limited."

The detective's eyes, as warm as two chunks of frozen slush, stared at Greenfield. Greenfield's eyes, as placid as twin forks of lightning, stared back. When Pratt finally spoke, it was with the restrained sound of a cop who has decided not to risk a charge of police brutality.

"Did you leave any instructions for her, such as putting out the garbage or accepting delivery of a parcel?"

"No instructions."

Pratt turned to me. "You?"

I cleared my throat and said, in a voice vaguely reminiscent of my own, "I told her not to open the door."

"Why did you do that?"

Greenfield slammed both hands down on the arms of his chair. "Just a whim, Detective. More than two dozen homes have been burglarized in the area in the past six months. And the thieves, I might add, are still walking the streets."

Pratt's frozen gray eyes slid to Sergeant Walchek and back to Greenfield before he managed to unclench his teeth. "I asked Mrs. Rome."

"That's why," I said. "The burglaries."

"You told her not to open the door. But she opened it. She must have. No sign that anybody forced their way in. And according to you the only two keys to that door were with you and Mr. Greenfield. So she opened that door. Why do you think she opened the door, after you told her not to?"

"It's possible," I said hoarsely, "she didn't understand me. Her English was not very good."

"She opened the door," Pratt insisted, "and let them in.

She let them go all the way up to the top floor. You sure you didn't tell her to expect somebody? A repairman?"

I shook my head.

"Obviously," Greenfield said, "she knew whoever it was who came to the door."

Pratt's bleak gaze traveled back to Greenfield. "You telling me she was tied in with these burglaries?"

Greenfield got out of his chair with exaggerated deliberation, thrust his hands into the pockets of his corduroy slacks, and glared down at the detective. "I am theorizing," he said very quietly. "I know absolutely nothing about this young woman. I don't know where she came from, her family background, the people with whom she associated. It's *possible* she knew thieves. It's also possible she did not. There are any number of possibilities. The only possibility I rule out is Peter Pan flying in through the open kitchen window with a block and tackle for removing the loot." He crossed to the armoire and contemplated the empty shelves.

"If they were friends of hers," Pratt went on in the same dead voice, "why did they fracture her skull?"

Without turning around, Greenfield said, "The girl has no future, and not much of a present, but she must have had a past, pristine or otherwise. If there's an answer to your question, that's where you'll find it." His humility, such as it was, was selective; he would have been diffident in the presence of Matisse or Casals, but would have no compunction about instructing MI5 in the fine points of espionage. The Sloan's Ford police, apparently, gave him no pause.

Pratt tapped one foot quietly against the floor. Something beyond Greenfield's hubris was sticking in his craw. An uneasy silence settled on all of us, and in my mind images succeeded each other like quick cuts in a film: Mathilda nodding to me as I explained how to clean the armoire, "Yes, yes, yes." Mathilda's high-heeled sandals, tight jeans, the leather jacket she still hadn't removed when I left, Mathilda getting out of the van—

"Oh!" I said. "That woman—" I turned to Pratt. "The woman who brought her here—she'll be coming to pick her up. Somebody has to tell her—"

"What's the woman's name?"

"I don't know." He regarded me skeptically. "She drives

a cream-colored van.''

"What time was the girl due to be picked up?"

I looked at my watch. "She could be there now."

"Mapes," said Sergeant Walchek, and Officer Mapes disappeared down the stairs.

Detective Pratt rose from the wingback chair like a great gray whale rising from the ocean depths. "Windows to the fire escape locked," he said, "and not broken. Drop from the open kitchen window, thirty feet. No marks on the windowsill. No marks on the downstairs door. She let them in." He nodded to Sergeant Walchek and moved to the doorway, speaking as he went. "If you happen to think of anything you forgot to tell me, you let me know." He turned and directed his glacial gaze at Greenfield. "If you happen to think of *anything,*" he said carefully, "or if you find out anything—anything at all—you let me know."

And then I knew what it was that was making the detective so unhappy. He was convinced we knew something we weren't telling him. He was remembering a case two years earlier involving a hit-and-run driver, when Greenfield had instituted his own investigation without portfolio, designated me assistant sleuth, and succeeded in establishing unbreakable alibis for the police department's only two suspects. Apparently it still rankled.

I heard police-feet thud on the stairs and the distant click of the downstairs door.

Greenfield took a disc from his collection and stood looking at it. He had nothing on which to play it. In order to hear it he would have to go down two flights of stairs, around to the front of the house, and up the other staircase to his office. If he moved the office stereo to the living quarters he'd have nothing on which to play his tapes during the day. He looked like a man who'd been knocked down by a bus and then, for good measure, kicked while he was lying there.

I went to the window and looked down at the street. Down below a patrol car was pulling away from the curb. An elderly woman walking up the street carrying a bulging knitted shopping bag, had stopped to watch it and look up at the house. The van in which Mathilda had arrived that morning stood a little farther up the street, and Officer Mapes was speaking to the woman behind the wheel and pointing off in the direction the patrol car had taken. I caught a glimpse of the woman's shocked face as she leaned out to see where he was pointing. Mapes went out into the road and held up traffic while the woman in the van made a clumsy U-turn, then he got into his car and took off, the woman following.

"They're taking that woman to headquarters," I said.

Greenfield abandoned the wake he was holding beside the armoire and sank into his wingback chair.

"Pratt," he said, "was either so busy worrying about any information we might be withholding that he couldn't think straight, or he actually believes this is just another in a string of burglaries. One thing's certain—it wasn't a delicacy about flaunting his keen deductive powers that kept him from pointing out the obvious discrepancies."

"What discrepancies?"

"Maggie. Think."

"I'm not in peak condition."

"If they were burglars—and she didn't know them—and all they wanted was to get into an empty house—any empty house—to steal some valuables and make a quick getaway, and if, to that end, they rang the doorbell to confirm there was no one in the house to make difficulties, then why, when the girl opened the door, didn't they simply make some excuse and leave?"

I thought about it. "Maybe they realized she didn't speak English too well and thought they could . . . could get away with pretending they had some legitimate reason to be here. And came in to . . . look around, see if there was anything they could take that wouldn't make her suspicious. Like the stereo. She might think they were taking it in for repairs."

"Why bother with anything that complicated when all they had to do is go away and find a completely uninhabited house—there are plenty to choose from during the day—where they could scavenge at their leisure?"

"They might have thought you had some very valuable things."

"A natural conclusion to reach, given the grandeur of this edifice."

"They were petty thieves."

"If they were petty thieves, why didn't they take the cash under the begonia while they were at it? The silver chafing dish? My gold cuff links?''

I worked on that for a minute or so, pacing the floor, clutching my middle as though the pressure of my arm would soothe it.

"If they went for the stereo first," I said finally, "and Mathilda suddenly got suspicious and decided to make trouble . . . and they hit her to keep her quiet . . . and then realized"—I took a long, shuddering breath—"realized they'd killed her, they could have . . . just panicked and run . . . without looking for anything more. Do you have something around here that would soothe my stomach?"

Greenfield got up and headed for the kitchen and I followed. He took a bottle and a glass from the cabinet, ran the cold water, and said, "A couple of raw-brained, small-town desperadoes, hearing about some old miser living alone with his fortune in uncut gems and gold bullion stowed under the mattress, work their way into his house in his absence by passing themselves off as honest workmen to the pretty young servant girl who, though simpleminded, suddenly develops the wit to see them for what they are when they proceed to dismantle and carry off a large item of value, but as she is about to raise the hue and cry, they dispose of her with a few vicious blows—what did they use, by the way, or do they normally carry a length of steel pipe on these adventures?— and she falls dead, at which the ruthless ruffians gaze in horror at their handiwork, not having meant to kill her at all, even though she was a witness who could subsequently have described them to the police. . . ." He extracted a tablet from the bottle. "It sounds less like the reconstruction of a suburban smash-and-grab than the libretto for an unsuccessful seventeenth-century French opera." He handed me the tablet and the glass of water. I very nearly threw the water back at him. On his behalf I had been subjected to violent trauma, been grilled by the police, and suffered a severe gastrointestinal upheaval. Now, insults!

I popped the pill into my mouth, swallowed some water, and said coldly, "If you don't like my solution, what's yours?"

"Solution." He started back to the living room. "We don't even know the nature of the puzzle."

I picked up my bag. "I'm going home. I'm going to bed. I'm going to cower under the blankets for a few days." I got to the doorway before his voice stopped me.

"You can't cower tonight. It's Friday."

Friday. I heard myself telling Shirley Oliver I'd see her Friday night. I turned and looked at him in dismay. "We're not going to play *tonight*. Not after *this*. My God, Charlie, this is no time to tackle a Schubert trio!"

"You took a pill," he said, "I'm going to take a trio."

It was a rebuke of sorts, and I accepted it as I went down the stairs. It hadn't occurred to me that there was more to Greenfield's reaction than a sense of outrage. It hadn't occurred to me, either, that the alternative-scenarios folderol, the intellectual puzzle-solving, had been, in part, an attempt to buffer the visceral response to the horror.

I was about to turn the car toward home when I realized that Elliot would be back from Richmond that evening and there were no vegetables to go with the leftover roast chicken.

Food. In an attempt to keep my gorge where it would be most comfortable, I tried to think of vegetables as mere objects, without the attendant tastes and smells. I pictured them painted on canvas: eggplant, tomatoes, summer squash— a still life, inedible. It seemed to work, and I thought I could manage a few minutes at the market.

The Farmer's Market was a mile out of town, an open-air, mom-pop-and-kids affair sheltered only by three walls and a roof. It remained open for business from Memorial Day to Thanksgiving, and the produce, trucked in daily from their own upstate farm, was fresh, ripe, crisp, and expensive, unlike the fruits and vegetables in the supermarkets which, though just as expensive, were soft, limp, and rotting, or hard, unripe, and sickly pale.

I sped along the market road with the windows wide open, shivering with the chill but determined to breathe as much fresh air as possible. The road was lined on either side with dying wild flowers and fading privet, with trees whose leaves were tentatively turning to pale brass and russet. I worried that the drought would keep us from a deep, rich autumn. Any old subject would do to distract my mind from the memory of a girl on a rug.

When finally the market came into view, it provided the only burst of color in the landscape: the pale green clapboard structure, open along the front, spilling over with bins of orange-red tomatoes, dark green and yellow squash, wine-colored apples, stacks of golden pumpkins.

I pulled into the wide graveled stretch provided for parking and joined the handful of shoppers moving from bin to bin, carrying the blue canvas baskets provided by the market. Blindly I filled my basket with pears, green peppers and grapes, a head of escarole and some huge tomatoes, and stood uncertainly, looking around, knowing I was not really concentrating on the job at hand. I heard a squeal of tires on the road and a sound like BB shot, and looked up to see a shower of gravel go flying as a battered, coffee-colored station wagon made a breakneck turn into the parking area and screeched to a stop.

Jessie Lucas emerged from the car with smoke billowing from her nose as though she, and not the automobile, had raced the mile and a half to the market. She ground out her cigarette in the gravel and, coughing prodigiously, picked up a blue basket and headed in my direction. I wondered if she were going to make conversation, and if so, what I would find to say. ("How are you?" "Not too well, I've just come from a murder.")

I didn't really know Jessie. I'd been introduced to her once at a party (she was alone, no husband), admired her vibrant manner, the way she spoke with a flourish, as though she'd sprung from different soil, had more dramatic roots than the majority of suburban women. She couldn't be more than a few years older than they were, but seemed to have lived harder. I'd been told she was both actress and painter, and asked if I could interview her for a "Profile" piece. She'd gaped. "Good God, me? I don't *have* a profile. I'm a dabbler. I dabbled on the stage when I was young, now I dabble in paint. There's no one to write about. The words would vanish from the page as you put them down." No interview, but we kept meeting in passing, brief exchanges at the bank, in the drugstore.

She was still coughing when she saw me. "If I could only sing," she called out, "what a Mimi I'd give them! 'No Teresa Stratas,' they'd say in the grand tier, 'but just listen to that cough! She hits a C below middle C, that's a pretty neat trick for a soprano.'"

I smiled wanly and looked at the string beans.

"I would love to be able to blame it on pollen or tuber-culosis," she went on, inspecting a bunch of celery, "but the truth is I have a weak and self-indulgent nature. And besides, what the hell, how much longer can I last, the old girl's about ready to pack it in anyway. No woman," she admonished the sky with the celery, "should be forced to live on after fifty. There should be kind people going around with questionnaires asking one's preference and seeing to it that one departs gracefully and without pain."

An unfortunate topic. As my uncertain hands filled a bag with string beans I spilled some on the earthen floor, stooped down, gathered the spilled beans, and stood clutching them, not knowing where to put them. Jessie pulled another plastic bag from the roll and held it open while I emptied my fist of the dirty beans.

"You don't look glorious," she said. "I have seen livelier faces being wheeled out of an operating room. Why don't you go sit down somewhere and let me finish your shopping?"

I shook my head. "Thanks, I'm finished." I made my way to the cash register presided over by the sharp-eyed mama of the family, and from there back to the car, but as I opened the hatchback and deposited my parcel, Jessie reappeared at my elbow.

"If you're not fit to drive, lock up and come with me. You can come back for your car tomorrow."

"I'm fine. I think it's just that I haven't eaten all day."

"You don't look like a skinny junkie."

"It wasn't deliberate. Something happened and I forgot."

"Forgot to eat! That has *never* happened to me. I wonder what it's like. I ate when I was in love. I ate when the final decree came through. I don't think anything short of murder would make me forget to . . ."

I must have turned chartreuse or periwinkle blue because she obviously saw, in my face, that she had scored a direct hit.

"Don't tell me—" she began, half-laughing and then suddenly looking uneasy. "Has something awful happened?"

"Yes it has," I said, not meaning to say it at all, but

evidently needing to expunge the knowledge by sharing it. I found myself telling her that burglars had got into Greenfield's house, that a cleaning girl had been beaten and killed.

"They *killed* her? What did they hit her with, a piano?"

"It was so . . . inadvertent. She was only there on loan. Charlie's woman left and I borrowed this girl. From Dina Franklin. If I hadn't been so bloody helpful . . ."

"From Dina . . ." Jessie murmured. "Poor . . . girl." And, with a sudden change of voice, looking out over a field that stretched beyond the market, " 'Murder, though it have no tongue, will speak with most miraculous organ.' " After a moment she slapped the hood of the Honda and said, "Let me drive you."

"No, it's all right, thanks."

She gave me a last look, went back to the market, lighting a cigarette, and I saw her pick up an eggplant and examine it. I got behind the wheel and drove home.

5

HOME WAS A sprawling, much-used gray house with peeling white shutters on Putney Lane, a testament to twenty years of uninhibited living by two boys now leaving their mark on respective college dorms, and to the antics of an exuberant red setter named George who, for the past six years, had made a number of territorial claims which tended to give the place a certain derelict charm.

It was dusk when I pulled into the driveway. I looked, automatically, for George to come bounding to the fence, but there was no George. I scanned the yard; no sign of him. At this time of day, unless he knew I was in the house, he never failed to watch for me, never failed, even when otherwise occupied, to hear the car. I found myself gripped by a cold, throat-stopping fear. One terrible thing had already happened: these things come in threes. . . .

Pulse pounding, I carried the groceries to the front door and inserted the key. And stopped, realizing that the comforting British expression, "safe as houses," had become obsolete. Houses were no longer safe. Not even here, forty miles from the urban rot, on a peaceful, upper-middle-class suburban street inhabited by relatively decent, family-oriented, sensible people who bought season tickets to the opera and the ballet and discussed the editorials in *The Times* at their dinner parties, a street of well-cared-for lawns and excellent garbage pickup, of dogwood trees and healthy kids on bicycles. There were no longer any safe houses here. I could open the door and walk in on a "burglary in process" and get bashed over the head like Mathilda. It could already have happened to George, to silence him, as he barked his head off, protecting his territory.

On the other hand, George could have seen a particularly desirable female retriever and cleared the fence in one ecstatic leap, a thing he had never done, but there was always a first time.

I turned the key quickly and opened the door. The house seemed undisturbed, breathing normally. My Liberty of London scarf still dangled from the hall table, the copper bowl of slowly expiring marigolds still sat on the piano in the living room, green bananas still hung from the kitchen ceiling in a tiered straw basket. Nothing to fear but fear.

I looked into the mud room off the kitchen and there was George, sleeping. I let him in, wondering if he was getting old, went cautiously upstairs, and made a quick reconnaissance. All untouched.

A glass of sherry, some dry toast, George fed and padding around the house after me, Fauré's *Pelléas and Mélisande* suite on the record player, and life was not as threatening as it had seemed a half hour before. I washed the fruit and vegetables I'd bought. The phone rang. It was Elliot. He'd run into a problem, he wouldn't be back for another twenty-four hours.

"Everything okay?" he asked casually.

No, everything is very bad. Something incredibly bad has happened, and I don't want to be alone in this house tonight, I don't care what the problem is, come home!

"Same as usual," I said.

When I replaced the receiver I stood by the phone, immobilized by the sudden return of fear. Where should I sit? What was the most strategic position to be in, in the event of a break-in? How quickly could I get from the living room to the front door? What if George refused to run with me? Should I put the lead on him now, let him trail it around so that I could grab it the moment I heard a sound?

In the end I turned on lights all over the house, dragged an armchair to the entrance between hallway and living room, and sat there turning Le Carré's pages, reading without seeing, not a single word reaching the part of my brain that translated the little black marks into words, images, ideas. The record player repeated Fauré over and over. I kept my ear alerted for the sound of illegal entry.

Burglars. Burglars had forced their way up the stairs into Greenfield's rooms and killed Mathilda, no matter what "discrepancies." Burglars had broken into Carl Spector's house, into Gordon's neighbor's house, into Dina Franklin's . . . Mathilda had worked for Dina. Had she worked for Carl Spector? For Gordon's neighbor? Was there a connection? Why, then, had they killed her? But other houses had been broken into. Mathilda couldn't have worked for them all. The lady who drove the van? Was she in on it? Was it some organization of petty criminals? Not so petty now. Murder is not a petty crime. I hunched in the chair, waiting for the night to pass.

When the sound came I jumped as though a dentist drill had touched a nerve. Frozen, all previous schemes and strategies forgotten, I sat there clutching the book until I realized the sound was the telephone ringing.

"Gordon and I," Greenfield said, "have been waiting for twenty minutes."

He really was determined to drown murder in Schubert. Had he told Gordon? I wouldn't put it past him to say nothing that would disturb the Friday-night music. It was only fair to let him find relief where he could, but how could I leave the house and come back later, much later, at midnight, to the empty house, and turn the key in the lock: "Charlie, would you and Oliver consider coming over here instead? I'm—ah—waiting for a call."

They brought the music and the music stands. I let George out into the yard, we struggled through the first two movements of the Schubert. I made coffee. The calm, warm blood of ordinary living flowed again in my veins. It was only when they prepared to leave that I felt a constriction in the chest.

Idiot, I told myself. Elliot has had engineering problems that kept him overnight in every one of the disunited states, burglars existed then as now, and you managed to survive. The only difference is *thinking* about it.

I dredged up a good-night smile as we went to the door, but somehow it didn't pass Greenfield's inspection. He left his cello in the hallway while he carried the music stands down to Gordon's car, and when he came back he went right by it into the living room and sat down in the honey-colored armchair.

"You're nervous," he said accusingly.

"Gosh, no," I said, assuming a carefree pose on the sofa. "Murder is run-of-the-mill stuff these days. Common gossip in the supermarket. 'Oh, by the way, so-and-so got murdered last night.' 'No, really? And we were going to have the bridge party at her house. Well, well.' "

"There's a cure for nerves. I'm not sure there's one for facetiousness."

"A cure? I'm surprised at you, pushing tranquilizers."

"I think I preferred you throwing up." He put a hand to his forehead and rubbed it slowly. "I'm not significantly more tranquil than you. Same cause, different symptoms. Person or persons unknown invaded my house, helped themselves to my property, and murdered a girl who was working for me. I'm suffering a typical reaction of impotent rage. The rage is acceptable, the impotence is not."

I began to recognize a familiar psychic landscape: a garden path, down which I was being deviously and firmly led.

"To feel helpless in the face of violence is often a

matter of choice,'' my guide continued. ''The violent man's alternative is to arm himself with a physical weapon which, of course, only escalates the violence. There's also a sane alternative.''

The ''cure,'' what else. Find out who and why, and see that they're put out of circulation. I read it plain on his face, an implacable determination to get at the truth. C. B. Greenfield had mounted his mental charger, and he had a second horse waiting for me.

I stood up, to achieve superior altitude, if not superior force. ''Charlie, if you're going on another crusade you go alone. I hung up my lance and my shield after the last one. I'm not equipped to tangle with burglars. They take drugs. They're unstable. Count me out.''

''The first step''—he ignored me—''is to find out whatever we can about the girl. We need to know more about her.''

''Not me. I need total ignorance. Total disengagement. Removal, that's what I need. Preferably to the Costa del Sol.''

''The burglars will only follow you there.''

''*Follow* me? What do you mean, follow me? That's bizarre!'' I began to wonder if they would.

''They'll speak Portuguese. Or Dutch, or Arabic, even Swiss. Crime is pandemic.''

''Well, that's that, then, isn't it? We can hardly launch a global investigation.''

''You, no doubt''—he stood up, the better to look down—''would see no point in bailing out the canoe because there was a lake full of water waiting to come in.'' He paced the room.

''Burglars are police business. We *do* have police.''

''In a country where even children carry revolvers to school, also knife each other in the playgrounds, it seems obvious that the police are overworked and understaffed and need any help they can get. In Sloan's Ford they may not have the school problem, but on the other hand, we are not equipped with a handful of the most brilliant graduates of the police academy. Detective Pratt is no fool, but he's a man whose concern for a healthy society—if he ever had one—has atrophied from lack of successful application. His fighting spirit suffers from apathy. He's also understandably reluctant to probe too deeply into the behavior of local respectable families. He'll be very happy if he can trace this incident to a group of Hispanic friends of this girl, without having to interrogate a single Sloan's Ford inhabitant. The police have their training, their weapons, and a knowledge of the rules—none of which may be applicable in this case. Whereas mental agility is always applicable.''

"In that case you won't need me. As I recall, mental agility is your department. Mine is just running my feet off. Charlie. Seriously. Forget it. We're not talking about a little clever snooping around in the aftermath of some otherwise respectable person's one moment of madness. These are *real* criminals.'' He raised his spiky eyebrows. "You know what I mean.''

"You're obviously bucking for promotion to my department. If you already know they're professionals, you've deduced more than I have.''

"I'll put this as plainly as I can. I decline your kind invitation to a suicide mission.''

Greenfield looked at his watch. "What time is Elliot getting back?''

"He's not. He's stuck there overnight.''

He studied my face, measuring the degree of trepidation. He glanced at the sofa. He frowned.

"I'm fine,'' I lied. "I have George.''

"You lie,'' he murmured, "so badly.'' He went to the sofa and poked it with his fingers. "If the entire house were impregnable and bulletproof, you'd still spend the night with your eyes wide open. I'll camp on the sofa.''

"The house has three bedrooms, if anyone needs a place to sleep. You don't, so take your cello . . .''

"Fine, I'll use one of the boys' rooms. Elliot wouldn't object; he knows by now we long ago rejected the possible pleasures of seduction for the certain joys of exasperation.''

"Elliot has nothing to do with it. I don't want you here because it would make me feel incompetent and neurotic.''

"That alone would be worth the discomfort. What kind of neighbors do you have?''

"Neighborly. Go home."

"Tomorrow's Saturday. I'll leave at dawn, none of them will be awake. I'd be grateful for a toothbrush." He took off his jacket.

"You're not staying. I'm perfectly capable of spending a night alone in my own house."

"But not, apparently, of making a few inquiries in the light of day."

"The odds are different."

He draped his jacket over the back of a chair. "I find your symbols of dignity a little arbitrary. You won't lift a finger for self-respect when you've been victimized, but staying alone in the house is a point of pride."

I took the jacket off the chair. "My symbols are my own affair. I don't want you staying in my house to protect me."

"Well, I'm certainly not going to stay outside, patrolling the perimeter."

I tossed the jacket to him and marched to the front door. "Good night, Charlie."

The argument went on for another ten minutes, Greenfield resolute, Maggie adamant. Finally, with a parting shot about the wrong kind of courage, he took his jacket and his cello and left. Just to spite me. He must have known I didn't want him to take me at my word.

I let George in and checked the doors and windows six or seven times before going up to bed to lie there, quivering like a plucked violin string, straining for the sound of a stealthy movement anywhere within a hundred feet of the bedroom. My eyes began to burn, my neck muscles became rigid, my legs twitched, the hours passed, I sat up, turned on the lamp, and became very, very angry.

Not to be able to sleep secure in my own home? Where was I living? In what barbarian-ridden, godforsaken, murderous desert? In what scabrous, reptilian human jungle? Police sat at a desk less than two miles away while thugs prowled the streets, their presence violating peace of mind, making a hash of freedom, slaughtering the existence of haven, massacring trust! For this I sweated my way through college? Suffered the slings and arrows of finding a mate? Went twice to the delivery room, ministered to mumps and chicken pox, put up wallpaper, paid taxes? For this?

Something had to be done.

6

MY ANGER HAD, if anything, increased with the morning light and the sight of the puffiness around my eyes, and I headed for police headquarters with a view to venting it.

Surrounded by those grim green walls, confronting Sergeant Walchek across a high wooden counter, I let loose, demanding adequate protection for the innocent citizens of Sloan's Ford. Squads of police, I ordered, cruising the streets twenty-four hours a day in unmarked cars, automatically operated alerts between headquarters and every house in the village, state troopers, bloodhounds, and, if need be, the National Guard.

"Why," I clamored, "are we paying exorbitant taxes to live in fear? Why is the world only safe for criminals? Why does bureaucracy have a thousand reasons for expecting our support and another thousand for not giving it when we need it?"

Walchek's square and sturdy gaze never faltered. Armored in insensibility, his handsome head outlined against the shelf of athletic trophies on the wall behind him, he said they were working on it.

"Not good enough!" I cried. "Immediate action!"

"Ma'am," he said, steadfastly refusing to use my name which he'd known for some time, "it's no use getting hysterical. We've got a big problem these days. This isn't the only community that's being hit."

"This is the community you're supposed to protect!"

"The best advice I can give you is have a burglar alarm

installed."

"What makes you think *that's* a solution? Don't you think criminals know how to bypass a burglar alarm? Don't you know they've all attended Southern California University of Crime and Violence, six months of TV and you get a masters in Violent Crime? Any ten-year-old *child* knows how to get by a burglar alarm!"

"They've been a deterrent in a number of cases."

"Swell. And what about people who can't afford them?"

"All I can tell you, ma'am, is we're doing everything—"

A buzzer buzzed. Walchek pressed a button and a disembodied voice began to squawk. "No, we got that one," Walchek told the machine. The voice squawked again. "Down on the hill. Right." A door behind me opened and a patrolman holding a sheaf of papers crossed the floor to the area behind the counter. The machine buzzed again. "We're a little busy here right now," Walchek said to me, indicating dismissal.

"So are the criminals!" I shot back, and left, wondering if my name had gone down in a little black book marked Local Troublemakers.

The police were busy. Busy on the hill. Busy elsewhere. Busy—when they had the time—"working on it." Greenfield was right.

I stopped at the drugstore for a large bottle of aspirin. The pharmacy counter was thick with people buying allergy remedies. A woman in elegant mushroom-colored slacks and a dark violet sweater was waving a prescription blank at the pharmacist counting out pills behind his low glass partition: Naomi Gardner.

"Jesus," she was murmuring, "I'll never get out of here. Walter! Walter, could you just take this and send it up later? I can't wait!" With a smile and a shrug and a "Listen, I'm compulsive," she tore out of the drugstore, cheeks flushed, eyes burning.

A few minutes later at the shopping center she was streaking out of the bakery, a long loaf of French bread sticking out of the bag under her arm. In a moment she had vanished into the supermarket.

Naomi was not worrying about burglars. She didn't

have the time for it. She, too, was busy.

I retrieved a pair of Elliot's slacks from the cleaner's, went back to the car. Naomi whizzed by, a purple blur in a black Mercury with a tan top. In a parked Chevy a woman sat behind the wheel counting her change while the car radio blared the hourly news.

"Thirty-year-old man suspected of shooting three persons near the East River will be arraigned in . . . police searching for two youths seen running from the subway platform where the young medical student had been attacked . . . surrounding the post office building in Lacon, South Dakota, where a sniper on the roof has been . . . "

The woman in the Chevy scrambled out of the car to greet a friend.

"Lin*da*! Did Connie tell you about the *ban*quet? Aren't you ex*cited*? Are you going to wear a *gown*?"

The radio continued its matter-of-fact litany of sudden death in the same neutral voice in which it announced the traffic conditions. No one listens, I thought. The stopper may be unplugged and intelligent life on earth slowly gurgling down the drain; nobody hears it. Preoccupation? Defense mechanism? Or simple stupidity?

You, no doubt, would see no point in bailing out the canoe, because there was a lake full of water waiting to come in.

Not that much difference between myself and the lady in the Chevy. I heard, and complained, and worried, and nothing more. I drove to Poplar Avenue to surrender.

In the driveway next to the old white house with its long shallow front porch, Greenfield's Plymouth glinted in the noonday sun. I parked behind it and walked across the weary grass to the front door. Saturday it might be, but Greenfield would not be in his living quarters when the only available stereo system was in his office.

But there was no music floating down from the second floor. There was, instead, a woman, and what she was doing could not be called floating by even the most generous extension of the imagination. She seemed, in fact, to be descending in loosely joined sections: a pair of large and baggy maroon slacks and above that, but not connected, a round-faced, kerchief-wrapped head and sweatered shoulders, followed by a rather beefy midsection which came bumping along after. I stood aside and she gave me a quick, furtive, sidelong glance as she passed. The facial features had an unmistakable Latin cast and I'd last seen them looking fearful, framed in the window of a van.

I went up the stairway. Greenfield was in the swivel chair making notes on a memo pad in his lap and sipping coffee from the cover of a thermos that stood on the desk on a paper napkin next to a wedge of Gouda and a half-eaten apple. Camping out in the office. He glanced up briefly as I came in, and continued scribbling.

I made room on one of the armchairs and sat. He stopped writing, gazed thoughtfully at the thermos cover in his hand, and murmured, "The rug has gone to the cleaner's, Mrs. Lacey has gone to Detroit, and the stereo, no doubt, has gone to some slimy fence in New Jersey. I'm homeless." He ran his hand over his head to make sure the crown of thorns was there for all to see.

When he got no response he swiveled to look at me. I gazed steadily at a fly buzzing against the window. Let him figure out why I was there. Putting it into words was too much to ask; my presence was compliance enough.

He gestured to his picnic lunch. "The cheese is slightly above mediocre if you'd like some." I shook my head. He put the pad and the coffee on the desk and went to the hive of stereo tapes set against the wall, and I could see by his face that he'd seen the white flag flying. Whenever he recognized the signs of capitulation in an opponent there was a subtle change in his normally slightly pained expression; nothing as definite as a smile or a glint in the eye, only a suddenly refreshed look, as though he'd splashed his face with cold water. While I watched the motes of dust dancing in the shaft of sunlight from the window, he fiddled with the machinery and the warm rich sounds of a Boccherini cello concerto drifted across the room.

Back in his chair he cut into the cheese with a fruit knife, speared a section on a fork and bit into it, eyeing me carefully. He wanted verbal confirmation.

"Maggie," he said finally, in that slow voice, so mild you barely feel the sting, "I find it hard to credit that you came down here in the middle of a Saturday just to show me your imitation of a Lest We Forget poster. When I left you last night you seemed to have no difficulty speaking. If you've subsequently lost the use of your vocal chords, why don't you just write out your message?" He handed me the pen and the memo pad from the desk.

I twirled the pen idly between my fingers. "On the way up," I said, " I passed a woman taking the separate parts of herself down the stairs. The woman who drove Mathilda. How did you manage to find her?"

"I sat here," he replied, "and waited for the law of survival to take effect. Grief seldom blinds a working-woman to the need for hard cash."

"You mean she came here to sell information? She knows something?"

A faint groan. "The way your mind works. The girl had money coming to her for the work she did yesterday, and the woman came to collect."

"She told you *something*. You were making notes." He gestured to the memo pad in my hand. I glanced down at it and read what he'd written there: " 'Lucas, Moss, Bryce, Gardner, Franklin,' and an address. What's this, a list of people who've been burglarized?"

"Employers," he said. "According to the woman, those are the people who employed the girl one day a week."

I looked at the list again. "I don't think the lady knows what she's talking about. There's only one Lucas in Sloan's Ford and Mathilda never worked for her."

"You have firsthand knowledge of that?"

"No. It's just a logical deduction. If I met you, as a casual acquaintance, at the market, and told you a certain girl had just been murdered, and it was a girl who worked for you, would you receive the information by calmly quoting a line from Shakespeare and picking up an eggplant?"

"If you walked up to a woman shopping at the market, whom you know only casually, and announced a murder, I'm surprised she didn't call the state mental hospital to find out if they were missing a forty-seven-year-old female inmate."

"It didn't happen that way. She saw I was upset, and she asked . . . Just take my word for it, she didn't doubt what I was telling her, and that was her reaction. Moderately horrified, but completely detached."

"The woman who gave me these names drove the girl to each of her jobs; it's unlikely she'd be mistaken, and why would she lie about it?"

"You've led a protected life with Mrs. Lacey. You haven't been exposed to the broad spectrum of devious behavior among cleaning women. What else did you find out?"

"Only her address. Her understanding of English diminished rapidly the more I questioned her." He reached for the telephone book. "Where Mrs. Lucas is concerned, there's no need to speculate." He turned pages, found a number, and dialed. I heard it ring five or six times, and Greenfield was about to hang up when a voice answered. He introduced himself, told Jessie Lucas he was going to run a story in the *Reporter* on a crime that was committed yesterday and would like to include some comments from employers of the victim. "Mathilda Guiterrez. I understand she worked for you." There was a pause and the voice spoke again. "Not on the phone, Mrs. Lucas. I'll send a reporter whenever it's convenient for you. I appreciate it." He replaced the receiver. "Detached she may have been, but employ her she certainly did." He copied Jessie Lucas' address from the phone book and handed me the slip of paper.

"When?"

"Now."

I looked at the address and sighed. "I'm not doing this wholeheartedly."

"I trust your heart won't enter into it at all. Eyes, ears, and nose will do."

I gave him a look to let him know that regardless of my conscience-prompted collaboration, whatever happened from now on was fundamentally his responsibility.

7

JESSIE LUCAS LIVED on the outskirts of Sloan's Ford, south of the village center, in a section that could be reached only by one road, and that road ascended vertically for more than a mile before flattening into a wooded and meadowed plateau. More country than suburb, it was sparsely dotted with houses, the architectural style eclectic: contemporary fortress, ranch, farmhouse.

At Jessie's number there was a graveled forecourt separated from a small inner courtyard by a five-foot-high stockade fence of gray weathered palings. Wild rosebushes climbed up the inside, trailing their branches over the top of the fence, a few small pink flowers here and there, prolonging the season. The front of the house was low, of whitewashed stucco, with a door of paneled wood that looked as though it had been blackened by centuries of peat smoke. It needed only a thatched roof to belong in the Cotswolds, or Scotland, or Wales. The roof, though, low for a distance of twelve feet, then rose sharply to accommodate a second story, and there seemed to be a great deal more house at the back than appeared at first glance.

At the door I lifted a knocker made of a stone griffin from the crumbled cornice of some Roman villa, and knocked. Jessie's voice sang out, "The door's open!" I stepped into an entryway where old straw gardening hats and yellow slickers hung on wooden pegs on the wall and a huge Victorian urn held an assortment of umbrellas.

The entry opened into a vast, wandering space in which the furnishings for leisure, for work, for cooking, for dining, all flowed one into another without the interruption of walls. In the middle distance a couple of nineteenth-century sofas stood talking to each other, there was a scattering of tables, tiered, pedestaled, galleried, round, oval, and square, covered with framed photographs in antique frames standing among ancient candlesticks, ornate table lamps, glass bowls filled with pearled marbles, pinecones, dried wild flowers. One complete wall was covered with bookshelves where the massive collection of books was punctuated here and there by colored glass bottles, satin-and-ivory fans, antique cooking utensils, earthenware bowls and goblets, and an old lute.

· At the far end, to one side, the wooden counters and cabinets of a kitchen area were visible, and next to that a large round pine table and ladder-back chairs stood near a raised hearth on which a black Franklin stove squatted decoratively. On the other side of the hearth the ceiling rose, and in an L-shaped section under a skylight, Jessie Lucas stood peering at a canvas resting on an easel, a brush heavy with yellow paint in one hand, a cigarette in the other. She wore a voluminous, blue, man's work shirt, the sleeves, rolled to the elbow, spattered with blobs and smudges of yellow, brown, and white. Daubs of the same colors appeared on her arms, her jeans, and her hair.

She stepped back from the easel and stuck the brush into a jar of dirty-colored liquid standing on a nearby workbench laden with tubes and jars and paint-smeared rags. She gazed with feigned ecstasy at the canvas, lifted her arms in mock tribute to the painting in front of her, and exclaimed, "Rotten! Really rotten! A genuine fraud! It's so bad it might even sell." Puffing on the cigarette and coughing a little, she turned to me and smiled, "So. You've come on a mission for Mr. Greenfield."

"I've just scrapped that in favor of another one. Promise me that when you move you'll sell your house to no one but me."

She laughed. She had a generous laugh, and generous Renoir proportions, and a face like the one in Degas's *Woman with Chrysanthemums:* clever, humorous, knowing—and secretive. For all her easy familiarity, I could never now delude myself, knowing she had known Mathilda, that what Jessie said was any barometer of what she felt.

"Have some coffee." She gestured me over to the pine table. "I grind my own coffee beans in this expensive machine my once-husband once bought, and it's probably the worst-tasting brew since the stuff Chaplin made from boiling his old boot." She poured coffee from a steaming pot into two stoneware mugs and set one in front of me with a spoon, a sugar bowl, and a cardboard container of milk. "I can't join you at the table," she said, carrying her mug with her to the refrigerator, "because I have to make a bouillabaisse. I love bouillabaisse but it's a god-awful time-consuming bitch of a thing to prepare and if it weren't for the prodigal son coming home I'd dine happily on pickled herring." She took a bowl of celery and peeled onions from the refrigerator, slapped them onto a piece of butcher block, stubbed out her cigarette, and washed her hands at the sink. "My son, Joshua by name, is currently inhabiting one quarter of a railroad flat in the brothel-and-health-food section of the Lower East Side, and every so often he decides to come home for a weekend respite from the rigors of directing an exceedingly off-Broadway, pseudo-Brechtian drama. As for Mathilda, what do you want to know? Did I kill her? The answer is no."

Jessie could throw a curve with the best of them. I swallowed my mouthful of coffee with difficulty and covered confusion by picking up a startlingly beautiful, unsymmetrical wooden bowl sitting on the table.

"This," I said, "did not come out of a factory."

"Good God, no. That's art you're handling there. I found it in the shop of the man who made it, up in Ruys-kill. That's spalted maple, that is. And it's a brand-new acquisition, I haven't had much time to enjoy it, so be careful with the coffee."

I put the bowl down, finding it difficult to take my eyes from the unusual grain of the wood that swirled around the bottom and up the sides of the bowl as though it were alive and moving. "I was surprised," I said, back to business, "to find out that Mathilda worked for you. I wouldn't have guessed it from your reaction. Yesterday, I mean, at the market."

"Oh," she said, chopping up celery and onions, "you expected me to shriek, or grow pale and swoon away?" She looked around the counter for her cigarettes, found them, and lit one. "Well, that's not what I do when I'm shocked. I disappear. I become someone else, jump right into a character from Chekhov or O'Neill, grab lines from any old play I can remember. When Lucas told me he was going to live with someone else I answered him in Noel Coward. He was very put out. It's the only way I can keep from fainting. Shakespeare, of course, is most useful. Old Willy is loaded with lines you can use in almost any crisis. And everybody does."

I had a feeling I was being conned, but there was nothing to be gained from pursuing it. "What kind of girl was Mathilda? Did you like her?"

"Like her? I didn't think of her in those terms. She wasn't a bosom buddy, any more than the plumber. She was nice enough. Didn't clean worth a damn—her cleaning was on a par with my coffee. But then"—she looked around the vast room bathed in a sepia light, with its collection of ornaments and oddments—"I'm not sure this place is capable of being cleaned properly."

"Was she flighty, serious, dependable—"

"Flighty, no. Dependable, not very. She was slow. She lied. But that's par for the course. She was a bit of a scavenger. I'd find her going through the wastebaskets, picking out the odd discarded earring, or a perfume bottle with a drop still left in the bottom. But she didn't steal anything that wasn't already thrown out. And she was cheerful. Singing all the time." She rinsed a skillet under the tap and added, rather irrelevantly, "And of course she was young and pretty."

"Had she been up here long? I gather she was South American."

"Central. Guatemala. But if you're going to take this information seriously, consider the source. Some of these people are here illegally and lies are automatic." She dripped sesame oil into the skillet and added the chopped vegetables. "According to Mathilda, she came up to live with her cousin—from past experience I can tell you a 'cousin' is anything from a sister to a virtual stranger whose name was passed on by a friend of a friend of a relative back home—and that—also according to Mathilda—was only about three or four weeks before she came to work for me, which makes it early last spring.''

I remembered the awkward way Mathilda had worn her big-city disguise and thought it was likely, at any rate, that she hadn't been lying about how recently she'd arrived.

"This 'cousin' she lived with is the woman who drove her to her various jobs?''

"I would imagine." Jessie pushed a strand of hair off her forehead with the back of her hand. "I had no interest in trying to untangle the knotted skeins of the Central American underground." She took the cover off the stockpot simmering away on the gas range and added something sticky from a frying pan, scraping at the bottom with a ladle. "Okra," she said, "was invented by the man who failed to come up with a workable bubble gum.''

"What about her social life? Did you get the impression she had a man around? A husband? A boyfriend? Did she ever get telephone calls while she was working here?''

"She got calls. She also made calls. An employer's telephone bill should exceed your own or what's a cleaning job *for*? She would jabber away in some dialect— Castilian it *wasn't*—I couldn't catch more than one word in fifty, and not for lack of trying. But whoever she spoke to was not male—you don't have to understand the language to get *those* overtones.'' She pressed garlic into the vegetables in the skillet and stirred. "Actually, I'm the wrong person to ask about these things. You should ask Naomi Gardner. Before she lets anyone into her house she collects a file on them the FBI would envy. Or Dina Franklin, who makes a point of knowing everything about everybody, as all good politicians do. Dina is a misnomer. It should have been Diana. Goddess of the chase.''

"The moon, isn't it? Or the forests?''

"The forests, maybe. Diana the huntress. She stalks the ultimate trophy through urban jungle and suburban swamp, her quiver filled with the powerful arrows of youth. I often think Dina would be so much more *acceptable* if someone could arrange for her to have a few consecutive years of *failure*." She spooned the stock into a roux in a saucepan, stirred it, poured the mixture back into the stockpot, and plunked on the cover. "That's it," she said, "the fish goes in later. And there's nothing more I can tell you about Mathilda. Must go out for my run now. Once a day I have to go out and inhale something other than cigarette smoke. It's in the contract I made with God."

"What's God's part of the contract?"

"To see to it that when I die it will be in December, so at least I won't have to go through another winter."

My time was up, and I had an uneasy sense that I was leaving unfinished business behind. There was something I should have asked, or something she'd said that raised a question I'd lost track of in the cascade of her monologue. Trying to remember it, I bought myself a little time.

"Do you—um—have a rule about not showing your paintings to people who don't know anything about painting?"

"It's those who *know* something about it that bother me. But, yes, as a matter of fact, I detest putting them on display and standing by while people wriggle around in intense discomfort trying to find something intelligent to say about them. And then the banalities! I paint two ways—one to earn a little spalted-maple money—greeting-card level—and then, for myself, for a reason to get out of bed. If you're really curious you can look at the stuff that's here"—she gestured to the alcove—"while I get my running shoes. But only on condition that you make absolutely *no* comment."

She went off across the room and up a flight of open stairs leading to the floor above. I went into the alcove planning to use the time to recall what it was I should have asked, but the intention disappeared with my first glance at the canvas on the easel. This was certainly no pretty little greeting-card landscape.

It seemed to be a depiction of the interior of some macabre Madison Avenue shop. Against an acid-yellow background the separate, unconnected sections of a female figure appeared in various grotesque contexts: a pair of voluptuous breasts were cradled in the pearly tissue paper of a gilt-covered gift box, rosy buttocks reposed against dove-gray cloth in a glass display case, a pair of long, elegant legs reclined on a shelf covered in green velvet, and lying discarded in a wire wastebasket was the head, mouth open in protest. Slick, smooth-edged liquid shapes of a Dali.

What on earth did it mean? Was it a passionate statement about something, a flippant comment, what?

I turned to the paintings standing on the floor with their faces to the wall, and picked one up. Totally different in style: a humid garden awash in roses, reminiscent of the suffocating romanticism of Fragonard. A young woman, her perfect bosom spilling out of the gauzy draperies of her bodice, sat on the grass. Her wasp waist was circled with a daisy chain, one seductive ankle peeped from beneath the folds of her skirt, one alluring arm rested on the lush green grass, her lips, slightly parted, were luscious, the golden ringlets that curled around her head were lustrous—but the space between her mouth and the top of her head was a hole. Instead of nose, eyes, forehead, and whatever presumably lay immediately behind them, there was only a neat, round aperture through which the rose-strewn garden stretched to a blue horizon.

I put it down and picked up an innocent-looking depiction of a church wedding in the pastel palette I associated with eighteenth-century Britain: bride and groom standing in a shaft of ethereal light, the diaphanous bridal veil resting on brown curls that circled a blank, skin-colored oval, the groom gazing blissfully at the naked torso of the faceless bride at his side.

Mama mia! I was no stranger to the frustration of staring in vain at paintings whose message totally eluded me, but this was something new. It was not a lack of response I was experiencing, but a confusion of responses. Was this a simple mischievous impulse to parody past masters? An expression of anger? And if so, against what, or whom? What was the significance of the absent or discarded female faces? Or was there any?

I lifted the last painting from the floor: still another style, this time a Quattrocento Madonna—Fra Angelico or one of those guys, complete with solid-gold halo, except that the Madonna was seen from the back, standing, holding, instead of the infant, her own head, halo and all, just visible in the crook of one arm. She was naked from the waist up and skintight jeans outlined her suggestively postured backside. I thought immediately of Mathilda, and felt an uncomfortable tightness in my throat. Why Mathilda? There was no resemblance between the haloed head and Mathilda's. Jeans alone do not a woman make. Or is that what Jessie was saying? Or was I receiving messages that hadn't been sent?

Jessie came down the stairs wearing sweat suit and running shoes. "Here we go," she said, "*sans mene in corpore sano,* though I'm fast losing the latter, and lost the former years ago."

As I backed out of the forecourt, I saw the navy blue sweat suit disappearing up the road at a slow trot. I descended the near-vertical hill with my foot on the brake, thankful that Jessie had put a ban on comments. The one that came to mind was, in keeping with the paintings themselves, a paraphrase: who'd have thought the woman had so much hate in her?

8

I HAD CIRCLED my house on foot before entering, checking all the doors and windows for signs of forced entry, and wondering if I could get used to living in Reykjavik. Then I remembered that Iceland was a country relatively untouched by crime precisely because it didn't allow foreigners to live there. Open the door to me and my compatriots and it would probably be knee-deep in criminals within a year. I abandoned Iceland without too much regret, preferring safety in a warmer zone, if there was such a thing. What were the statistics in Tahiti?

Sitting at the kitchen table, a plate of toast-and-tunafish crumbs at my elbow, I studied the list Greenfield had given me and pondered my next move. "Moss, Bryce, Gardner, Franklin." The list suggested nothing but a list; possible approaches were not written there. The straight-forward request for information about a crime victim was reasonable enough for Jessie, who had already known about Mathilda, thanks to me. But the others (Dina was in St. Louis and I doubted the news had reached her there; in any case I was not about to fly to St. Louis to ask questions), the others might or might not know what had happened the day before, and if they didn't, I would not be the one to tell them. If I'd known Mathilda worked for Jessie I certainly wouldn't have told her. Today, as I had good cause to know, empires could crumble for lack of domestic help, and I had learned long ago in history class that bearers of bad tidings often left the imperial presence in a horizontal position from which they never recovered. While I hardly expected that drastic a consequence, I saw no reason to expose myself to whatever wailing and flail-ing there might be.

Alternative approaches? The most obvious was the excuse that I was looking for a cleaning woman and had heard the one they employed might be available. Two things against that: one, if they knew what had happened to Mathilda, they also knew where it had happened; two, if they didn't know, and thought it was an innocent request, it was a matter that would logically be taken care of in a phone call, it offered no plausible reason for me to invite myself into their homes for a chat. Phone calls were a waste of time; a few cold facts and excuse me, I have to go, there's someone at the door. The important stuff seldom made it over Ma Bell's wires: the unguarded facial expression, the casual gesture that said more than any verbal reply.

I put the lunch dishes in the sink and went for a walk, with George on his leash sniffing at every twig and bush by the side of the road. This being a Saturday, there were actually people visible on the street, going in and out of the houses, raking leaves, jogging. A crisp autumn day, but surely by now we should have had more color. Were the trees so dry that they hadn't the energy to blaze? Oh yes, there was the odd patch of apricot, a sprinkle of pinkish-red, but it all looked so tentative, so reluctant.

I remembered an October years ago, in Vermont and New Hampshire: mountainsides showered with the colors of pomegranate and plum, pimiento and the deep purple-brown of aubergine, clouds of saffron, fountains of cranberry and cinnamon, sweeps of banana-yellow and dark, dusty winesap-apple red against the midnight green of pines and the slender stalks of silver birches. . . .

I wrenched my mind from nostalgic glories. Concentrate. How to open those closed doors? I needed face-to-face confrontations, and for that I needed an alleged purpose that was not only logical, but so compelling they couldn't resist talking about it.

This is one problem, I thought, addressing myself mentally to Greenfield, the police wouldn't have. "Detective Pratt. Like to ask you a few questions." And in they went, with all possible cooperation. Well, my alleged purpose was always simple enough; I wrote for the *Reporter*. The *subject* was the tricky part. As it was beyond reason to suppose my powers of invention would come up with three different usable ideas, I'd simply have to think of one subject of equal fascination to all three women. From what I knew of Gardner, Moss, and Bryce, it would be easier to find one subject of common interest to Coco Chanel, Susan B. Anthony, and Mrs. Cotton Mather.

I had discarded three or four embryo ideas when I turned a corner and started down the hill to Glenbrook Place and there, sitting where it had sat for eighty-odd years, its boarded-up windows overgrown with ivy, was the subject.

They had all attended the meeting; they would all, obviously, be interested.

I jog-walked home, released a panting George into his yard, opened the front door forgetting to worry about burglars, looked up Gardner in the phone book, and dialed the number. A teenage girl's voice told me her mother was out shopping and would be back in an hour. Roberta

Moss's line was busy. Agnes Bryce answered the phone in a voice so self-effacing it was a strain to hear what she said. Fortunately the strain was relieved by the fact that what she said was short, and mostly monosyllabic. When I asked to see her in regard to an article I was writing about divided opinion on the sale of the school, she said she had nothing to say on the subject.

"But you were at the meeting Monday night. You must be interested in the outcome."

"I go to all the meetings. I do live in the village."

"But you must have an opinion about the sale."

"I have no opinion."

"You mean you don't care one way or the other?"

"I don't want to discuss it."

"Mrs. Bryce, the point of the article is to give a sense of the feeling on this issue among responsible citizens in the community." When on shaky ground, confuse with verbiage. "I'll be quoting a number of influential people in the village and it would be a glaring omission not to include the comments of someone as active in local affairs—"

She said something, faintly.

"Sorry, I didn't hear—"

"I said I have nothing to say."

There was a timid click as she replaced her receiver. I looked into the mirror above the telephone table and a bewildered face looked back at me. You'd think I'd asked the woman for intimate details of her married life! (Did she have any? Was she capable of intimacy? Submission, yes, that I could believe. Part of the bargain.) I was so intrigued by Agnes Bryce's unreasonable, not to say paranoid response to questions about the school sale, that I'd forgotten my primary purpose in calling her. Well, I'd ruined any chance of that, now. Whatever Agnes thought of or knew about Mathilda would remain locked behind those small, careful lips as far as I was concerned.

I dialed Roberta's number again, this time it rang, and a jokey male voice said, "Hello, there!" I asked Jordan Moss if I could speak with his wife.

"Oh, she's a very busy woman, my wife. Darling? Have you finished composing your address to the United

Nations? Hold on, I *think* she can spare you a minute.''

He left me listening to faint noises like mice scrabbling behind the walls, and then Roberta's soft, breathless voice said, ''Yes!'' implying she had been waiting decades for the call that would change her life, and who knew but that this was *it*.

I told her who I was and what I wanted.

''You want me to—you want *my* comments? For the paper?''

''I'd be very grateful if you'd expand on what you said at the meeting. You seemed to be taking a firm stand.''

''Oh. Yes. Well, I do—um—I do have strong feelings about it. I mean, it really is an important issue, don't you think? Well, obviously you do or you wouldn't be—um—the thing is, I don't think people are aware how the whole—um—structure of a community can be affected by . . .''

''Could you remember what you were going to say until I get there? I take better notes without a phone in my hand.''

''Oh. Of course.'' A pause. ''Of course. Um—we're a little—there are *things* going on—you know—Saturday—but I'm sure we can find a corner—''

Ten minutes later Roberta opened the door of the woodsy, contemporary house that jutted out here and there, both at ground level and the one above, as though good ideas had come just too late to be ideally incorporated. She admitted me to an Amazonian jungle of potted and hanging ferns where Jordan Moss was on his way out into the chilly autumn in white shorts and T-shirt, zipping a case over his graphite tennis racket: October holds no terrors for those who are fit.

''Manners, Roberta,'' he said. ''Introduce me so I can say 'charmed' and kiss the lady's hand.''

''We've met,'' I said briefly, ''at a party.''

''I must have been sloshed.''

''Maggie Rome,'' Roberta put in quickly.

He kept the hand just a fraction too long. One of those. Made a vow no female would die in ignorance of his charm.

He swung out the door and leaned in again to say, ''Darling, you will find time to call the Shaws and make sure they'll be ready at five fifteen? I mean, in the midst of your preoccupation with all those matters of international importance?"

Roberta finally showed a spark of rebellion. "*I will call them*," she said, underlining each word with exasperation.

While she went, apologizing, to make the phone call, I sank into a foam rubber chair that closed around me like some giant amoeba, and spent the time looking around at the household furnishings. A bold Italian sofa, Early American coffee table, contemporary Swedish rug, old brass andirons next to an ovoid fireplace, pewter mugs on a single shelf, a large Japanese watercolor on one wall—the house seemed to have been assembled in spurts, separated by intervals during which the temporary enthusiasm for one period or style of decor had been abandoned and another embraced.

Roberta came in bearing grapes in a cut-glass bowl. She walked bent slightly forward, like someone not quite certain of the strength to remain upright.

"These," she breathed, setting them down carefully on the coffee table, "are Malaga grapes. They taste Mediterranean. I like to experiment with food, don't you? We all sort of fall into the habit of the same . . . *routine* kind of diet. You miss so much that way. Last summer I joined a discovery group—we met once a week in the city and made a tour of the small ethnic food stores. It was . . . really . . . quite a revelation. Out here we don't really take *advantage* of all the . . . the *diversity* of the city. So much to learn, if only people would—well, for instance, this architectural history tour—the marvelous old buildings we never even *see*, running to the theater or the restaurant—there was an article in *The Times* about the young man who conducts these tours; I clipped it out and last week I said 'Why not?' He took us down to Canal Street and we really *looked*, you know, studied those old buildings. A sense of . . . history—the history of the city—well. You wanted to ask me some questions."

With a fistful of grapes I was about to launch into the first of the obligatory school-related questions when a dark-haired boy of about seventeen, with his mother's large eyes and intense expression and his father's athletic body, clattered down the stairs from above and into the room, announced that he was late for the game, that he'd be back "sometime" and was gone.

Roberta called after him, "Take your key! And— Ricky—you won't stay out too late—?" The slam of the front door answered her. She sat twisted around, looking at the spot where she'd last seen him, her mouth still slightly open, then she turned back with an uneasy laugh. "I shouldn't do that. They resent being told. Especially these days, when they . . . *mature* so quickly. By the time they're fifteen they're . . . crystallized." She seemed to be in perpetual pursuit of the *mot juste*, as though every utterance were part of an oral exam on which she was being graded. "And they're so . . . busy. They're involved in so many activities. They have so many . . . commitments. I don't remember being so committed at that age. My daughter's completely absorbed in political science; she doesn't *think* about anything else. Greg went right into premed without any . . . hesitation. Michael knew he wanted architecture before he even got to Columbia. Their goals are so . . . defined. Not one of them ever . . . floundered." She looked half-proud and half-bewildered. "It must be their father's genes."

I thought of my own two undergraduates, swinging like pendulums from medicine to musicology to geology to acting.

"Don't knock it," I said, and before her train of thought could run onto another siding, I got down to my alleged interest in her position on the sale of the school property.

She wound her spasmodic way through a long, involved, and not very coherent explanation of why and how the property should be used for a senior citizens' residence. Admittedly I was not terribly interested, merely whiling away the time until I could somehow bring up the subject of Mathilda, but even in my apathy I recognized that Roberta was not, actually, a passionate believer in the senior citizens' cause, and had very little basis for assuming it was a viable plan. Her eyes wandered and she changed her position constantly as she searched, not only for words, but for justifications. It all sounded a little like a nun who had wandered into the wrong lecture hall and been asked to say a few words on the Importance of Fashion.

When she ran out of steam I thanked her and looked around with what I hoped was an appreciative expression.

"This house is so neat. So polished. I don't know how you do it. My place always looks as though I'm getting ready to move." A slight exaggeration, but how could she know?

"Oh," she said, immediately stooping and picking a thread off the rug, "it's all . . . it's a surface job. The . . . the tip of the iceberg. The house is falling apart. I haven't had very good cleaning help."

"Good God, you were lucky to find any at all. How did you manage that?"

"She . . . um . . . came to me through a friend. A nice girl. Very . . . very . . . cheerful and pleasant, but she . . . well, she cheated. I shouldn't say that; I don't blame anybody for cheating on housework, it's such a . . . demeaning job, nobody respects you for doing it, even if you do it well. It's the most thankless work in the world. Even *women* look down on the women who do it, we've all adopted the male attitude, what you do in the house isn't really *work*. You'd get more respect if you were a gas station attendant."

"I gather she mended her ways, though."

"Who?"

"Your cleaning help. You said 'she cheated.' Past tense."

"Oh." Roberta's prettily curved mouth snapped shut and her large eyes grew larger. She plumped up a cushion on the sofa, moved a book on the coffee table.

She knows, I thought. But if she knows, then she must know that *I* know, so why not say it? Unless . . .

"She left," Roberta said, with an odd little laugh. "Last week. She said she couldn't work for me anymore, because she was going to school on Tuesdays to study English. That was a lie, of course, because I heard later that she was going to start working for Phyllis Bianco on Tuesdays. That's the fourth one I've lost, and they all lied about why they were going. *I* know the reason; I don't have a job to go to. They don't want the lady of the house hanging around to . . . *supervise*. They just want to rush through the house in an hour or two and take their money and go. If you're home they have to spend at least four hours doing *something*. I tried staying out of the house while they were here, but buying groceries doesn't take that long, and how much time can you spend at the library? How many department stores can you go to, when you don't really *need* anything?" She gave a shuddering little laugh. "It's really . . . ridiculous. You pay them a fortune and—I was always so *nice* to them—listened to their family troubles—with Mathilda I even . . . pleaded with her to stay. Isn't it stupid to . . . humiliate yourself that way? She wasn't even very good. But at least she was *something*." She straightened up, a resolute look sitting awkwardly on her face. "I've got to have *someone*. I am not going to be a cleaning woman. I've wasted enough of my life. Everybody's doing something interesting. In a few years it'll be too late to start. It may be too late now." She sagged again. "Skills. You have to have skills."

She was so distraught, sitting there rearranging the grapes in the bowl, thin fingers, thin wrists sliding out from under the sleeves of a teal-blue shirt, that I had to make an effort to force the conversation back to where I wanted it.

"I had a cleaning woman once," I prompted, "who spent all her time on the phone with her boyfriends."

"Yes," she said vaguely, "some of them do that. Not Mathilda. I don't think she had a boyfriend. She hadn't been up here very long. When I asked about her weekends, it was always a family outing. To the beach, or to visit relatives. The one before that had a man who sometimes picked her up after work. But Mathilda always drove with—what's her name—a big woman. Of course, you never really know much about them. They tell you what they think you want to hear."

"I suppose, in a way, we're the enemy. That's why some of them have no qualms about stealing things from the people they work for. Though I've never had one who did. Have you?" Subtle as a bulldozer, Maggie.

"No," she said, "not stealing. Unless—well, you could

say that cheating is a kind of stealing. And walking out on someone who depends on you. For no good reason. No good reason at all." She tore a cluster of grapes with such force from the central stem that loose grapes from the bowl were scattered over the coffee table, rolling about on the brown wood like tiny, pale green balloons. As she scooped them up, clucking at her clumsiness, the telephone rang and she went to answer it, clutching grapes in both hands.

I stood up to go. I had learned little about Mathilda and more than enough about Roberta, but there didn't seem to be any prospect of an improvement in the ratio, or in the value of the information.

"How big a platter?" Roberta was asking her telephone. "I have one that's—oh, definitely big enough for that. No problem, I'll—no, I'll bring it over—we'll drop it off on the way to pick up the Shaws."

There was a clatter of china, and she returned, minus the grapes, carrying a large platter that looked very much like Royal Worcester. I wondered how our quaint suburban customs would appear to foreign eyes: borrowing the neighbors' china, all social plans an open book— Did they do that sort of thing in the outskirts of Alexandria, Auckland, Madrid?

"Well, thank you," I said, "for your time and your comments."

"I hope I didn't . . . say anything that . . ." She made a little face. "When you know something you said is actually going to appear in *print*—"

"I'll send you a copy beforehand. If there's anything you don't like, we'll strike it," I promised, thinking of the phone call I'd have to make saying Greenfield had scotched the article. What a life of deception I led, worse than any cleaning woman.

She followed me into the front hall, carrying the platter. "I'd better leave this here so I don't forget it. Naomi's having a dinner party. We had to . . . decline because we have theater tickets. I hope Jordan doesn't mind the detour. He's so . . . obsessive about timetables."

"Naomi Gardner?"

It had often occurred to me that coincidence is much

more rampant in real life than in fiction. In my case the coincidence was usually to my disadvantage, and this was a pleasant novelty. "I drive by the Gardners' on my way home. I could easily deliver it for you."

9

IT WAS FOUR blocks, north and east, to the Gardners'. I drove carefully, one eye on the platter bumping along on the seat beside me. It was a pretty platter, traditional, pleasant, a little sentimental. I wondered to what extent people are defined by their possessions.

A flagstoned path, bordered by dormant azalea and hydrangea bushes, climbed the long slope to the Gardners' front door. Backed up against a considerable rise of wooded land, the long, low, many-windowed house, with a sun deck at one end and three chimneys in a row, looked somewhat like a small redwood ocean liner unaccountably beached among dogwoods and maples standing in beds of pachysandra.

I was still a few yards from the door when it opened and Leonard Gardner's tall and solemn presence filled the opening. He stood half-turned toward the house, one hand on the outer knob, and said to someone inside, "I didn't hear you. Pick up what?" He stepped back into the house, leaving the door open, and I could still see the back of his tennis sweater and slacks, and the racket case he carried. (Do *all* husbands play tennis on Saturdays until the snow falls?)

"Naomi. You were just down there. You bought everything in the store." Leonard somehow gave an oracular tone to the least elevated subject. "How did you manage . . . to overlook a six-pack of tonic water?"

A very brief reply from inside.

"We'll manage without tonic water. We have plenty of ginger ale. There's nothing wrong with ginger ale. We also have club soda. This isn't a bar, Naomi. We're not running a bar here. We don't have to stock every drink under the sun. If they don't like what we're serving they'll just have to make do. When we go to someone else's house we drink what's available. Nobody's going to sulk because they can't have tonic water. In fact, I'd be very surprised if anyone even *asked* for tonic water. It's not the time of year for tonic drinks. It's not as though this were summertime, when people drink vodka and tonic or gin and tonic. I'm just going to be making an unnecessary trip for six bottles of tonic water that nobody's going to drink. I guarantee, when the party's over I will have to carry six bottles of tonic water downstairs and nobody will look at them until next summer. I'll go if you insist but I *know* you're not going to need it. Unless you want it for yourself. If you have an urgent need for tonic water then say so, but if . . ."

Leonard's speech patterns, familiar to me from frequent Village Board assignments, had the unfortunate effect of filling me with a terrible ennui. His habit of playing endless dull variations on the same dull theme made my mind wander. I was afraid if I stood there much longer I'd simply let go of the platter and it would smash into fragments on the flagstones.

"Then you *don't* really need it. I thought so." Leonard turned and came through the doorway, looked down at me from up there behind his tinted glasses, with the small, impersonal smile a high priest might bestow on a vaguely remembered acolyte. I wondered which had come first: had his height given birth to his pomposity, or had some Messianic delusion in early childhood urged his hormones to keep pushing him upward?

"I have something for Naomi," I said.

"Oh. Fine. She's inside." He waved me in and proceeded on his long stalks of legs down to his two-car garage.

I stepped into a small foyer hung with a few framed Impressionist prints and turned right, through an archway into a long living room carpeted in Mediterranean blue, with traditional sofa and armchairs in complementary shades of blue and violet, a bricked, brass-screened fireplace, discreet lamps, large circular brass coffee table, a picture window, and French doors slatted by vertical blinds, looking onto a terrace and the back garden. The fabric of the sofa was worn in places and the chairs could have used re-covering, but there were new embroidered cushions in peacock colors stacked in the corners of the sofa, a bowl of perfect yellow chrysanthemums stood on the coffee table, and everything that could be was polished and shining beyond the call of duty.

It was a room in which someone with fastidious standards but no time or patience for home decorating had made a hasty but intense effort to compensate for its flaws.

The fireplace stood between two archways, one the entrance from the foyer, the other an entrance to some room from which came the rattling of silverware, interrupted by the sudden ring of the telephone. I heard Naomi's voice: "Mr. Pinestra? About time. Listen, that shower you supposedly fixed is leaking again; I want you to come over and get it *right* this time. Any evening. Next Saturday, then. You don't work on weekends? Hey, good for you, Mr. Pinestra. *I* don't have *any* days off, so I'll be here next Saturday waiting for you." She clicked the phone. Rapid heel-taps passed over linoleum.

I rounded the fireplace and went through the far archway into a room with cantaloupe-colored walls featuring a long walnut dining table laid with brown woven place mats and more chrysanthemums. Through a doorway at the far end I saw Naomi peering into an open oven, poking with anxious, hostile stabs at something from which rose an appetizing, steamy smell of clove and garlic and beef juices. She pushed it back, shut the oven, shot from counter to sink to refrigerator with containers and utensils, slamming, shoving, jabbing, as though repelling an enemy attack. Suddenly she rushed back to the phone, dialed.

"Jeff? How are you, any better? Getting your medication? Listen, don't waste time while you're in there, write me a novel called 'Life in a College Infirmary,' and I'll get it published. I found you some more sweat sox.

Anything else you want me to bring you? No, it's not, that's what 'mother' means. Go to sleep. Get lots of sleep. I'll see you tomorrow."

A timer went off with an insistent burr. She sprinted to the stove, turned off the flame, put the pot on a cool burner, marched into the dining room and grabbed up the silverware she had dropped earlier. Stained shirt, wrinkled jeans, hands rough, nails chipped, face patchy with tension, lion-colored hair a little greasy—I could hardly believe this was Naomi Gardner.

She froze, incredulous at the sight of me, her eyes going from my face to the platter and back again with wild lack of comprehension.

"From Roberta," I said quickly. "I happened to be there when you called and I was passing by—".

"Oh. Oh. Wonderful. Thank you." She flashed her friendly smile, dropped the silverware once again and took the platter from me, gripping it like a passenger on a roller coaster clutching the safety rail.

"Leonard let me in." (I don't go barging into people's houses.)

"Fine. Thanks." She was breathing quickly and shallowly, wasting no words because every breath counts, take one too many and you might find yourself short when you need it most. With a taut, jerky movement, she put the platter down on a wheeled serving cart. The telephone rang. She whisked out of the dining room to the phone in the kitchen.

"Yes! Milly? What happened? Actually agreed to put him on? You're sure it was Cavett's office? Great! Really great. Bob going to play shepherd? Not me, Milly. Impossible. I have to carry that DeWitt woman over to the Francis show. Yes, Tuesday. Eleven forty-five. Total clash. No. I promised. She trusts me. Won't leave the Alexander without me. I'm the one got her safely to every engagement for two weeks. She doesn't believe anyone else knows which way the streets run."

There was the sound of someone hurtling through the house and a girl of about sixteen, in a bathrobe, her wet brown hair streaking her face, burst into the kitchen from some unseen aperture.

"Dad?"

"He's gone." Naomi hung up the phone and quickly went for another look at the oven.

"Gone!" the girl wailed. "Oh *God*! He's got my *hair blower* in the car!"

"Use a towel, Amy."

"A *towel*! God! They're picking me up in twenty minutes! God!"

"Amy!" Naomi's voice flew out of control but she caught it and stuffed it back into its cage, where it beat its wings against her throat. Quickly she put an arm around her daughter, kissed her cheek, led her out whence she had come, with a few murmured words, and returned just as the phone rang again. She grabbed the receiver, free hand clenched into a fist, a muscle twitching in her jaw.

"Directions? Of course. Marvelous at giving directions. Dinner may not be much, but directions will be superb. Leonard is out and he's custodian of directions. He'll call you, okay? Looking forward."

She raced to the sink, turned a faucet, flung open a cupboard door, took a bottle from a shelf, a pill from the bottle, filled a glass, drank down the pill, checked a pot on the stove, hurried back into the dining room, besieged, and saw me. Still there.

"Can I help?" I asked, to account for my presence. "I couldn't be more sympathetic. I'd rather walk from here to Boston with pebbles in my shoes than give a formal dinner party. Especially without help."

"Help?" She gave a short, high-pitched laugh, like a dog's yelp. "Help! There's no such thing. Where've you been? They promise by every saint in churchdom they'll be here when the day comes. . . . ." She flung out an arm. "You see anybody helping? Oh, it's marvelous." She mimicked a self-pitying whine, " 'Mrs. Gardner, I can' come tomorrow, I have to go with my cousin.' *Every* week for *six* weeks I reminded her about today. 'Oh yes, I be here. Yes, yes.' Listen, it's a lovely world we live in. Terrific setup. If you're conscientious, responsible, moral, ethical—you get stuck, you get a knife between the ribs. If you're deceitful, self-indulgent, amoral—you've got it made. Next time they hand out the sense of responsibility, I'm going to pass. Next time around, I swear I'm going to be a domestic or a plumber.''

"Roberta said your domestic was a nice girl, she was sorry to lose her. It *is* the same girl?''

"Everybody's nice when they're young and healthy, nobody but themselves to think about, do what they like, *when* they like, *how* they like.'' She stopped suddenly and gave me a puzzled look. "I didn't know you and Roberta knew each other.''

"Actually, I was there on business. I'm doing an article on the sale of the school building.''

"What did she say?''

The question surprised me. She of all people would know Roberta's views.

"More or less what she said at the meeting. As a matter of fact, I was hoping to get some quotes from you—but this is hardly the time.''

"I'm not in favor of selling to the Brant Institute, I can tell you that much.'' She plunked down a final fork, suddenly remembered something, whispered, "Son of a . . .!'' raced into the kitchen, flung open the refrigerator.

I left, my offer of help disregarded as I'd expected it to be: everything had already been done, every inch of that house had been cleaned and polished and straightened, every flower arranged, every carrot scraped, every green bean Frenched, every mushroom trimmed, by Naomi Gardner alone. In less than two hours she would be dressed to the teeth, velvet-skinned, silken-haired, wafting a trace of Je M'en Fou through the room, and filled with implacable anger.

She doesn't want to be there, I thought, as I went down the flagstone path, doesn't want to be in that house, doesn't want to be entertaining guests, and works all the harder for fear her attitude will show in a slipshod meal or a speck on the rug. Naomi's fanatic effort to appear the perfect hostess she never wanted to be reminded me of Graham Greene's description of a character's "disguised poverty": *The effort needed to polish his shoes, to press the suit. . . . He couldn't, like the young, let things go.* Naomi couldn't, like the happy hostess, let things go.

No wonder she raged at Mathilda's eleventh-hour

desertion. I wondered how she would feel about her harsh words when she discovered what had happened to Mathilda. And how Roberta would feel. And why it was they didn't know: why Jessie, who had shared the girl with them, who obviously knew them more than casually, hadn't called to tell them.

An unlikely trio in any case. Jessie, Naomi, Roberta. What could possibly have made companions of three so diverse personalities?

10

"VOLUMES," I TOLD Greenfield over the phone, "I have learned volumes. Anything you want to know about Jessie Lucas, Naomi Gardner, or Roberta Moss I can tell you. About Mathilda, nothing new or startling. She has lied, she has cheated on the housework, which means leaving dirt under the sofas and dust on the picture frames, she has let people down, made promises she didn't keep— all perfectly normal, as you would know if you hadn't been spoiled by Mrs. Lacey. On the other hand, she didn't steal, just picked discarded things out of wastebaskets, and there's no evidence of a boyfriend. Do you happen to know if there's anything fishy about the Brant Institute?"

There was a silence and then Greenfield said dryly, "How about a few statistics on the state of the British economy? Or the names of the ships currently in port in Hong Kong? There are any number of irrelevant topics we could discuss."

"It's just that I've had some strange reactions to the business of the school sale—never mind why it came up."

"If the Village Board had discovered anything sinister about the Brant Institute, the proposal wouldn't have reached the stage it's at."

"Leonard Gardner is *on* the board, and it was his wife who made the insinuation."

"What did she say? Exactly."

"Well, it wasn't so much *what* she said. Never mind. I'm probably seeing scandal where there isn't any."

"You haven't mentioned Mrs. Bryce."

"I haven't seen Mrs. Bryce. And I'm not likely to. I think Mrs. Bryce is computerized. I think she's dressed and instructed by some programmer in the morning and goes through the day repeating the same two dozen words in different combinations."

"This is all very colorful, but hardly enlightening. I'm leaving in a few minutes. I'm going visiting and I won't be around until Monday."

"Have a nice time." Visiting. That could mean one of his three grown daughters, or Madame X, the sometime companion of whose existence I had no concrete proof, but nevertheless knew he had hidden away somewhere; not so much a necessity as a comfort, an occasional pleasure, like a favorite sweater or a special dish.

"You're going to transcribe your notes, I hope, before you forget what they mean?"

"I *never* forget."

"Debatable. Include everything. Not only the conversation, not only what was said about the girl. I want those 'volumes' you learned, however you learned them."

"About Lucas and Moss and . . . ? Why do you want that? I mean it's interesting, if you're planning an ethnographic study of Sloan's Ford, but it's not going to tell you anything more about . . ."

"Just leave it on my desk when you're finished."

"That's going to be a lot of typing!"

"Not all of life is pleasant."

"You know, Mr. Greenfield, *The Times*, the *Post*, and the *News* have all offered me big money . . ."

"You wouldn't be happy with them." He hung up.

I took the typewriter and the Eaton paper from their hiding places in the hall closet. One of these days when the first of the boys had reached the inevitable need to shake the dust of Putney Lane from his heels, Elliot would insist on turning his room into a proper study for me, with a desk of my own, and shelves for all the tools of my trade. And I would still use the dining room table, because I liked being able to look out at George in the yard, rolling in the grass in some private happiness, or just sitting snootily surveying his domain. And George, of course, would always be there. Anything else was unthinkable.

After an hour of typing I got up to stretch, and found the niggling curiosity about the Brant Institute had been lurking in a back corner of my mind, waiting for an opportune time to sidle up and give me another poke. I could not bear unanswered questions. It wasn't, alone, what Naomi had said, it was Roberta's artificial sponsorship of the senior citizens, it was Agnes Bryce's utter refusal to discuss it—and that led to another question. The one I'd forgotten to ask—earlier that day.

I went to the phone and dialed Jessie Lucas' number. A low, gravelly voice said, "Lucas Car Wash and Art Gallery, we also cater American Legion picnics and interracial weddings." I asked for Jessie and she came to the phone.

"The prodigal son?" I asked.

"Still suffering an occasional sophomoric hangover, poor thing. What can I do for you?" The words "this time" hung in the air unspoken.

"I forgot to ask you something. Not really relevant, but it bothers me. How did Agnes Bryce get into the picture where Mathilda is concerned? I can't see that kind of communication between Agnes and you, or Naomi or Roberta."

"I don't think I know how— Oh yes I do. That woman—that 'cousin' of Mathilda's—used to work for Agnes and they had a row and the woman walked out and passed the job on to Mathilda."

"Oh, that explains it. Thanks. By the way, I took your advice and saw Naomi and Roberta, but I didn't say you sent me, and I sort of came in the back door because I wasn't sure they knew what happened to Mathilda. And Naomi said something as I was leaving that makes me wonder if there's something dubious about the Brant Institute."

"What did she say?"

That question again! "Just that she was opposed to it. She was pressed for time so I never found out why. I assume there's something not very kosher about it."

"Not that I know of. Could be, of course."

"Then that's why you were against the sale? At the meeting?"

"Me? Oh, I just like to shoot my mouth off. Old actresses never die, they just wait for public meetings. Josh! That's not white wine, it's vinegar!" Her voice came back to the phone. "Good Lord, do you suppose they drink *vinegar* in the East Village? I knew about tofu, but— Well, I must take a bath."

I cradled the receiver and stood there staring down at it. Maybe I was wrong and there *was* nothing to find out about the Brant Institute. But something told me there was, and that everyone knew but me. It shouldn't have bothered me. I've always wished to be the kind of person who is so clearly above the concerns of ordinary folk that not to be privy to the current gossip is merely a further mark of my distinction: my own person, going my own way. But there you are, God made Gauguin and George Sand, and then, after He'd run out of that particular material, He made me.

Back at the typewriter, I mulled over Jessie's allusion to old actresses. That was one aspect of her life I didn't know anything about, except that it had been an aspect. When, for how long, and why no longer? Curious. At this rate Greenfield would get his report sometime around Halloween. I attacked the typewriter.

Forty minutes or so of peaceful quiet, working away steadily in the slowly darkening house. And suddenly the silence was shattered by the sharp ring of the doorbell. I stopped with my finger on the M key, the entire day instantly wiped from my mind, replaced like a slide in a projector by the fear I'd all but forgotten. The house was dim, lifeless to an outside eye, no light visible from the front. The car was garaged. George had gone into the mud room; I'd heard his metal swing door clang a few minutes earlier. An apparently deserted house. Who could be ringing my bell at this hour on a Saturday evening but someone testing to see if the house was empty?

The bell rang again, sending cold needles along my nerves. Obviously it made sense to let it be known someone was home, but the thought of opening the door to some cold-eyed monster with a possible length of pipe in his pocket turned my every limb to lead. I went stiffly, slowly, carefully, toward the front door, like a drunk trying to simulate complete sobriety. I switched on lights as I went; possibly that would send them running before I reached the door.

It didn't. There was a shadowy figure out there, head bent, shoulders moving, searching for something. A weapon? With fingers like pieces of frozen dough, I quietly put the chain across the door and switched on the outside light.

It was Elliot.

I undid the chain and threw open the door.

"Elliot!" I cried in amazement.

He looked mildly surprised. "I told you I'd be home around this time."

What could I say, "I forgot"? One doesn't say that to one's husband.

"I know, I know, it's just—I'm so . . ."

He picked up his old brown suit carrier and briefcase and came into the house, leaning forward to brush my cheek with a kiss. "Thought you were out. I was just looking for my key. You look as though something's scared the hell out of you." He said it comfortably, taking off his rumpled jacket and yawning. "Air travel is no way of life for a tired man. Heard from the boys?" He sorted through the mail on the hall table.

"Not since you left, but they're fine. Everybody's fine, I'm fine, George is fine, the house is fine, the car is fine." I quickly took care of all his primary concerns. "But, Elliot, our whole world is crumbling. I don't like this part of the century. I want to go back to those days when people sat on their front porches with mockingbirds singing in the honeysuckle vines, watching Tom Sawyer whitewash his fence."

He rubbed at his gray-flecked, tightly curled hair and yawned again. "Another burglary?" he said.

"Oh, God, you're so far behind! Never mind, I'd better get some food together."

I postponed the lurid details of the last twenty-odd hours until after dinner when he was sitting in his big chair in the living room with George leaning against his leg periodically licking the knee of his slacks in ecstasy at his return. He listened quietly to the whole story, every so often unwrapping a chocolate mint from the dish at his side and popping it into his mouth.

"Well," he said finally, "if it will make you feel better, we'll have an alarm system installed." And then, in response to my silence, "Did I say the wrong thing?"

"The alarm is only a—a *gesture*. It's not a solution. Good God, people are breaking into our neighbors' houses and—committing *violence*! Aren't you—doesn't it make you *angry*?"

"It makes me concerned," he said calmly. "That's why I'm going to spend a thousand dollars or more on some equipment that's probably not worth more than fifty."

"But to have that kind of thing going on—here—to *live* that way—doesn't it make you . . ."

"Of *course* it's appalling. But it's a police matter, after all. There's not much I can do," he said peaceably. He was altogether a peaceable man, took things as they came. I never did understand it. What would he say if he knew that his wife was even now setting about to uncover the criminal? Probably shake his head peaceably and decide to call home at intervals during the day.

"Elliot, do you have some hidden aggressiveness? Something that only shows up on the job? Some characteristic I don't know about, that gets your adrenaline going?"

He smiled. "What a question, after twenty-three years." He yawned. "I keep telling you, there's an advantage to having a practical approach. It makes life much simpler."

Later, as I was sinking gratefully into sleep, and realized that the knots in my shoulder muscles had dissolved for the first time in two days, I wondered at the amazing sense of security provided by having one other human body beside you. One that belonged there.

"G. K. Chesterton," I murmured.

From Elliot's pillow beside me there was a faint "Mm?"

"Your 'practical approach.' Baloney. That comes from being hung up on science. Like the man said"—Greenfield would spit if I used "like" for "as," I thought sleepily—" 'It may be conceded . . . to the mathematicians . . . that four is twice two . . . But two is *not* twice one . . . Two is two *thousand* times one. . . .' "

His hand fumbled through the bedclothes to rest on my arm and he snored gently.

11

MONDAY MORNING BROUGHT a sky of uneven gray, sweeps of slate mingled with patches of pearl. On a distant hill a plume of tangerine and dull gold foliage burned somberly against the gray. There was a faint, smoky dampness in the air and the forecast spoke hopefully of showers.

At nine A.M. Greenfield arrived at my front door in brown tweed jacket, green-and-brown plaid shirt, the brown corduroy pants, and a thoughtful, not to say bemused, expression. He'd read what I'd left on his desk the day before (using my key and running into and out of the empty office in record time) and was on his way to Superior Sound in what he was certain was a vain attempt to duplicate the unique qualities of his stolen stereo.

"A few things to discuss with you," he said, and sat himself down at my breakfast table in the kitchen, absolutely refusing coffee or anything else. "The police, so far, haven't been able to come up with any connection between the girl who was killed and any individual or group who might possibly have committed this burglary. And I'm fairly certain," he added, not without satisfaction, "they never will. Apparently the girl had no relatives in this country. The woman who called herself a cousin is merely a compatriot from the same town in Guatemala. And that woman's whereabouts at the time have been verified by whoever employed her that day. The girl lived with the woman and the woman's three young children, paying, no doubt, a good few dollars for room and board. The girl hadn't been here long enough to make friends of her own, especially as she worked double shifts five days a week—in the evenings she and the woman cleaned offices in Manhattan—this woman could one day conceivably *own* offices in Manhattan—and on weekends the girl helped the woman around the house. Social life consisted of going to visit the woman's brother and his family. The police—to use their quaint phraseology—are checking him out, but he lives and works in Queens, and I can't see the advantage in his making a round trip of eighty miles, with the price of gasoline what it is, for anything less than a bank robbery." He watched me eating sprouted wheat toast and marmalade. "Sweet domestic glop?"

I showed him the Chivers label on the marmalade jar and he took a piece of toast and spread marmalade on it.

"Marmalade," he said, "without the rind, is like Balzac in a translation by Walt Disney."

"The police *gave* you all this information?" I asked. "How did that happen?"

"I'm a crime victim. I have a right to know what they're doing to recover my property."

I gave him a look loud with disbelief. "I think they're buying your cooperation. You traumatized Pratt two years ago and he's afraid you're going to do it again."

"You can't traumatize a boulder. In any case they're telling me only what they don't mind my knowing. They're going to waste a lot of time 'checking out' those people in Queens. I *told* you Pratt was going to squirm around hoping to find a solution to fit his preconceptions. He's far from ready to admit that what happened has nothing to do with the local burglaries."

I was just as far from it as Pratt. I looked down at my cup, swirling the half-inch of Sanka left at the bottom. "Charlie—I've been through these investigation rigmaroles twice before. It may add a fillip to my relatively uneventful life, but it also adds a lot of wear and tear. If I'm going to run around making enemies and it doesn't lead to catching the burglars . . ."

"You'll at least have the comfort of knowing the worst that can happen is loss of property, inasmuch as the local burglars have never been violent."

"So far."

"The earth," he said with elaborate patience, "hasn't bumped into the sun . . . so far. The West Coast hasn't broken off from the continent and drifted out into the Pacific . . . so far. I can give you a long list of things to worry about, if that's how you want to spend your time."

I immediately saw California becalmed in the middle of the Pacific Ocean, all those power-crazed executives at M-G-M and Columbia wondering how they were going to make the red-eye flight to New York in time for their breakfast meetings in the Oak Room of the Plaza.

"So far," Greenfield continued, "the only violence was committed on Friday, and it was no burglary. The stereo was taken for the same reason a fugitive wades into a river—to confuse the pursuing pack. I agree with Pratt that the girl must have opened the door. And I'm convinced she opened it because she knew the person who rang the bell. She didn't know that many people. Who, of the ones she knew—aside from the self-styled 'cousin'—was in a position to know she'd be at my house that day?" He brushed toast crumbs from his fingers, reached into a pocket for the typed pages I'd left on his desk, put them on the table, and looked down at them. "I can think of five possibilities. These four, and Dina Franklin."

My impulse, of course, was to say, "You can *not* be serious." But why bother, of course he was serious. Hadn't he twice before come up with a list of suspects that made me wonder if there'd been a disturbance in his cerebral cortex?

I knew by now that my knowing, or even liking someone, did not automatically render that person incapable of committing a crime. But *this* crime? I chose my words carefully. "You're talking about five sane, rational, ordinary, respectable suburban women."

"I'm talking about"—he tapped the first of the typed pages—"a woman who spends a good deal of time executing grotesque paintings full of a profound hatred of something or someone"; he flipped a page; "a woman you described as being programmed by a computer"; flipped another page; "a woman so low in self-esteem she's convinced that everyone else is superior, even her cleaning woman"; another page; "a woman so angry and paranoid she can barely unclench her teeth"; he put down the typed pages; "and a woman so full of her own importance there's nothing she would consider beyond her ability or her right." Wryness raised one corner of his mouth. "Try describing them again."

I shook my head. "Not murder."

He snorted. "Nothing triggers such murderous anger as the treachery of someone on whom we depend for our well-being. It's no accident that in the unexplained death of a husband the wife is the prime suspect. And, of course, the other way around. Children kill their parents. And the other way around. Employees have been known to shoot—or stab—or bludgeon—their bosses. And sometimes—the other way around."

I still shook my head. "There are some things certain kinds of people can't do. It's a matter of . . . background, training, social orientation, a way of thinking. Not a cleaning woman. Never. They could *feel* like killing her. *I* have. But they couldn't, actually, do it."

"Mencken," he said, "had the only answer to a baseless conviction: 'You may be right.' The fact remains, if we're going to go on with this we have to use what information we have, and what we have is the knowledge that any of five women, familiar to the girl, so that she'd open the door to them, could have known where that girl was on Friday."

"True. They all could have known. Friday is a good day to have help, just before the weekend. Everybody wants Friday. Any of them might have asked her to switch her day to Friday. Especially knowing Dina was going to be out of town. Incidentally that eliminates Dina."

"If she was actually out of town."

"Oh come on, Charlie!" I laughed. "All that compli-

cated planning in advance? Telling everybody she was
going to be out of town in order to establish an alibi?
Even if you accept murderous anger at a cleaning woman
as a motive, it doesn't last that long!''

"You make so many categorical statements." He stood
up, looked at his watch. "We can worry about Franklin
later. Gardner, Moss, Bryce, and Lucas give you plenty
to start with."

"Start *what* with?"

"You're becoming moderately crafty at this kind of
thing; it shouldn't be too difficult to find out where they
all were between ten and one on Friday."

I waved my hand airily. "Don't give it a thought. I
could probably find out where Judge Crater went if I had
a week off."

Greenfield started for the front door. I followed.

"First of all," I said, "Naomi Gardner couldn't have
been in the neighborhood, she has a full-time job in the
city. Secondly, even if she took a day off, the police must
have been to see all of these women by now, and if they
didn't know about Mathilda before, they do now, which
means they also see through that baloney about the article
on the school sale, and doors will slam in my face with
the speed of light, never mind the natural resistance to
divulging one's timetable to anyone who has no business
asking! And as for Agnes Bryce, she wouldn't even let
me get near her *before* this! So my question is—how?"

"When it became clear to Crusoe," he said, opening
the door, "that there was no Hilton Hotel on the island,
he discovered an attribute called ingenuity. It's still
around." He went down the walk.

Crusoe. I shut the door. Anybody can build a *shelter*.
Let's see him trace the movements of four highly mobile
suburban women without their knowing about it!

I cleaned up the remains of breakfast, distressed by
Greenfield's assumption that any of those women could
be suspect. All the theories and statistics ever formulated
or compiled could not convince me. But rage; rage had
certainly been evident in Naomi's dining room. And in
Roberta's tearing of those grapes. Genuine rage. People
don't rage against someone who's no longer among the

living. Unless they were doing it to mislead me, make me think they didn't know about Mathilda. False rage based on genuine rage. Were they suspect after all? If Jessie hadn't told them about Mathilda, was it because she knew the information would have been superfluous? And had she warned them I might show up to ask questions? Had they been giving me a performance? And if so . . . I took George's leash from its hook on the mud room wall, and went for a walk.

We strolled up and down the quiet hilly streets, the roadway speckled with fallen leaves, shreds of rust red and walnut brown that had drifted gently down, in the mild moist air, from the old, wide-branched overhanging trees.

The streets were very still: no cars, no kids, no sign—except for the postman in his blue-gray outfit with the mail sack swinging from his shoulder—of human presence. The flat top of a privet hedge had been adorned with a paperback copy of *The Scarlet Letter*. Picked up from the road, no doubt, where it had dropped from some student's overloaded arms and placed on exhibit by some suburban archaeologist; relic of a vanished community. A community of unattended houses. A perfect target for thieves. Or killers. For whoever had gone up the stairway to Greenfield's rooms carrying something short, heavy, and potentially lethal.

One thing was certain: Greenfield would have to abandon his theories about those women if I proved they were elsewhere at the time. Where could they have been?

Naomi had been at work. No problem there. All I had to do was call that small independent publishing firm she worked for (What was the name? Someone had told me once. "One of those new outfits—five or six people doing the editing, the business end, the PR work, everything themselves." Garson King? Griffin Cowan? Something like that). Call the company and say I was the police and wanted to know where Mrs. Gardner had been between ten and one last Friday. A snap. Once I joined the police force. As for Jessie Lucas and Roberta Moss . . .

A black-and-white cat sitting on someone's front steps stiffened at sight of George and ran silently across a patch of bare ground, sending up a small cloud of dust. When was it going to rain?

I jogged down a hill. I was going to need every bit of vital capacity I could accumulate. Just *thinking* about trying to discover where Jessie and Roberta had been was a severe drain on my health. Neither of them had any fixed routine. Roberta's life was so unstructured and her interests so varied and unpredictable that she might have been doing anything from shopping around for a set of cloisonné-handled spoons to trying out group transcendental meditation. Jessie could have been painting, could have been jogging, could have gone to the city to see a rehearsal of the play her son was directing. Or to a museum, or a gallery, or a movie, or a marathon.

The most likely answer was that they had both been at home alone with no witnesses, cleaning out the refrigerator or hunched over a table writing long-overdue letters. Go prove it.

As for Agnes Bryce— The more I thought about Agnes Bryce the more I wanted to forget her. Where, oh, where, would Agnes Bryce go? To church to help with some cake sale? To the dressmaker to have one of the First Lady's dresses copied? To a meeting of the Committee for the Abolition of Alcoholic Beverages, Sex Education, and Singing in the Streets?

What a marvelous exercise this was going to be in how to waste time while increasing the blood pressure.

Glenbrook Place was as empty of life as the other streets. Jessie, Roberta, Agnes, myself: anomalies. A handful of homeowners left behind in the daily exodus.

I turned off Glenbrook to circle the big, abandoned school building standing there on its three controversial acres, surrounded by hills, and remembered the woman at the meeting who was so worried about children crawling through broken windows and being trapped inside. There were no broken windows, front, back, or sides, only the solid-looking boards and the aging brick and ivy. I pulled George away from a half-eaten pretzel hiding in the grass and started back to the house, trying to review, mentally, the things I'd seen and heard in the respective homes of Jessie, Naomi, and Roberta, trying to find some helpful allusion I might have overlooked, some casual remark, some reference, some object.

By the time I reached my driveway I had garnered three crumbs. One of them meant a trip upstate and one a trip to the city. It was too late in the day for either of those, but a trip to the library was easy enough.

I made the routine tour of what Greenfield called the "perimeter," went into the house, took off the old, comfortable navy blue pullover of Elliot's that I liked to wear for walking, got out of my flat, comfortable Wallabees, substituted heels and a heather-gray pullover of my own, and brushed my hair. I would have done none of this if I were going to the Sloan's Ford library, where the personnel consisted of people who had seen me in all manner of dress and condition: shapeless and bundled to the eyes in winter, sagging with the heat in summer, my hair drenched with rain, my nose red with a head cold; they already knew the worst. But the Sloan's Ford library was as yet too small and impoverished to provide the service I needed, and I would have to go to the Gorham library, which was older, larger, wealthier, and made no allowances for unseemly appearance.

I got into the Honda and headed north, the road a gray ribbon through the painted, wooded hills, the somber, broken gray of the sky backlit by a faint brassy light that turned the patches of autumn foliage to copper and flame.

The Gorham library, set like a jewel in a bed of green velvet lawn, had a chaste New England look: pinkish brick, white trim, large, bay-windowed reading rooms with soft armchairs and fireplaces; Wedgwood green walls of bookshelves, a smell of old, quiet money. I spent forty-five minutes sitting at a small table peering at the microfilm machine before I found what I was looking for, and then it was a disappointment. I learned the time and place where the daily architectural history tour began, the name of the tour guide, and the price of the tour, but no telephone number. The only way to speak with Ira Samuels was to appear at two P.M. at the corner of Canal Street and West Broadway, forty-odd miles away.

As I was leaving the Gorham library, a woman who could have posed for the female figure in *American Gothic* was returning a novel with a flamboyantly romantic jacket. What steamy depths of passion, I wondered, were concealed behind that relentlessly austere facade?

I saw the Gorham post office opposite as I left the library, and remembered that we needed a roll of stamps. Imposing flight of shallow stairs leading up to a suggestion of Greek Revival frontage, but the inside was not too different from the dinky one in Sloan's Ford: the Stamps window was closed and all customers were lined up at the Parcels window. I took my place, fourth in line, behind a T-shirted man with a black mustache and a tattoo on one bicep. The small, round-cheeked man attending the window had a jaunty manner and a penetrating voice and was obviously given to brightening the corner where he was. He flirted at top volume with the young woman he was serving and when she left he accepted a parcel from the woman next in line with boisterous goodwill.

"Well, well, what have we here! 'R. Bryce, Seaview, Florida!' Land of sunshine and oranges. I remember it well. Had a brother-in-law down in that area, very fancy, Palm Beach and all that, there's the place to be all right, how do you want to send this, my dear, regular parcel post is my advice, unless you want to pay a fortune— parcel post? *Very* good.''

I peeked around the tattooed bicep and it was Agnes Bryce, all right, neat dark suit and tidy little purse under her arm. Did she come here often, I wondered, like for instance last Friday between ten and one? Did she go to the Gorham library and take out novels with passionate jackets? She walked briskly on her way out, carefully tucking her change into her wallet. I decided she probably didn't read anything but cookbooks. I doubted she even had a library card. But then, I would have doubted the same of *American Gothic* if I hadn't seen her with the evidence. Preconceptions, as anyone but Greenfield would put it, are counterproductive.

Rolling south again on the gray ribbon, the hazy shape of an idea was forming, and by the time I reached Sloan's Ford it had come into focus. It all depended, of course, on the pertinence of the theory that a pressure cooker cannot keep its lid on without a vent.

I pulled into the parking lot beside the Sloan's Ford library, a small, boxlike space set in cement, where the low tables of the children's section crowded up against the librarian's desk and mobile carts were carrying the overflow from the inadequate shelf space. Funds for the building of a new library, long years in accumulating, were constantly being sought from government bodies, private industry, and the pockets of the local public, via benefit concerts and book fairs, the latter an imminent event yet again.

I walked through to the back, past a white-haired gentleman waiting to check out Thomas Mann's *Buddenbrooks,* past a young mother searching the floor for a lost yo-yo while two tiny preschool girls stood by clutching thin, flat picture books, past a bushy-haired woman in a plaid cape stooping intently over the card index. In a room at the back my friend Arlene was busy with the accessioning machine, stamping numbers on the pockets of new books and on the corresponding book and inventory cards.

"Kreutzer," she said, examining a book with a shiny white jacket splashed with black-and-green daubs, "you ever hear of a Solomon Kreutzer?"

"No, only a Sonata Kreutzer."

"It got some good reviews," she said, mystified. "I'm not going to take it home. I can't cope with sentences that are two pages long. I lose track." She stamped the pocket.

"Could you check," I asked her, "and see if someone named Agnes Bryce owns a library card?"

"I've had some strange requests in my time! What's this all about? Secrets, secrets!" She went to look and came back. "Yes, she has a card. So?"

"Arlene, I have to ask you an enormous favor." I told her what it was and she looked at me warily.

"This is a gag," she said.

"Serious."

"I can't do *that*! It's illegal—I think."

"I promise you'll get it back in two days. You can cut it up and throw it away. Nobody's going to use it. There's no risk."

"What if that woman comes in here and makes a fuss?"

"Say it was a mistake. Say someone with a similar name lost her card, came in to get another one, and that new girl at the desk thought she said 'Bryce' instead of 'Rice' and made it out from the Bryce registration in the file. When the lady pointed out the mistake, the girl made out still another one, in the lady's correct name, but left the Bryce card lying on the desk, and when I took out a book I picked it up instead of my own."

"I never knew you had such a diabolical mind."

"A recent acquisition. Arlene, come on."

She shook her head. "I can't."

"I wouldn't ask you if it weren't *very* important. You know that."

"What *is* it?"

"I can't tell you now. But I will, someday."

She looked unhappy. "I don't know—it's so *complicated*."

Ten minutes later I left the library with a card bearing Agnes Bryce's name. I had no qualms about using it as I planned. For Agnes to receive a phone call from Maggie Rome asking questions about the Brant Institute, followed only days later by Maggie Rome in person with questions about a library card, might be a little hard for Agnes to swallow—except for the fortunate fact that while it was my business to know *her* by sight, Agnes had no reason to associate my name with my face.

Somewhere beneath my sense of accomplishment was the knowledge that the small piece of plastic with its typed paper name tag might not get me the specific information I needed. But I decided, with Scarlett, to think about that tomorrow.

12

IF THE ALEXANDER HOTEL had been one of those commercial vertical cities with twelve hundred rooms and half the businessmen of Cincinnati, Des Moines, Seattle, and Montreal going back and forth at all hours, life would have been a lot simpler.

The Alexander was a small, genteel hotel just east of Fifth Avenue, with a hush over the cream-and-lavender lobby with its pastel chairs, Oriental vases, and potted trees, that disdained the vulgar clamor in the streets outside. In such hotels the staff knows immediately whether or not someone belongs in that cloistered establishment, and what's more, cares. As I made my way across lavender carpeting, the man presiding over the cream-colored reception desk, who had sparse sandy hair and a pale mouth like a fish, glanced up with a minatory frown, and I fully expected him to stop me at any moment and demand credentials.

When at a disadvantage, I told myself, pretend you own half of Connecticut. And proceeded with what I hoped was haughty self-assurance to where a tall, elderly couple, beautifully dressed and exuding the perfume of a large portfolio of stocks and bonds, stepped out of a noiseless elevator. While they tottered grandly to the reception desk, distracting the fish-mouthed reception clerk, I slid into the elevator and pressed the button for the fourth floor. Two minutes later I was knocking at the door of number 402, congratulating myself on having guessed correctly that it would be wise to call Laura DeWitt in advance from a corner phone booth and tell her Carson Griffith could get her a mention in an astrologer's column but he had to know her room number and Mrs. Gardner, who knew it, wasn't around.

The door of 402 opened. I don't know what I'd expected, but what opened the door was not it. I'd seen ads for Laura DeWitt's novel, *Janone:* huge quarter-page ads featuring mosques, oil wells, sinister male and female faces, and adjectives such as Lusty, Gigantic, and Riveting in boldface type. The face that appeared in the crack to which the door opened was pale, puffy, lined, weary, timid, and bewildered. It belonged to a small, plump woman in her late fifties whose chestnut hair coloring clearly had not been applied in a Madison Avenue salon. I thought perhaps this was the chambermaid, until I saw the checked flannel bathrobe.

"Ms. DeWitt?" I asked, taking no chances on status, married or single.

"Yes?"

"Hi! I'm Pat Goldman. From Carson Griffith. May I come in?" I hadn't seen Pat Goldman since we'd switched tank suits in high school.

Laura DeWitt opened the door cautiously. "I don't understand."

"Ten-oh-five," I announced, bouncing into the room, "we'd better hurry if we want to get to the taping by ten thirty."

"Ten thirty?" She clutched her bathrobe at the neck. "Oh, no, they said eleven forty-five. I'm sure they said eleven forty-five. I can't *possibly* be— Where's the other one? The other woman—what's her name?"

"Mrs. Gardner?"

"She was supposed to pick me up at eleven fifteen. I don't . . ."

"Are you sure? Somebody must have fouled up. I was told to be here at ten. Let me just check." I crossed the room with authority, sat down on a powder blue chair, opened the briefcase I'd brought with me, and shuffled the stack of papers inside. "Now where . . . ? Here it is. Don Corey show, studio six, ten thirty A.M." I slammed the briefcase shut just as Laura DeWitt moved closer to see for herself. She blinked, frowned, and looked worried.

"Didn't I already *do* the Don Corey show?"

"You couldn't have. It's right there on my schedule."

"I'm sure I did it the other day. A thin man with glasses. We had trouble with the microphone. I thought I was doing Arlene Francis today. I could have sworn . . ." She sat down wearily on the rose-strewn bedspread of the powder blue bed, shaking her head. "I have trouble remembering what day it is. If only I could go home. I had no idea it would be like this. It was hard enough just *writing* the book. It took five years. I was exhausted when I finished it. Then they told me I had to go on the road. 'We can make this book skyrocket,' they said. In the past three weeks I've been to fourteen cities. I'd never been out of Virginia before that. In Los Angeles they forgot to send a car for me and I was late to the interview. In Chicago the airport was closed in and we circled for two hours. In Indianapolis they put me in a bookstore to sign autographs and nobody came to the table except to ask if the store had a ladies' room. In Boston my flight was delayed and I had to sleep sitting up at the airport. In Minneapolis they lost my luggage. My stomach's upset. My clothes are all wrinkled and dirty. I'm too old for this."

"I'm terribly sorry about this mix-up, Ms. DeWitt, but we do have to straighten it out. Now they must have given you a copy of the schedule."

"Oh—yes—" She got heavily to her feet and went to a powder blue dresser covered with containers of hair spray, dusting powder and hand cream, loose change, face tissue, two copies of *Janone*, a box of corn plasters, and scattered sheets of writing paper. "Yes," she said, nervously pushing the papers around with two fingers, "I know they gave me a schedule, though I've never bothered with it because they're always calling me up to remind me in advance— Yes, this is the one."

I opened the briefcase again. "I think the quickest way to find out where we went wrong is for me to check your schedule against mine. Just read it out and I'll check it off, day by day." The logical procedure, of course, would have been for me to read it for myself, but that would leave her free to look over my shoulder while I presumably checked it against my own schedule. I really didn't think it a good idea for her to see the letter from the telephone company that was passing itself off as a schedule. As I'd hoped, she was too tired to question the arrangement. She read, and I made quick shorthand notes of the days, dates, times, and locations. After she'd given me Thursday's schedule she skipped to Monday.

"You left out Friday," I said.

"There's nothing here for Friday. Did I do anything on Friday? No, I remember. They said take the weekend off. I think I slept most of the time."

Thanks a lot, Laura DeWitt.

I snapped the briefcase shut and gave back the schedule. "Well, this is a worse mess than I thought. None of it checks with mine. Somebody got the signals crossed, or this was an earlier schedule that was later changed and no one told me. It's no good trying to do anything over the phone. I'll have to go right back to the office and straighten things out."

Laura DeWitt retied her bathrobe with clumsy fingers, searching my face anxiously. "What about the other woman? Will she be here at eleven fifteen? Is the Francis show still on?"

"Somebody will definitely be here," I promised her. "I'll take care of it in five minutes once I get back. You just relax."

I went to the door, marveling at the mysterious alchemy by which a diffident, unadventurous, untraveled, middle-aged woman was metamorphosed into the author of a "Lusty, Gigantic, Riveting" novel. The same dichotomy, I supposed, that would have the *American Gothic* lady taking it out of the library.

At the door I turned and said, "By the way, I'm sure you've heard this from a thousand people about your book, but I *literally* couldn't put it down."

Her tired face flushed pink and her eyes almost sparkled. "Why *thank* you," she said.

At least, I thought, going down in the elevator, the visit hadn't been a total waste of time for *one* of us. And I hadn't actually lied: you couldn't put down something you'd never picked up. Poor Laura DeWitt. I decided Naomi was in a self-defeating business. The goose that laid the golden eggs was the author's reflective nature.

Reflective natures are not meant to hustle in the market-place. But the eggs have to be hustled, and so the goose is violated. Eventual result: dead goose, no more eggs.

I held my breath, crossed my fingers, clutched my bag, and took a subway to Canal Street. It was an experience not unlike, I would guess, that of crawling through the sewers of Paris. I emerged begrimed and gasping for air. And as far, ethnically, economically, and emotionally, from the Alexander Hotel as pizza is from pâté. They should have saved those adjectives for Canal Street. Lusty. Gigantic. Riveting.

American history seemed to be etched into every old brick, every gaudy storefront, every ironstone facade, every second-story window scrawled in Greek or Hebrew or Chinese, that lined the swarming street. Selling was what Canal Street was all about: belts and borscht, screwdriv-ers and sandals, leeks and socks and baskets and pea pods, padlocks and underwear and saucepans and egg creams, knishes and scissors and seaweed and buckles—a gargantuan, panoramic market sweeping from river to river across the width of Lower Manhattan.

I made my way along the thronged sidewalk to the southeast corner of West Broadway, where three women and two men had gathered beside a hand-lettered sign proclaiming that Architectural History Tours started here. Fee paid and name and address given for future mailings of interest, I shuffled along with the others as Ira Samuels led us to our first historic site. He was a bony, balding, eager young man with a wide smile over a receding chin, brown eyes burning with intelligence behind thick eyeglasses, and a navy blue pinstripe suit that flapped around his thin legs as he walked. And he walked. And he talked. And he walked again. And we followed. To learn that there actually *had* been a canal once, where Canal Street now stood, which was lovely for the Dutch colonizers who were naturally less homesick as a result. To be shown gambrel roofs, and dormers, and federal lintels, and the eight-panel front door and leaded-glass transom and wrought-iron railings of the Henry Street Settlement. To have pointed out to us cornices and shut-ters and Flemish bond bricklaying. And more. Much more.

Two burning, blistered feet more.

When he finally bid us good-bye, back at the corner of West Broadway, I succeeded in snaring him for coffee and a sandwich by revealing that I was a reporter for a suburban magazine (which existed but had never heard of me).

"Doing a story," I said, looking without enthusiasm at the fried egg between the two slices of rye bread, "about commuter discoveries. Unusual activities that attract people in the suburbs to the city; not the ordinary theater-restaurant-concert stuff." I took a small bite of the sandwich: not bad. "And what I really want to get are a sampling of the reactions of people who have taken this tour—fascinating tour—I enjoyed it immensely." Not too much of an exaggeration, bar the feet.

"Everybody enjoys it," Ira Samuels assured me, picking at his Danish. "You see—it's *real*. It's the way people lived. It's reassuring."

"Of course, but I want to get it in their own words. Now if you could give me a few names—from different tours—say different days of the week—not too far back, so their memories will be fresh."

"Well, I do the same tour every day."

"Yes, but weather conditions, the number of people—it all makes a difference. Just four or five lists, say beginning last Wednesday, and I'll pick the names."

"Hey, listen, I don't know—this could be invasion of privacy or something."

"I'm *only* going to call and ask. They don't have to talk to me. Most people jump at the chance to get their names in print. And the publicity won't do *you* any harm." Something about the city seemed to sharpen my least endearing qualities.

When, eventually, he agreed, I expected him to say he'd mail it to me, but he opened the scarred and peeling black leatherette shoulder bag he carried, removed about a ream of paper, and proceeded to search through the sheets. Architectural Tours was a compact business.

"Thursday," he said, handing me a sheet. I scanned it quickly; no Roberta Moss. I took out my notebook and wrote down some name.

"Monday." Well, that didn't interest me at all. I wrote down another name.

"Friday." I grabbed it. No Roberta.

"Wednesday." There was Roberta. Wednesday.

"Is that enough?"

Yes, quite enough. More than enough. Two screaming feet and nothing to show for it. I wrote down a few more names for the sake of appearances, thanked him profusely, and went back down into the Paris sewers.

The train ride home from Grand Central, airless, endless, and creaking though it was, seemed like a canter through the Tuileries by comparison with the subway.

I stopped in at the office, not because I had anything to report, but in the hopeless hope that Greenfield might be on a new tack. In the downstairs office Helen was typing and Calli and Stewart Klein were arguing about who was responsible for the final sentence of his last piece not quite making it before the bottom of the page intervened. "I don't chop anything!" Calli declared. "Probably it got a blue pencil!"

Upstairs Greenfield had both elbows on his desk, one hand holding up his forehead, the other the telephone receiver.

"I'd say you have a cause for concern," he was saying, "not necessarily for alarm. If you can find the time, I'd appreciate your letting me know when you get news. No trouble."

He replaced the receiver, swiveled slowly away from the desk, to the usual screeching accompaniment, and looked me up and down.

"You look," he said, "as though you're about to ride to the hounds." This was a reference to the tweed suit, rust-and-black ascot, and mahogany-colored boots.

"Naomi Gardner dresses this way all the time," I said. "Most women dress this way every day in cosmopolitan circles. You've become accustomed to the boondocks, where we tend to go to seed and end up owning nothing but six pairs of jeans that all bag at the knees." I made a seat for myself among the stacks of news clippings and periodicals in one of the slowly decomposing armchairs.

"And what, other than wearing different clothes, were

you doing in cosmopolitan circles?"

"My job. Without success. You'd better call in Robinson Crusoe."

He seemed not to hear me. "In your opinion," he said slowly, "is Dina Franklin the kind of woman who might treat herself to an illicit weekend?"

"What?"

"Just give me an opinion."

"You know her better than I do," I said dryly. "You get private messages."

"I don't *know* her at all," he growled. "What's your opinion?"

"I'd say it depends. If you're talking about last weekend, no. If there was business to be done in St. Louis, no mere romance would keep her from it. Men may be necessary as spectators, but winning is all. Why, isn't she back yet? She could have been delayed. Things come up."

"That phone call," he said, "just before you arrived, was from Mr. Franklin. He said he'd found a note on her desk to call my office before she left for St. Louis. He wanted to know if I'd spoken to her on Wednesday. I told him she'd spoken to you."

"What's the problem?"

"She hasn't been home. What's more, he called the people she was supposed to see in St. Louis. They say she never arrived."

13

DRIVING THROUGH THE village the following morning toward the road that would take me north to Ruyskill, my mind was on Dina Franklin, but my eyes were on a group of men gathered around some surveying equipment at the end of a cul-de-sac formed by two facing rows of stores slightly angled in toward each other like an inverted V with a flat, rather than a pointed top. It was at the flat top, with its waist-high cement wall separating the street from the bank of the Sloan River, that the men were standing, and I could guess what it was all about: this end of town was in a hollow and on several memorable occasions the Sloan, swollen by sudden heavy rains, had overflowed its banks and flooded the nearby stores. Veal chops were drowned, loaves of bread submerged.

I pulled into a parking space, got out of the car, and went to see what I could find out. (I was still, when I had time for it, working on the *Reporter*.)

I noticed, among those present, Mr. Farnham from the hardware store, Jim Gillis from the luncheonette, and Fred Bryce, making points, with gestures. The hardware store and the luncheonette were in the disaster zone immediately adjacent to the river, but Bryce Realty was safely at the other end of the village. Was Fred Bryce involved only from a sense of community responsibility? Very laudable, if so.

One figure in the group was a head taller than the others: Leonard Gardner had evidently postponed whatever business awaited him in his city office in order to be in on what was happening here. I had a feeling it was less that he was a conscientious board member than that he liked to feel he was running things.

I learned from Jim Gillis that there were men here from the state Department of Public Works, and a district engineer, and that Fred Bryce had been responsible for forming a Merchants' Committee to demand state assistance to prevent future flooding.

"Good man, Fred," Jim Gillis said, and Farnham said, "He sure got them off their butts—excuse my French."

But Fred Bryce, civic hero, had been temporarily superseded. I heard Leonard Gardner's apostolic voice: "This river must be dredged! There are tons of debris in this river. Dead trees fall into it. Live trees fall in and root in the mud. In a bad storm the detritus from upstream floats down; pieces of sheds, tables, chairs, float down. They get stuck downstream and the water backs up and floods this area. The stores here have to shut down for weeks. There is enormous water damage . . . "

"I've already told them," Fred Bryce said in his quiet drawl. He flashed his winning Little League grin at the men from the state. "Nobody wants our merchants going out of business. Right, boys? It wouldn't look good for the state."

"So what you want here," one of the men said, "is a little dredging and maybe a short retaining wall?"

"We don't want a *little* anything," Gardner intoned. "We need an alternate flood basin, pumps to regulate the flow of water from that low-lying area upstream, not to mention a dam, and retaining walls at least twelve feet into the riverbed."

One of the state men laughed shortly. "How about the moon while you're at it?"

"There must—" Leonard Gardner looked down at his elbow where Fred Bryce's hand was clamping it.

"Let these boys figure out what we need. Leave it to them," Bryce said, in a pleasant tone that brooked no contradiction, like a door-to-door evangelist with muscles.

With a look of cold incredulity, Gardner jerked his arm free. His face flushed, his mouth and nose pinched, he looked the embodiment of Old Testament wrath: one did not dismiss Leonard Gardner with impunity. I suddenly realized he could be a nasty man when crossed.

"Leave it to them," he spat out, "and we'll get whatever plan requires the smallest appropriation of funds!''

"They wouldn't be here at all," Bryce said carefully, "if I hadn't arranged to get them down here."

"Did you get them down here," Gardner breathed fire, "to prevent flooding? Or to make political capital out of getting them down here?"

Bryce went very still, a half-smile caught in the dead white of his face. He slowly stretched his neck and his small eyes glittered, like a cobra about to strike. Gardner had aimed unerringly at Bryce's Achilles heel: the civic hero's good name had been attacked, in public. Malignity seemed to flash in the air between them. It was a tossup which one, at that moment, was more dangerous. They stared at each other, The Unassailable versus The Irreproachable, each ready to slay the other to protect his own image.

Flood control was now, obviously, of secondary importance; the contest of egos was not going to make way for newsworthy items for quite a while. I decided I'd had enough of simmering anger. There were entirely too many angry people around. I went back to the car, and set out again for the road to Ruyskill.

My thoughts, as I drove, veered back to Dina Franklin and the fact that she had never reached that office in St. Louis. What could have happened? There was so little to go on. When I'd called Howard Franklin to give him all I could remember of my last conversation with Dina, he'd said, with an admirable control that didn't quite mask his anxiety, that he'd checked hospitals, relatives, and friends, and nowhere had anyone seen or heard from her.

Disappeared? People don't disappear. Unless they're kidnapped. On the way to LaGuardia? On the way from the St. Louis airport to wherever she was expected? No one would kidnap Dina. In the first place she was no heiress, celebrity, or Italian politico. In the second place she wouldn't let them. No, Dina, while waiting for her plane, had met some Arab dripping oil profits, who had offered her an opportunity to design an entire city in Saudi Arabia, and the two of them had switched airports and taken off on the next flight to the Middle East. So caught up in the blazing professional status she would achieve, Dina didn't even pause to wire her regrets to St. Louis. What was an insignificant shopping mall on the Mississippi when visions of an entire sugarplum metropolis danced in her head? And she knew Howard would not be home from London for several days and so she hadn't sent him a cable until she'd reached Riyadh, and everyone knows about cables being lost in transit, especially in the Middle East where they have a few other things to worry about.

The fantasy became so real to me that I clearly saw Dina returning eventually to give a big dinner party featuring Arab cuisine and a colorful account of being driven across the desert in a gigantic Rolls-Royce replete with swimming pool and dancing girls.

Perhaps it would be just as well not to mention this explanation of her absence to Greenfield.

The highway to Ruyskill was an old state road, running through and becoming the main street of a series of small villages and towns, seedy and jerry-built; gas stations, luncheonettes, billboards, and supermarkets their main attractions. Ruyskill, though, was a museum piece. It had, in the nineteenth century, been a posh upstate resort: elegant white-painted hotels, their long porches lined with wicker rockers, spacious gabled houses, lush green lawns. Originally settled (as what wasn't?) by the immaculate Dutch, it was immaculate still, the hotels and houses freshly painted, the sidewalks neat and cared for, the storefronts sparkling, all of it having achieved a fine, period patina.

As a nostalgic curiosity, it attracted a good deal of domestic tourism from spring through fall, and it followed as the night the day that some enterprising young artists and artisans had set up shop on the outskirts. Here the well-preserved center of Ruyskill straggled off into countryside in diminishing density and prosperity, giving way to a scattering of modest old houses, clean but sagging, a row of small stores, and a few barns. The barns were neatly but cheaply converted for commercial use, with the word ANTIQUES either painted in large block letters on the side, or lettered quaintly on a hanging sign, the grass plots in front dotted with birdbaths, bentwood chairs, old settees, braided rugs, oil lamps, and cartons of chemists' bottles.

Nowhere did I see a sign of what I was looking for, but if I had to make inquiries the old, sagging houses seemed the most promising. One advertised Handmade Pottery, another, Fine Arts Gallery, a third, Soft Sculpture. I parked in front of a small grocery in the row of stores and walked back to the house that displayed in its bay window a variety of large squashy objects made of patterned cloth or materials of a solid, vibrant color, artfully shaped into human or animal caricatures.

I crossed a lawn, opened the door, a bell tinkled, and I walked into a large front room filled with more Soft Sculpture, some of it on the walls, some sitting on stools or tables, some supine on the white-painted floor. In a corner, eating a large oatmeal cookie and sorting through a pile of exotic fabrics, a large, round-faced, pale-haired woman with no eyebrows to speak of looked up and said, "Hi, can I help you?"

"Help is what I came in for, not to buy, I'm afraid. I'm looking for a woodworking shop. Handmade bowls, that kind of thing. It's supposed to be around here somewhere."

"Oh, you want Gunnar. I *told* him that sign's invisible." She came forward, wiping her hands on her green smock, a cookie crumb stuck to her lip. "He's out in back. I'll show you."

We went out across a patchy lawn to where a dirt lane ran between the Sculpture house and the Fine Arts Gallery. She pointed down the lane to a garage in the rear, painted barn-red. "You have to wander around to find places here. It's quiet today, but we still get people on weekends, and sooner or later they find all the shops. There's a gallery in a shed behind Gunnar, and a basket store over the grocery. You take any space you can get. Come back again if you want to look around. No charge for browsing." An eye out for business, that girl.

I walked down the lane, noticing as I drew closer to the garage, a carved wooden sign over the door: Woodart. Through the screen door came the whine of a sanding machine, but when I opened the door and called "Hello" it stopped, and a barrel-chested man with brown hair hanging down over his forehead, looking more stevedore than artist, appeared at the far end of a room in which tables and shelves were filled with wooden boxes, trays, candlesticks, lamp bases, and bowls ranging in size from small to gargantuan, everything beautifully grained and satin-finished in a variety of wood colors from deep reddish-brown to amber.

He gave me the Ruyskill greeting: "Hi. Can I help you?" He wore dust-covered faded dungarees and a washed-out blue T-shirt that matched his pale eyes.

"I think this is where my friend found that beautiful bowl." I gave him a confiding, rueful smile: Maggie the ninny. "I'm in terrible trouble. I saw the bowl at my friend's house and I admired it so, she gave it to me as a gift. I took it home with me in the car and like an idiot left it on the seat while I went in to get some groceries, and it was stolen. Nothing's *ever* been stolen out of my car. I couldn't believe it. Anyway, you can see the position I'm in, what she'd think of me if she knew I'd been that careless. I absolutely have to replace it before she finds out. It was a small bowl. Spalted maple."

He smiled, shaking his head skeptically and revealing a wide space between two large front teeth. "You can look around. I have all kinds of bowls. . . ."

"I want the exact same bowl. The spalted maple."

He went to a shelf, picked up a deep bowl curved in at the top like an unopened tulip. "That's spalted maple." He put it down and picked up a shallow bowl with a fluted edge. "That's spalted maple."

"No, it was smaller than either of those, and completely smooth, and not completely round."

"They're all different. Why don't you just pick one you like?"

I registered dismay. "But I have to have the identical bowl. Look, if you knew what it looked like could you *make* me another one like it?"

He shook his head again. "I doubt it. I get the shape from working the wood, not the other way around."

"But you could try. Do you remember selling a spalted maple bowl last Friday? If you remembered the sale you might remember which bowl it was."

Shaking his head seemed to be a favorite pastime; he did it again. "We had a lot of people in over the weekend."

I couldn't believe he'd had that many at this time of year, nor could I believe he'd made that many sales if all he did was shake his head.

"You could look it up. You keep a record of your sales, don't you?" I watched his head, half expecting to see it move left to right. Instead, he shrugged.

"All it would say is spalted maple bowl. That's not a description."

"Maybe you could tell from the price. Would you humor me and look it up?"

He smiled resignedly and went over to an old lectern against the far wall on which rested a thick canvas ledger.

"Friday?" he asked, flipping pages. "What date was that?"

I counted back and told him. After running his finger down a page he said, "I sold a lamp base on Friday, and a pair of candlesticks, and a twenty-inch fruitwood bowl. No spalted maple."

Well, there it was. I'd learned what I'd come to find out.

"I *know* she bought it on Friday."

"Then I guess she didn't buy it here."

Hope sprang. "Are there any other woodworkers in Ruyskill? Or *near* Ruyskill?"

He shook his head, smiling.

"I don't understand it," I said glumly, feeling fairly certain the sale was recorded there in the ledger on Thursday, or Wednesday. It would fit the pattern I was establishing.

I walked back to where the car was parked, went into the small grocery store, bought a container of orange drink, a piece of cheddar cheese, and an apple, and sat in the car munching, drinking, and congratulating myself on having avoided success in three consecutive searches for confirmation. I doubted that any professional sleuth could do better.

I could check the other studios; having come this far, Jessie would not have confined herself to the one shop.

But even if they remembered her, she would have had to buy something to pinpoint the day, and how did I know what, if anything, she'd bought? She *had* bought the bowl, and there was no record of the sale on Friday, and unless Gunnar cheated on his income tax by recording only half the sales (and I doubted he had enough income to warrant it), that was that.

The orange drink tasted the way I imagine a cheap perfume would. I stuffed the apple core into the container, dropped it in a bin, made a U-turn, and started home. Three down, one to go. Depending on where Dina Franklin had been on Friday.

By one o'clock I had reached the turnoff to the road that led directly to the center of Sloan's Ford, from which a left turn up a hill would take me to my destination. But keeping a course dead ahead would take me to the market road that in turn eventually bisected a back road leading to the same place; there was an advantage to the latter. I kept on to the market road and made a stop to replenish our store of onions, zucchini, and Bartlett pears, remembering my last visit there, string beans on the ground and Jessie coughing and offering to drive me home. It seemed as distant as childhood.

The back road, when I came to it, led past a warren of development houses, past the far end of the high school and down a steep hill bordered on one side by a neat, well-tended, somehow impersonal cemetery. I wondered for an instant where Mathilda was buried, then quickly shut the mental door I'd opened and concentrated on the students straggling home in twos and threes, carrying books. Another half-day? It never ceased to amaze me how many half-days the school schedule included.

A right turn brought me into a pocket of prosperous older residences, substantial brick houses with glassed-in porches, stiff shrubbery, stiff drapes at the windows. I checked the numbers and stopped in front of the largest and most prosperous, sitting on a corner plot with a high wall of privet guarding the considerable backyard. I looked for a Doberman pinscher—it seemed the kind of place that might have one—but saw no sign of dog or any other creature, until a group of high-school girls came down

the street, spreading across the road in defiance of any
vehicle that might want to pass.

There was something familiar about their half-defen-
sive, half-arrogant manner. I'd seen these same girls
recently . . . then I recognized one of them, the one who
had fallen off the bicycle a week ago. She wore the same
tight jeans, the same fringed jacket, a lot of eye makeup
and lipstick—only the big, round orange pin was missing.
As I watched, the girl parted from her friends, shouting
"Walk slow!" (Greenfield would have torn up her diploma
if she'd had one.) She ran clumsily in her high heels up
the path and into the house I was planning to visit.

So that was the Bryces' daughter. My first thought was
that her flagrantly sexy getup was surprising for a member
of that family. My second, that it was only to be expected;
at sixteen it was automatic to gravitate to the opposite
pole from the family's. Still, I'd be willing to bet she'd
remove the face paint and change the clothes before Papa
got home.

I left the car and followed in her steps to the front door.
It was not precisely a front door, but a glass and alumi-
num guardian door, opening onto a small vestibule that
protected the front door and the floors and carpets that
lay beyond it from rain, hail, snow, and dirt. A mat on
the floor, guarding even the guardian vestibule, said Wipe
your Feet. An unsealed cardboard carton, the words For
Mailing written on the side with a marking pen, stood
beside it as though someone had attempted delivery and
then just left the parcel.

I rang the bell and waited. There was no sound on the
other side of the door until the thumping of high-heeled
slides on carpeted stairs brought the Bryce daughter to
open it.

"Oh," she said. "Yeah?"

"I'd like to see Mrs. Bryce."

"She's not home." She turned a knob on the inside of
the door, came out into the vestibule and pulled the door
shut behind her.

"When will she be back?"

"I dunno. I just got home. You better call her on the
phone later." She opened the guardian door and peered

anxiously down the street. "I gotta go," she said, and ran off, losing one shoe in the process, hopping back to get it and taking off again.

I looked down at the carton. The top flaps were folded into each other to keep them rigid. I bent down and eased them free. The box held two foot-high stacks of 8 X 10 printed sheets headed C.M.G. NEWSLETTER. Clearly not private and one never knows what will prove to be informative. I removed one of the top sheets, folded it, put it in the notebook in my bag, folded the carton flaps back together, and left the house. I was already in the Honda with my key in the ignition when Agnes Bryce drove carefully into her driveway.

She got out of her shining-clean blue Ford, with its bumper sticker about our right to protect our homes, meticulously rolled up the window, testing it at the top with a finger to make sure there was no crack through which rain from the cloudless sky could enter, checked that all the doors were locked, and came toward the house carrying a brown grocery bag.

Agnes' body was a soft rectangle on legs. There were no sharp corners, but neither were there any curves or undulations. From shoulder to knee the maroon knitted suit seemed to cover some ambiguous padding without recognizable sex or function. The legs, on the other hand, were shapely and ended in reasonably attractive T-strap sandals. I couldn't decide whether these were the one secret vanity for which she atoned by giving up so much in other ways, or whether she would have covered them up if she could do it and still wear a skirt.

When she saw me approaching, her small blue eyes seemed to bulge a little more and her tiny, cupid's-bow mouth drew in at the corners. Her face had the bland, anonymous prettiness of an antique doll, the skin looked powdered even where it wasn't, and the faint pink dab of lipstick was confined to the center of the cupid's bow, a fence-sitting gesture. (I know what's being worn, but I'm respectable.) Her pale brown hair was pruned to the same perfect lifelessness as the foundation planting around her house. She was like some unimaginative child's drawing of a woman: the intention recognizable, the result lifeless.

Only the eyes were alive . . . and alarmed.

"This is lucky," I said, taking a shortcut across the lawn, to her horror. "I was just about to leave."

"I'm very busy." She moved fractionally in the direction of the house.

"Oh, this won't take a minute!" I opened my bag. "There was a mix-up at the library and I went home with your library card instead of my own." I took out the small plastic square and showed it to her.

"*My* library card?" She took the card and examined it, pained to think that any possession of hers had reposed in someone else's questionable handbag.

"So you must have mine," I said cheerfully.

"No! How could I? The last time I was there I stood right there while she checked out the books, and took back my card."

"A moment's inattention," I suggested.

"I don't even remember seeing you there."

"I wasn't. I mean not when you were there. I got there at ten A.M., checked out some books, and then walked out without my card. Later on I opened my wallet to pay for something and realized I didn't have the card, so I went back for it. The girl looked around, showed me this card, and said that was the only card she had lying around, someone had probably given you mine by mistake. My card must have been lying there when you came in last Friday and you mistakenly . . ."

"I didn't go to the library last Friday."

"It *must* have been Friday. That's when I left my card."

"I was right here last Friday waiting for the cable TV people to come. We got it for the sports," she added hastily, fearful I might spread the word that the Bryces watched X-rated movies. "They put it in and then we had trouble with it and he said he'd come back Friday and he did, and I stayed here watching him."

"Not all day, surely."

"He didn't get here until two o'clock."

"You're sure that wasn't Thursday?"

"I went to visit my sister on Thursday. Well, this is silly. I *have* my library card. I can prove it to you. It's in my other bag." Standing up to people was not a thing

Agnes was accustomed to doing, but slurs upon her virtue were not to be taken lightly, and to be charged with having taken someone else's library card, even by mistake, was tantamount to being accused of theft. She disappeared into the house, closing both doors firmly behind her, leaving me behind on the doorstep like a delivery boy waiting for a tip. I hoped it didn't occur to her to wonder why I'd waited five days before taking care of the matter. Busy, I could say, but I trusted what I judged was her lifelong habit of not making waves to keep her from asking.

She returned with her own library card, held out to me triumphantly.

I assumed a puzzled frown. "I don't understand it. Then what happened to *my* card?"

"Well, *I* don't have it. I suppose"—she looked troubled, seeing a need for confrontation—"I'd better complain about this other card with my name on it. I must say they don't have a very good system."

"Probably a perfectly innocent mistake. Ask for Arlene Gordon. She gave me the card." No problem, Arlene, this woman's attack will be half retreat.

I went back to the car. Four down. And Agnes was the only one whose presence elsewhere could be substantiated.

14

"THIS WILL UNDOUBTEDLY go down in the annals of detection," Greenfield said, helping himself to more sautéed mushrooms, "as the polar opposite of the investigative coup."

We were sitting at my dining room table eating lamb marinated in lemon juice, ginger and garlic, a Greenfield favorite I prepared every so often when I had done badly in other fields of endeavor. Greenfield had a standing

Wednesday-night dinner invitation, a custom born in an impulsive burst of generosity during my first year with the *Reporter* because Wednesday was the day we went into print. There had been Wednesday nights he'd been otherwise engaged, or not in the mood, times when we had dined *en famille*, the boys being home, and times like this when there were only the two of us. Elliot that day had gone to Tennessee and wouldn't be home until late evening.

"Oh I don't know," I said, "it takes a certain talent to come away empty-handed three times out of four. You think it's possible Agnes Bryce lied, thinking we wouldn't check the cable people? I was hoping she'd tell me she'd been in Gorham, mailing a parcel. I'd have had her then; that wasn't Friday."

"She wouldn't lie."

"Probably not. Probably considers lying one step short of desecrating the flag, or saying something obscene about *Reader's Digest*. In any case I've done you a favor; if I'd found proof that Lucas and Gardner and Moss had been elsewhere, you'd be out of suspects. Leads. Whatever you want to call them."

"Those women. The three graces. Hate, Anger, and Fear." He caught my quick, aggressive lift of the head and said, "Don't *jump*. I'm not trying to define any person with a word. We're all susceptible to those emotions. Nevertheless, when you're looking for the roots of violence, you can hardly ignore such blatant suggestions. I suppose those women are all somewhere between forty-five and fifty?"

"That neighborhood."

He nodded, chewing.

"Charlie, do me a favor. Don't give me any prehistoric nonsense about women of a certain age."

He gave me, instead, a mournful glance. "Someday, your watchdog antics will convert me to the antifeminist view. When *people* of a certain age—male or female— first begin to sense a loss of power, they can become very fearful and very angry . . ."

"And take it out on the first cleaning woman who crosses them?"

". . . and have an urgent need to assert themselves, at almost any cost."

"But that's just what they're *not* doing. Roberta Moss can't even assert herself with her own seventeen-year-old son. Naomi does without tonic water rather than assert herself. Jessie— Well, maybe Jessie asserts herself on canvas. I still don't know what those paintings are all about, but she certainly doesn't have any *people* around to be assertive with. The only woman I can think of who makes a *religion* of asserting herself is Dina Franklin."

Greenfield scooped the last three mushrooms from the bottom of the bowl onto his plate. "Dina Franklin . . . I had a visit from Detective Pratt. On a *Wednesday*. I can forgive him his other limitations, but a detective, if nothing else, should have an ability to recognize a condition of crisis. I got rid of him in four minutes. In that time I gathered he's developed a suspicion that I know where Dina Franklin is."

"*I* know where she is. Saudi Ar—" I bit my tongue. Greenfield paused with his fork in midair, watching me with doleful speculation. I shook my head. "You're as bad as Pratt. You always think I'm withholding vital information. I was only joking."

"I never take humor lightly. '*In comoedia veritas*.' What prompted the joke?"

"I don't know. Just—the kind of thing that would be so attractive to Dina that she'd take off without notice. Something that would further her career—it's silly."

"Maggie. Evasions are not substitutes for details."

I told him. He looked thoughtful, contemplating the last mushroom. "What was she working on?"

"No idea."

"Something she was doing in connection with her work. It's as good a line of reasoning as any." He glanced down at George who had roused himself from his nap on the living room rug and come to place his chin on Greenfield's knee. "What does he want?"

"Attention. Like Dina."

The doorbell rang. My current reaction to the unexpected ring of the doorbell was instant paralysis. Greenfield's, apparently, was action. He pushed back his chair, stood up, and went out of the room, George at his heels.

I managed to call out, "Put on the chain!"

I heard him cross the hall, switch on the outside light, and open the door. No chain. Then the sound of a strange male voice, and Greenfield saying, "I couldn't tell you. You'll have to—wh—! COME BACK HERE! . . . Maggie!"

I flew to the door. It was wide open, a startled man in a business suit stood just outside, holding a clipboard and a sheaf of circulars, and Greenfield was nowhere to be seen.

"Your dog—" the young man said.

I ran down the dimly lit path to the driveway; to hell with the house, the young man, where was George? Where was Greenfield?

Greenfield was at the foot of the driveway, peering up and down the street, his dinner napkin clutched in one hand. George had bolted into the night. That female retriever had finally come by and George had finally bolted.

"You might have warned me," Greenfield muttered, coming back up the driveway.

"I did! I said put on the chain!" I rushed back to the house.

"You didn't say it was for the dog."

"For everything! I've got to go after him." I brushed the man with the clipboard aside. "Not now. Not now. I've got to find my dog," and barged into the house. "I don't even know where to *look* for him!"

"Can I just leave this with you?" the man said, handing me a circular through the door. "I called during the day but you were out."

I took the circular, threw it on the telephone table, grabbed my keys and a jacket.

"I'm blocking you," Greenfield said from outside. "I'll drive."

The man was still standing there as I locked the door, going on about basic cable service and choice of programs, as he followed me to the driveway where Greenfield was unlocking his car.

I got into the passenger seat wondering where to start looking, how I could possibly find him in the dark, what Elliot would say when he got home.

"I think he went to the left," Greenfield said, backing out of the driveway and turning. "At least I saw *something* going in that direction."

We drove up one dark street and down another. We saw dogs, here and there, out for a walk on a leash. I asked the man or woman holding the leash if he or she had seen George, but none of them had. Once I thought I saw him turning the corner of someone's house into a backyard, and jumped from the car and ran across dew-damp lawn, through a black tangle of bushes, calling, "George! George!" but whatever I'd seen was gone, and in the kitchen window a light came on and a man in shirtsleeves peered out into the blackness.

"Won't he find his way home eventually?" Greenfield asked when we'd been driving around for ten minutes.

"I don't know," I said miserably. "He doesn't run around on his own the way some dogs do. He's not used to it."

"He must know the area to some extent. You take him for walks. Where do you go when you walk him?"

My heart leaped. Oh God, yes. "The school! On Glenbrook. We've been walking down to the old school." Greenfield made a U-turn in the middle of a block, the most reckless piece of driving I'd ever seen him perform. "He likes it there," I babbled on, reassuring myself. "He finds things in the grass. Pretzels, rubber balls. I'll bet he went there. I'll bet he did."

We sped down the hill to Glenbrook, turned into the entrance, and stopped a short way into the grounds. Someone had knocked out the light in the playground, a not-infrequent vandalism. The streetlights of Glenbrook Place illuminated only the few yards immediately adjacent; the rest of the acreage lay in darkness so absolute it was impossible to distinguish anything but the mass of the building itself and the tops of large trees against the lighter black of the sky. I cursed the moonless, starless night.

"George!" I called. "George, for God's sake, are you here?"

Greenfield opened the trunk of the car, closed it again, and the beam of a flashlight hit my legs. He swept the light slowly up and down the grass. Some small animal scurried off down the dip of a hillock. We moved forward, a few feet at a time, playing the light back and forth, the hope I'd felt when I'd thought of the school slowly evaporating as I called, "George! George!"

"He *does* know his name, I trust?" Greenfield muttered.

"Of *course* he does!" I shot back. "He knows everything. He's brilliant!"

"But lost."

"George!"

And suddenly, from somewhere not too far away, there was a bark! Not just any bark, *George's* bark!

"George?"

He barked again.

"Back there!" I said, grabbing the flashlight and running toward the back of the school. "George?" Another bark, closer. I swung the flashlight crazily back and forth and it finally found George, standing in the grass looking faintly injured, as though *I'd* deserted *him*.

"I've got him!" I shouted.

Greenfield's tone of Joblike patience traveled clearly through several hundred feet of inky blackness. "If it's not too much trouble, could you send some light this way so that I don't walk headlong into a tree?"

I shone the flashlight in his direction. I had my hand under George's collar (forgot the leash, calm, collected person that I am) to keep him from running away, but he showed no inclination to leave.

"What do we do now," Greenfield asked, reaching me, "carry him to the car?"

"I'll hold onto his collar," I said, moving at a crouch. "Come on, George, home." I handed Greenfield the flashlight and in the arc the light made traveling from my hand to his, something gleamed, like glass. "Wait," I said, "I think— Shine the light on the windows."

With a sigh for his interrupted dinner, Greenfield played the light along the foundation, revealing two boarded-up windows and a third—

"They did it!"

The boarding had been split and pried loose so that the boards sagged away from the window almost to the ground.

The four center panes of the window glass and their dividing bars were missing, except for a few jagged shards projecting from the remaining frame. Fragments of glass glinted on the ground near the wall.

"That must have been done in the last two days. Nothing was broken on Monday. I looked."

"Why?"

"Why wasn't it *broken*?"

"Why did you look?"

"Oh, because some woman at the Village Board meeting was nervous about kids breaking in those windows and maybe climbing in." I looked at the window again. "You don't think . . . ?"

Greenfield went close to the window and shone the light through the hole, then he stepped back. "I can't see much. There may be a dead animal in there. Or the place smells that way from being shut up. I can't, offhand, think of an animal that wields an ax."

"An ax?"

"How else would you split those boards? Let's go." He walked, shining the light on the ground beside him.

"We'd better tell someone about that window." With my hand in George's collar, I followed Greenfield's legs back to the car. "It *is* possible, I suppose, that some child climbed in there. Maybe got hurt and can't get out. Not likely, though. If he'd heard us he would have shouted. Unless— Oh, I suppose not." I stowed George in the backseat and opened the front passenger door to get in.

"Wait here," Greenfield said, and started back the way we had come.

"Where are you going? George, stay, I'll be right back." I shut the door and went after Greenfield. "What are you going to do?" I knew what he was going to do. "I take it back. There's no injured child in there." He kept going. I followed the light. "And even if there is, the situation can't be so desperate that it can't wait another five minutes. Let's get the superintendent, or whoever takes care of this place—"

At the rear of the school Greenfield searched the grass until he came up with a chunk of fallen tree limb. With this he swung at the remaining glass in the broken panes until the hole was clear of shards, played the light through the opening again, gave me the flashlight to hold, carefully climbed through and reached an arm out for the light. I gave it to him and stayed peering through the hole. The smell was faint but putrid, reminiscent of an occasion when some raccoon or mouse had been trapped between the walls of our house and died there.

Through the opening I saw the flashlight flickering close by on walls, floor, a wooden bench. It dipped for a moment, as though Greenfield were stooping, then lifted as he straightened, and as his footsteps receded, it lit up, briefly, first a ladder, then a distant doorway. Then the light was gone. I waited, wondering if that woman's fears had been realized. Vandalism taken advantage of by an adventurous child: fallen over something in the dark in there; tumbled down a flight of stairs?

I leaned close to the window and called, "Charlie?"

Silence, then a distant clank as of a tin can striking a metal surface, then silence again. I was beginning to feel cramped and chilled, peered again into the dark interior, straining my eyes for the least flicker of light. Greenfield the hero. What nonsense. And it was my fault, as usual, conjuring up images of a helpless, unconscious youngster. Another faint, distant sound. Good Lord, what was he doing?

Finally I heard footsteps again, and saw the bobbing light approaching. Greenfield's arm came through the window with the flashlight in it. I took it and trained it on the window while he climbed through and dusted himself off.

"Nothing there, of course?"

He took the flashlight from me and started back to the car.

"You must have gone through every room in the building. I thought *snow* would fall before you got back."

No reply. He moved on through the grass.

"Charlie!" I grabbed his arm. "You found something."

He looked down at the spill of light at his feet, as though he were seeing a future of unending persecution. He sighed profoundly. "Twice," he muttered, "in less than a week."

"What?"

"We have now landed firmly, with our four feet, in the wet cement of Detective Pratt's quick-drying convictions."

"*What?*" I stumbled after him as he walked on. "Charlie?"

He reached the car and stopped, his hand on the door handle. "I can just see the sour satisfaction on that elephant-hide face of his"—he opened the car door—"when I tell him where Dina Franklin is."

15

QUESTIONS. ASPIRIN. THE ugly green police room. Grim Pratt. Grimmer Greenfield. Back to the school. Demonstrate. Yes, we can prove we were looking for the dog: three people had been asked, they would remember, the cable salesman was there when it happened. The woman was shot. The woman. Three bullet wounds. Looked like a .38 automatic. Back to headquarters. Questions. Statements. Home.

Elliot had just arrived, the note I'd left was in his hand. He asked if I would consider dumping my job at the *Reporter* and resurrecting a childhood ambition to become a concert pianist. I crawled into bed, worried that I hadn't been ill this time, as I had with Mathilda. Could one become conditioned so quickly? Sleep eluded me for interminable hours. Finally I thought about giving it up and going down to start the breakfast coffee. My eyes closed and when the telephone woke me it was noon.

"Your lady came to see me."

"Oh. Arlene. Any trouble?"

"Trouble? Don't be silly. I was magnificent. Even you would have believed me."

"Very grateful. Really."

"You'd just better tell me what this was all about. I'm *consumed* with curiosity."

"One of these days. Promise."

"Don't forget to bring in your contributions. And remember you promised to transport books next week."

"Won't forget." The Book Fair. I hadn't even begun to collect my discards.

Shot dead. With a revolver. Dina. Not possible.

I showered, dressed, drank orange juice and coffee, reviewing in my mind the statement I'd given the police, including a not-quite-complete report of that last telephone conversation on the day she was to have left for St. Louis. I told them she'd said she had an idea who might have broken into her house (Pratt perked up at this: burglars again), but I'd deliberately omitted something else. When it came to a choice between my loyalty to Greenfield and my obligations as a citizen, the odds were good that I would obstruct justice.

Now, though, I wanted an answer to a question Greenfield had avoided answering once before. I knew better than to call; he had an encyclopedia of ruses for aborting annoying phone calls, the least of which was claiming there was smoke ascending from the floor below. I'd go to the office. And while I was about it, I'd broach the possibility of taking a trip around the world by slow boat and donkey until the police had found and incarcerated the maniacs who were wandering around Sloan's Ford disposing of people.

It was an ugly day, even to the weather, the air an oppressive combination of chill and humidity. And still no rain. For days now there had been reports of storms in the West, and the weather had always, in my experience, moved west to east. The *bad* weather, that is. The sunshine they kept. The storms and the Southern California entertainment they exported.

A .38 automatic. Shot dead. No. Not Dina. Not possible.

Thursday was a half-day for Helen and Calli, so I was not surprised, when I reached the white frame house with the mansard roof, to open the front door on comparative silence. What did surprise me was the sight of a rather large female bottom in a black dress printed with tiny green and yellow leaves, and the soles of a pair of size 9 oxfords, facing me from halfway up the stairway to Greenfield's office. On the stair tread beside the oxfords was a can of floor wax, and from the tremor of the buttocks I judged that some vigorous polishing was going on. The downstairs hallway was adorned with a mop standing in a pail of water, a pile of rags, and a vacuum cleaner. Greenfield, by God, in the midst of chaos and carnage, had found himself another cleaning woman!

I called out, "Hold it!"

A face like a withered full moon peered around at me.

"No wax on the stairs," I said, ascending.

The woman hefted herself to an upright position. She was big-boned, wide-shouldered, full-bosomed, with thick wrists and ankles and large, rough, red hands, and her yellowish-gray hair was pulled into a bun at the back. She made a gesture in the direction of Greenfield's office above and said, "No. No," and shook her head. I followed the gesture, but not the comment.

"You're not supposed to wax the stairs."

She looked at me warily and then her faded blue eyes slid away as though to assess the possibility of escape should I prove unmanageable. She said a few words in some language not even remotely familiar, gestured again toward Greenfield's office, and said, "No," shaking her head.

Heaven help us, she only knows one word of English.

"Charlie?" I called. No reply. I went cautiously up the rest of the stairs, testing for slipperiness, and checked the office. It slumbered peacefully in the afternoon gloom, not only uninhabited, but neat and tidy, with all the circulars, magazines, clippings, reference books, and journals cleared off the armchairs and stacked in tight little piles on his *bare* desk. Had she thrown out the indispensable clutter of notes, memos, telephone numbers? Good thing she was a stranger to our tongue; the verbal flaying Greenfield would administer when he saw it would leave the average English-speaking person skinless.

Descending again to where she waited, watching me carefully, I pointed to the can of wax and then to the stair tread, shook my head and said "No." She followed my every move, but remained stolidly uninformed. Her eyes slid away from me again. How in the world had Greenfield managed to communicate enough to hire her, let alone tell her what he wanted done? I went through the pantomime again, she nodded quietly six or seven times, and said a few more words in Serbolithukrainian, having understood not a whit. And I had once been so good at charades. There was nothing for it but to remove the source of the problem. I had picked up the can of wax and started down the stairs, when the front door opened, admitting Greenfield. The woman immediately burst into voluble complaint.

And he answered her! I gaped at him.

"She says you don't want her to work here."

"I was merely explaining that since you're not heavily insured, she's not to wax the stairs."

"I already warned her about that. She was only polishing the railing." He explained my strange behavior to her and she said something in return. "She says she had no intention of waxing the treads. She says she's not a fool. That, of course, remains to be seen. Come up."

"I can't stay." Why should I be around, with my throbbing head, when he walked into that office and beheld the disaster that cleanliness had wrought? "I just want to ask a question."

"You can do it up there." He started for the stairs.

"She's working on the stairs. I've alienated her enough." I all but dragged him into the downstairs office and sat down firmly in Helen Deutsch's typing chair. He looked unhappily at the scarred and wobbly captain's chair that remained and propped himself against a table.

"What's your question?"

"I have two, now that I've heard you speaking fluent Liechtenstein. You have ancestors I don't know about?"

"When an English-speaking army journalist finds himself on the wrong side of the front lines in Europe, he's well advised to learn enough of the language to stay alive until his own side arrives."

"I'm very nearly awestruck. The only genuine Middle European workhorse extant in the Western world and you not only find her, you can speak to her."

"It's the nature of life to sprinkle drops of good fortune between the floods of disaster. Do you still have that piece of paper I gave you with the names of the women who employed that girl?"

It took a moment to realize he meant Mathilda. "Piece of paper? Charlie, that was in another *life*. I don't know where it is. Why? We know who they are. If nothing else, we know *that*."

"The names were written down in sequence, to correspond with the days of the week. I have to know which one of those women she was working for on Wednesday."

"What's Wednesday got to do with Mathilda?"

He shifted his weight, noticed a jar of wilted flowers on the table, idly picked it up, and went to the sink in the alcove. "I managed to pry some information out of the medical examiner's office. . . ."

That didn't surprise me. I remembered from our last foray into private investigation that he had a way with medical examiners.

"They tell me Mrs. Franklin had been dead for some days." He dumped the flowers into the sink. "Exactly how many they wouldn't say. More than three." He brought the jar back to the table. "This being Thursday, she could have been shot as late as last Sunday."

"Yes?"

"However, an unused plane ticket for Wednesday was found in the handbag she had with her."

"So?"

He looked at me as though the implications were obvious. "That plane ticket is a rather good argument for the theory that last Wednesday was the day she was—at least—removed from circulation."

"And? Where does Mathilda come into it?"

He was patient, an adult dealing with a not-too-bright child. "Unless someone has gone berserk, and these are random, motiveless killings, it's possible there's a connection between the first one and the second."

"Connection? Are you saying Mathilda killed Dina on Wednesday, and on Friday Dina rose from the dead and took her revenge?"

He lost patience. "Where did you put the piece of

paper when I gave it to you?"

I shrugged. "In my pocket. No, I didn't have pockets that day. In my bag, I suppose."

"Look."

I slipped the strap of the bag off my shoulder and opened the bag. "Do you know how many times I've rummaged in here since then? Stuffed things in, taken things out. I could have dropped it in the garbage with a wad of Kleenex." I dumped the contents on Helen's desk. Scraps of paper floated among the debris: two obsolete grocery lists, an old ticket stub from the theater, a receipt from the cleaner's, a supermarket coupon with which I could save forty cents on a twenty-five-pound bag of dog food. "It's not here."

Greenfield leaned against the table with the empty jar, quietly condemning me. "I never knew a self-respecting journalist who would throw away a list of names until five years after he'd received it."

I looked up furiously from my wallet, which had also produced nothing relevant. "I wasn't exactly working on a simple, impersonal journalist's assignment!"

"Somehow you'll have to find out where that girl was working on Wednesday."

"Certainly. Could you give me about twenty minutes?" I swept the clutter back into the bag.

"Along with murder and unfinished sentences, Maggie, tantrums make me irritable."

"Why don't you ask that woman who drove Mathilda, the one who gave you the names in the first place?"

"For a very good reason. Her name and address were on that piece of paper. I can't even approximate them."

I crumpled. "My head hurts."

If he heard me, he was in no mood to offer sympathy. "Pratt, of course, knows who and where she is. I think at this point he's certain I know who killed them both— or did it myself. He'd give me information about as easily as he'd give me the use of his badge."

I went to the alcove, opened the refrigerator, and took out the ice cube tray. "Well, I hope you've thought of a way for *me* to get that information without talking to any of those four women, because I would have to have a *very* legitimate reason for popping up again to ask them *any* kind of question. At this point if I asked them for a glass of *water* they'd think it was a trap." I emptied the ice cubes into the sink, picked up a cube, and held it against my forehead.

"People have been known to extract information in passing."

"Passing from what to what? 'Just happened to be in the neighborhood?' 'Just dropped in to borrow a revolver?' "

"You could think of a dozen plausible excuses if you'd take the trouble."

"My head is in no condition to deal with anything that isn't right out in full view." I removed the ice cube from my frozen sinuses and dropped it into the sink. "I'm going to go home and take a bottle of aspirin. I only came here to . . ." How did he do it? I'd come here to ask a simple question, straight as an arrow heading for a tree trunk, and somehow he'd got me whizzing all over the woods and out again without making contact. I sat down again. "Charlie, last night when Pratt asked me about that phone conversation with Dina last Wednesday, I neglected to mention the message she sent you. I asked you about it at the time and you glided right by it. And I didn't know what kind of Pandora's box I'd open if I mentioned it to Pratt, so I didn't. Now that I've perjured myself to protect you, I want to know. What did Dina mean when she said, 'Tell Charlie it's going to be all right'?"

He looked extremely disappointed in me. "Faith," he said, "is not something I advocate indiscriminately. But between the two of us I should think it was mandatory."

"I have blind loyalty, it's better than faith. But I want to know."

"Even if it's incriminating?"

"*Is* it?"

"Of course not! She was probably referring to the vote on the sale of the school. It was no secret to any of the board members that I had an interest in seeing the sale go through. After the meeting she apparently decided she was in favor of the sale, and if her mind worked the way

I think it did, she thought it might be useful for me to know she'd done me a favor. She's—she *was*—a politician. Politicians can always use . . ." He broke off, leaving—of all things!—a sentence unfinished, and stared fixedly at some spot halfway across the room. I turned and looked, but there was nothing where he was looking except worn linoleum.

"Use what?"

"A quid pro quo," he said slowly, and shifted his gaze to the toe of his brown loafer, examining it intently.

Quid pro quo. That was hardly a thunderbolt. Unless it meant something I was too pain-logged to comprehend. I got up to go and the woman with whom I couldn't communicate came into the room with mop and pail. She asked Greenfield something and he answered, all consonants, no vowels. I couldn't wait to tell Helen and Calli we were all going to have to take a course at Berlitz.

The woman took from her pocket a plastic orange disc and gave it to Greenfield. He examined it, showed it to me. It had two black plastic initials glued to its shiny surface, an M and a G.

"She found it in the bedroom," he said musingly, "under the bed."

"Mathilda. She could have dropped it while she was cleaning."

"Did you see her wearing it!"

"She still had her jacket on when I left, but she could easily have had it on her blouse; it's the kind of thing she might think was chic. Some new fad, apparently, among the high schoolers. I saw another girl wearing one just like it. Agnes Bryce's daughter, in fact."

He turned the pin over to look at the back. "The catch is loose." He fiddled with it, put it in his pocket, and followed me out to the hallway, then suddenly turned back and spoke to the woman again. She answered. "Krjyvdwztondk." He came back to the hallway.

"There's your excuse," he said, "for asking those women questions. She's free Mondays and Wednesdays." He started up the stairs.

Well of course. Right under my nose. "It's easy," I called after him defensively, "to come up with solutions when you haven't got a headache."

He turned and looked back. "That's why it took me so long," he said, and went into his office.

There was an ominous silence. No footsteps crossing the floor. He was standing there surveying the orderly damage. I left before the storm could break.

16

AN HOUR LATER, driving through the village after a visit to the bank (murder or no murder, bills must be paid), I saw a white Peugeot pulled up just beyond the pumps at Victor's Garage. A brassy sun had come through the lumpy clouds, glinting on the chrome bumper, and standing near the open hood arguing with Frank, the mechanic, was the thin, tense figure of Roberta Moss. I pulled in behind the Peugeot and got out of the car.

"We've been good customers here for fifteen *years*," Roberta was saying. "I think that deserves some . . . *consideration*."

"Any other day be glad to do it," Frank said in his nasal voice. "Do it today if you like."

"Saturday's the *only* day I can . . ."

"Can't do it. Saturday's a busy day. If it was something simple, a twenty-minute job, maybe. But an oil leak, I have to put it on the lift, find out where it's coming from. Could be engine oil, power steering fluid, brake fluid, transmission fluid, rear differential. Can't do it on a Saturday."

"Why not? Why *not*? You fix other cars on Saturdays."

"Look, we got customers who need the cars for business, can't get to work otherwise."

"Businessmen!" Roberta's small, breathy voice rose to a screech, quivering. "You don't take *women* customers on Saturdays, that's what you mean! Women go to the end of the line, they can come in when it's convenient for *you*, because they have all the time in the world, they don't have anything . . . *important* to do!''

Frank looked embarrassed and startled, like a man caught in an elevator with some religious fanatic who has suddenly begun accusing him of Godlessness. He carefully closed the hood and slunk back into the dark cavern of the garage.

"My time is just as . . . valuable as anyone else's!" Roberta screeched after him, her face pale, her jaw clenched, her fist on the fender trembling visibly. Roberta Moss asserting herself. Was Greenfield right after all? And was it, as he claimed, born of a visceral anger at aging, or was it merely the learned anger of a recent convert to feminism? It *looked* visceral enough. I wondered if it was a good idea to try subtle questioning on a person in emotional turmoil, but she turned and seemed to see me. I gave it a try.

"We spend our lives at the mercy of repairmen," I said. She looked at me blindly. "I was going to call you about the article. I'm afraid it's been scotched."

"Oh," she said blankly, "I'm—sorry. I'm a little upset. My car is leaking."

"I have some good news, though. I found a cleaning woman if you still need one."

She blinked rapidly. "Cleaning woman! Yes! Yes, I do. What . . ."

"She's free on Wednesdays—that's the day you had Mathilda, isn't it?"

"No, Tuesdays, but . . ."

"Really? I thought of you when she said she was free on Wednesdays because I thought— Maybe it was Naomi Gardner who said she used to come on Wednesdays." I waited for her to confirm or contradict. No luck.

"I'll take any day she has. Where can I . . . ?"

"I'll get the number and call you. Oh—she doesn't speak any English. Or any other reasonable language. It's something like Czech."

I could see Roberta's mind racing through the alternatives: forget it and be left without help, use gestures, get an interpreter. "I'll take the number anyway. And thanks.

Thank you. I—um—have to—I'm late." She got into her car and took off, leaking oil. I watched her careen out to the roadway, stop with a squeal of brakes just inches from the passing traffic, and make several hesitant attempts to gain entry before finally lurching out, too close for comfort to an oncoming truck, eliciting a long angry blast of horn.

What was it I had called her? Sane, rational . . .

Still, the encounter hadn't been so bad. Either she didn't realize she'd been tricked, last time, into talking about Mathilda by a woman who had known Mathilda was dead, or I'd given her the lollipop before she could attack me for that. I decided to try my luck with the one who lived at the top of a near-perpendicular road.

Jessie's war-torn station wagon stood in the forecourt facing the stockade fence, but when I went through the courtyard and knocked on the door with the gargoyle, no Jessie called to say "Come in" and no one came to open it. I knocked again and waited. The wagon was here, she couldn't be far away. Gone to a neighbor's, probably, to borrow turpentine. I leaned against the door, prepared to wait, and the door moved. Foolish woman, leaving her door unlocked.

"Hello?" I called. No answer. I walked through the cluttered room to the foot of the stairs and called again, wondering if she was the sort to take afternoon naps. Nothing but silence. I was debating whether to wait inside or out when the door swung open and Jessie came in, wearing her jogging clothes, red-faced, breathing noisily.

"Ah!" she said, gasping for breath. "What brings you? Somebody else been killed?"

I stood there dumbly, shocked speechless. The headache, subdued by aspirin, achieved renewed vigor.

"Sorry. Black humor. I despise it, actually." She collapsed onto one of the Victorian sofas. "Jogging . . . is suicidal . . . for one of my advanced years. But what the hell? Thumb the nose at death. Hemingway had his bloody bulls."

She mentioned death so often, so easily. Every time I saw her. Bravado? Or the actress in her? Or . . . ?

"You thumb your nose at a lot of things," I said, "leaving your door unlocked."

"Oh, yes, the burglaries." She said it as though I'd reminded her that an open window invites flies. "They've been piling up, haven't they? Three the other week, then Dina Franklin, then that ugly house down the road. I always mean to lock the door, but there are so many things to think about. Besides, I hate to live that way. A little sherry, I think, would be nice. Behind you, there, in that dry sink. Glasses in the cabinet above it. Be careful, the door sticks and if you pull too hard a glass or two will fall out. I lost a cranberry goblet that way."

Who was she playing now? I wondered, getting the sherry and glasses and bringing them over to a piecrust table at her elbow.

"I come bearing a gift, of sorts," I said.

"A gift! God, how I need a gift. I'm so glad I suggested sherry instead of being bitchy and telling you to come back some other time, which I very well could have done, the way I feel today. A gift!" She handed me a stemmed glass with the amber liquid swaying in it. "Time was I had a gift every week. Robert Lucas was a lavish man when he had a letch. *There's* Robert." She gestured to a photograph standing on a nearby table in a tooled copper frame. "Boyish, ain't he? And every bit of forty-eight the day that was taken. Still and ever a boy. Robert's psyche solidified at the age of twenty-five. In thirty years he discarded nothing. He outgrew nothing." She sipped at her sherry. "He learned behavior, social accommodation, subtlety, the vocabulary of maturity, but at twenty-five his idea of the supreme emotional experience was a night on the town with something young, nubile, and willing. And it still is." She sipped again. "Sent Joshua a picture—do you believe this?—a picture of his little hideaway in Mexico, with his bikini-clad 'interior decorator' reclining on a chaise. 'Look what Daddy's got! Life in the old boy yet, my son!' I found it in Josh's shirt pocket. He throws clothes into the dirty-wash hamper without going through the pockets. Oh me, oh my, I need a cigarette." She got up and went searching among the bric-a-brac on the table. "Talking too much. A symptom of age. And loneliness. Old and lonely—virtually interchangeable." She found cigarettes in the drawer of a lyre table set against the wall under an old oval mirror, and caught sight of her image as she lit one. Regarding herself through half-closed eyes she said, slowly, "Pouched, pitted, and pasty. Wrinkled, runneled, and ravaged. Spotted and sagging and jowled. . . ." She struck a pose, tilting her head to one side and directing a mocking smile at the mirror. "What a beauty you are, my dear! How *could* your king forsake you?" Abruptly she came back to the sofa. "But then, Eleanor had the Aquitaine, and power is everything, isn't it? This"—a sweeping gesture around the room—"is hardly a rich French province."

Power is everything? And loss of power . . . I began to wonder if Greenfield had been interviewing these women behind my back. But how much of this was playacting?

"To listen to you," I said, "anyone would think you'd just left Shangri-La and the centuries had descended on your face."

She looked at me fiercely. It was the first time I'd seen her humorless. She really believed it, then, it was truly eating at her. She turned around, grabbed a small oval picture frame from the table backing the sofa, and thrust it at me. "Who's that?"

I looked down at a photograph of a radiant young woman of thirty or so, laughing on a riverbank in the sun, glorious roan-colored hair lifted by the breeze. She'd been very pretty. And now it was gone, and she couldn't see the attributes that were ageless, only those that were missing.

"It's you," I said.

"If you'd seen it in someone else's house you'd never have known!" She took it back, glanced at it briefly before replacing it. "Slender, too. Slender, by God. And why not? Lucas could always spoil my appetite, for good reasons and bad." She suddenly abandoned the mood. "So where's the gift?"

"At Greenfield's office. He's found a cleaning woman. And she's free Wednesdays, so you won't have to change your schedule."

She smiled. "How do you know my schedule?"

"I was trying to get Mathilda for Greenfield on a regular basis, and she told me she worked for this one on Monday, that one on Tuesday—I thought she said

Wednesday was Mrs. Lucas.''

"No, Monday was my day. Thanks for thinking of me, but I've decided to do without. They break my things. And besides, dollars aren't dollars anymore. I have to choose between help and tomatoes. Why don't you give her to Naomi? Poor Naomi needs all the help she can get, juggling all those responsibilities night and day. She works harder than anyone I know not to cheat *anybody*. Neglect is a word she doesn't have any use for. Her organs will make medical history."

"She must love her job to put up with all that strain."

"Love has nothing to do with it. It's fear that keeps her going. In a few years she'll be my age. That glorious time of life when salesclerks begin to ignore you, your children patronize you, and men's eyes glaze over as you approach. The beginning of that long, cold winter of the ego. Naomi is frantically rubbing sticks together to get a fire going against it." She grinned. "She doesn't want to end up like me."

I smiled, to show I could only take that as a joke, though I sensed it wasn't, and stood up to go. "Well, I'll tell her about the cleaning woman—if you think Wednesday would suit her." In my mind the reply was beautifully obliging: *Why not? That's when she had Mathilda.*

"Why not?" Jessie said, and drained her sherry glass.

I went to the door. "Thanks for the drink."

"De nada."

As I left I heard the telephone ring, and Jessie answered. "Ha! Just talking about you."

I drove back down the hill, my head buzzing with the memory of Jessie's scathing inventory of her physiognomy. Those paintings of pretty, young, headless girls: was it herself Jessie was decapitating over and over? Or all women who were younger and prettier than she?

Sane, rational . . .

I stopped for a light and realized I had no destination. Mathilda's Wednesday still had to be accounted for. She hadn't spent it with Jessie or Roberta; two other possibilities remained, and I only had to confirm one of them to get the answer. Another tête-à-tête with Agnes Bryce had all the appeal of a dental appointment. But Naomi would

not be available, she'd be at her job (and calling Jessie
from there! I wouldn't have thought those two could have
such a close friendship). There was one other means of
finding out about Naomi. It was a precarious one, depending as it did on unpredictable after-school activities. But
if the alternative was Agnes Bryce . . .

On the peaceful, tree-lined street where the Gardners'
house stood, a scattered procession of high-school students
meandered along the road, scuffling among the pale gold
and crimson of fallen leaves, but none of them was Naomi's
daughter. Perhaps she was already at home. I continued
down the street and into the Gardners' driveway, went up
the walk to the house, and was almost at the front door
when I heard from inside the violent slam of some inside
door, followed by a hoarse shout, a throat-tearing, vein-
popping yell.

"I—AM—TIRED!"

Again the door slammed. And slammed, and slammed,
as though it were repeatedly being opened for the relief
of sending it once more shuddering against the frame.
"TI-RED!" Slam! "TI-RED!" Slam! "TI-RED!"

The scream was wild, savage, a wounded jungle animal,
trapped and thrashing. Naomi? But Naomi must be at
work in the city. I went back to the driveway and peered
through the garage window. The black Mercury with the
tan top was standing inside. That wild animal was indeed
Naomi. There was no second car in the garage, Leonard
was not at home. Was she alone? Was the daughter with
her? Should something be done?

The slamming inside had been replaced by a repeated,
hollow, metallic crash, a sound as of someone pounding
the rings of a gas range with a heavy skillet.

"NO . . . MORE!" Crash! Crash! "NO . . . MORE!"
Crash!

I went quickly back to my car. I was not the person to
handle this, whatever it was. I'd call someone. Jessie.
Then I remembered that Naomi herself had just called
Jessie. Minutes away from screaming, and slamming, she
had called her. About what? I backed out of the driveway,
drove halfway down the street, and pulled in to the curb.
All these "sane, rational, ordinary" women exploding

simultaneously, all these volcanic eruptions of one kind or another within the space of an hour. And all from three women who seemed to have a good deal to do with each other. I found myself thinking of movies about men on old sailing vessels, months at sea in the torrid zone, crowded together belowdecks with rats and scurvy, simmering with resentment. Mutiny.

Nonsense.

Should I wait around on the chance of catching the daughter on her way home? On the whole I didn't think she was in the house with Naomi; I didn't think it likely that Naomi would give way with such elemental abandon in the presence of anyone else. Particularly her own child.

I had decided to give it another five minutes when a white Peugeot came streaking up the street leaking oil, and swooped, I saw, turning around to the rear window, into Naomi's driveway. I barely had time to wonder if she'd been summoned, when Jessie's rattletrap station wagon went jouncing past me and pulled up behind the Peugeot. Gathering of the clan. For aid and assistance— or something else?

I heard Greenfield's withering comment: "And it didn't occur to you to find out?"

Of course it did, Charlie. It occurred to me to whip up a disguise, ring the bell, and say I was collecting for the United Fund, and hope they wouldn't notice that I didn't leave after I got the money. It occurred to me that she had plenty of chimneys, and I've had no experience at climbing into them. It occurred to me . . .

But inevitably he'd have an answer: "The telescope would never have been invented if a Dutch astronomer had wasted his time telling himself there was no way to find out what was going on in the sky." Or some such thing.

I got out of the car and walked reluctantly back up the road to the Gardners' driveway, wishing I had one of those diabolical devices that make life so simple for double agents in spy novels when they haven't had time to get inside and bug the place. Some little gadget you apply to the exterior of a window, that's tuned to the frequency of the human voice and activates a computer which then

records the vibrations onto a disc which, when slotted
into a special recorder, will break the code and play back
the conversation in whatever language you happen to speak,
and all that malarkey.

Short of that, using my ears for eavesdropping was all
I could think of, and that would only work if there was a
convenient open window, or if all three of them had now
resorted to the earsplitting screams I'd heard earlier. Also
to be considered was the small matter of being caught at
it. The whole idea was distasteful. Gathering information
and impressions by question-and-answer was one thing,
listening in on private conversations quite another. These
were, after all, women whose sherry I'd drunk, whose
grapes I'd eaten; these were my peers, my neighbors.

"And what," Greenfield said via telepathy, "if one of
them is guilty of a crime? Have you, all by yourself,
established a new system of justice? Decided which type
of criminal shall be pursued and which shall be left alone
to get on with the paintings and the dinner parties?"

In the interests of justice I stared at the house, trying
to remember the layout of the ground floor. The living
room, I remembered, had French doors leading to the
back garden. I suppose that in a pinch I could explain my
furtive presence at the back of Naomi's property: "Came
to leave a message with your daughter, had dog in car, he
jumped out and ran off." Known as fiction based on fact.

I went quietly around the end of the house, past borders
of periwinkle and beds of chrysanthemums. The back
lawn was bordered with shrubs and well-tended flower
beds all put to bed for the coming winter. There was a
screening of fir trees separating the Gardners' plot from
their neighbors on each side, and at the back the land
rose, sharp and wooded, to an unseen plateau. An oblong
terrace with wrought-iron railing ran along the back of
the house level with the bottom of the French doors,
which faced due south, the blinds closed against the
southwest afternoon sun. I moved nervously up to the far
edge of the French doors where I would cast no shadow
on the blinds, and immediately heard Jessie's voice.

"Of course not! I wasn't there long enough. Just dropped
it and . . ." The voice faded as though she'd moved

away, and another voice spoke, muffled by distance, the words impossible to make out. Then Naomi's voice, hoarse but controlled, as, apparently, she approached the French doors and walked away again.

". . . home on Tuesday night . . ." The voice faded and then returned, as though she were pacing the room. ". . . never run into that girl . . ."

For a while all the voices were muffled, and then they faded, and then ceased, as though the speakers had moved to another room. I waited a few minutes to see if they would return, my skin twitching with the desire to be gone, but the silence continued, and finally I left the terrace, and the garden, and went as quietly as speed would allow, back to the Honda.

Bloody lot of good my eavesdropping had done me. Three incomplete sentences signifying nothing I could decipher. I wrote them down in the notebook I had in my bag, and drove off down the street. I'd gone a block and a half when two girls with their arms full of books appeared in the distance. I slowed and stopped, got out of the car to peer ostentatiously at the numbers on the houses, and when the girls were close enough I walked up to them and spoke to the one who was Naomi's daughter.

"I have an address here," I said, consulting my notebook, "that seems to be wrong. The people I'm looking for are called Salsbury and they're supposed to be at Sixty-one Chestnut Drive, but they're not. I was going to try Sixteen. Do you know a Salsbury around here?"

"Salsbury?" the Gardner girl said. "Nope, never heard of them."

I looked at her with elaborate sudden recognition. "Aren't you Naomi Gardner's daughter?" She smiled and nodded. "Well, that's lucky. You can give her a message for me. I've found another cleaning woman, if she's interested. I don't know if she's available on the same day your mother used to have Mathilda—Wednesday, wasn't it?"

"Thursday. The day I have student council meeting after school—like today."

"Well, tell your mother if she doesn't mind what day she gets, there's a lady available." I gave her my name and went back to the car. Thursday, Naomi. Monday,

Jessie. Tuesday, Roberta. Friday, Dina. Now, if everyone was telling the truth, it was obvious where Mathilda had been on Wednesday.

17

STEWART KLEIN, BUSHY of head and upper lip, had one hip resting on the edge of Greenfield's desk (a grade-B-movie pose that annoyed Greenfield as much by its source as for the casual intimacy it implied), and with all the breezy arrogance of youth, was giving Greenfield the benefit of his superior vision.

"You could attract more advertisers, expand to maybe twenty-five pages, the *Reporter* could become a significant paper, a force in the county. You could have real impact. And from there, who knows? The whole picture is changing. How many big papers have folded in the last twenty years? Metropolitans are in trouble—look at the London *Times*. Listen, Charlie, it's *not impossible* that the future lies in community news. And somebody like you, with your antennae, who picks up on a public danger a couple of light-years before these other clowns . . ."

"Come in, Maggie," Greenfield murmured.

I moved into the room. Stewart threw me a "Hi" and continued his sales pitch.

"Believe me, get a computer proofreader—I mean, this system is antediluvian—subscribe to a news service— you have to change—you have to *grow*."

"I," Greenfield interrupted quietly, "am constantly

growing. When *you* have grown, as much as *I* have grown, you might possibly stop confusing change with progress. Go find out about that route thirty-seven bypass, I have business with Maggie.''

"You don't understand what's happening, Charlie." Stewart went to the stairs.

"I suspect it's an enviable position." Greenfield watched Stewart's bushy head disappear and muttered, "How does he grow all that *hair*?" He got up to put a couple of Bach Brandenburgs on the machine.

"I have to tell you," I said, "I am not happy in your chosen hobby. I don't like what I'm doing. I'm spending my time lying and eavesdropping and that's not quite the career I had mapped out for myself—"

"Eavesdropping?"

"What are my sons going to tell their children, if they ever have any? 'Your grandmother was a snoop'? Charming."

"Eavesdropping on whom?"

"A fine legacy to hand down from generation to gener . . .''

"Maggie."

"I feel shabby."

"On your own time. If you have something to report, report." He sat down. The chair whimpered. It would make noise if a *leaf* settled on it.

I took a deep, petulant breath and settled on the arm of a chair full of the *Manchester Guardian*. "I met Roberta at the garage and found out her day was Tuesday. Went to Jessie's, her day is Monday. Went to Naomi's to see what I could find out from her daughter because I thought Naomi was at work. She wasn't, but I didn't think it was a good idea to tackle her so I waited for the daughter. On the street. Then Roberta and Jessie showed up and went into Naomi's house and I eavesdropped from the terrace. This is all I heard." I tore the page from the notebook and handed it to him.

He held it without looking at it, his sardonic gaze on me. "That," he asked, "is your report?"

I shrugged. He gazed. Caesar's last look at Brutus was jolly by comparison.

"A dull twelve-year-old," he said finally, "with a vocabulary of twenty words, who hasn't done his homework, would do more justice to a description of the plot of *War and Peace*."

He was right, of course. I'd given him the verbal equivalent of a stick-figure drawing. But I *was* feeling rotten.

"I found out what you wanted to know. I even stuck my ear to a French door like some sleazy informer, and conned an innocent adolescent into giving me information. I have spied on my neighbors. It's been a full and sneaky day."

There was a long pause while I studied the worn carpet and Bach performed his contrapuntal wonders with the viole da braccio. I waited for Greenfield to launch one of his long-suffering speeches, but instead he held up the page from my notebook, tore it in half, dropped the pieces into the wastebasket, and swiveled to the desk to busy himself scribbling.

After a stunned moment I got up, picked the pieces out of the basket, and put them on his desk. "That, I take it, was a demonstration of gratitude for my labor under stress?"

"I don't run a psychological sweatshop," he said, infinitely reasonable. "If the conditions are hazardous to your conscience, we'll abolish them. No doubt the police will unravel the mess in their own good time." He stapled two pages together, pushed a slip of paper in my direction. "There's a craft exhibit at the school. Woven wall hangings and clay pots. You can cover that."

A craft exhibit! I tore the paper neatly in two and dropped it in the basket. He swiveled away from the desk— John Cage fought briefly with J. S. Bach—leaned back in the chair, extended his long legs, and crossed his ankles, revealing strange oatmeal-colored socks that looked as though they'd been hand-knitted. A gift from Madame X?

"I have a paper to get out," he said calmly. "Are you working on it? Are you working on *anything*? Or have you joined the world's nineteen-year-olds and made soul-searching your full-time occupation?"

"Every priest, minister, and rabbi I've ever met has

been over forty."

"You think the clergy spend their time soul-searching? They're the backstage crew in a spiritual production. They're busy moving the scenery that creates the illusion." He closed his eyes. "Maggie, I'm feeling relatively fit at the moment, but I'm not getting any younger sitting here, so if you have anything to tell me, the immediate future would be the best time to do it."

I crossed to the far end of the floor-through room, stood looking out at Greenfield's garage, the uncompromising white clapboard structure looking like something out of 1900 New England, with the branches of a crab apple tree gently shedding leaves onto its roof, and thought about someone waiting out there for the right moment to cross the grass and ring the bell that would bring Mathilda down to open the door. I went back to the chair, shoved the *Manchester Guardian* to one side, sat down, and gave him a blow-by-blow account, in detail, in depth, and minus the editorials. When I stopped he sat for a while, watching his socks.

"Bryce," he murmured finally, looking annoyed. "So the girl was at the Bryce house on Wednesday."

"If she went to work that day."

"Why wouldn't she?"

"Charlie, there's nothing as boundless as a cleaning woman's ingenuity in finding reasons for not going to work."

"Mrs. Lacey . . ."

"Mrs. Lacey was to the average cleaning woman what Julia Child is to a fast-food chef."

"Who is Julia Child?"

"A character in *War and Peace*."

He spent two seconds on a critical glance and then his brows came together, a shelf of quills over his eyes. "In that case we'll have to find out first if the girl was there."

"From Agnes Bryce? *That* should keep me busy until Christmas."

Downstairs the doorbell rang.

"And if the girl was there," he continued, "we have to confirm that Dina Franklin was also there."

"Dina! Why would Dina be at the Bryces'?"

"I have no idea."

Calli Dohanis' voice accompanied stiletto heel taps up the stairs. "Charlie! A man wants to talk to you!" She appeared, wearing a tight gray flannel skirt and an emerald green blouse with football shoulders. "He's from cable TV, they give you new channels."

"Tell the man I'd rather keep a poisonous snake in the house."

Calli put her hand on her hip and glared at him. "You don't keep up with the world, you know that? How can you run a newspaper if you don't know what's going on?"

"Fortunately I have you to keep me informed. I'm busy, Dohanis."

"All right, be ignorant!" She clattered out and down the stairs.

"The world according to Klein and Dohanis." Greenfield swiveled back to his desk as the telephone rang. I picked up my bag and went to the stairs as he spoke into it. "Yes, I know. Yes, monstrous. A tragedy and an outrage. The board? Obviously the decision will have to wait until another trustee is appointed. The mayor does that, and I'm afraid he has a mandarin approach to time; he measures it in decades."

I went down the stairs.

That evening, emptying the wastebaskets at home, I came across the literature forced upon me by the man from cable TV just after George's jailbreak the night before. The night before. And tomorrow, possibly, while I was driving somewhere, while Greenfield was working at his desk, while the mayor was looking for another trustee, there would be a grief-stricken gathering somewhere, in some cemetery.

I emptied the basket quickly and made conversation, telling Elliot that Greenfield, too, had been solicited by the cable TV man, and wondering idly how many homes in Sloan's Ford were going to subscribe and which of our neighbors would be watching X-rated movies in the privacy of their . . .

The thought struck me in midsentence and I left Elliot to his politely lowered newspaper, and went to the phone.

It rang before I could lift the receiver to dial, and it was Greenfield.

"Maggie"—the quiet, deliberate manner was tinged faintly with satisfaction—"repeat what Mrs. Bryce said to you when you went there with the library card. All of it."

"Yes," I said, "you're right. That's what she said, and it already occurred to me."

A pause. "That's an encouraging sign," he said. "I thought you might still be involved with sackcloth and ashes."

Next morning I looked up the telephone number on the cable TV literature I'd retrieved from the garbage, dialed it, was passed on three times from a functionary of one department to a functionary of another, and after giving the last one a few imaginative distortions of fact, learned what I wanted to know.

By ten A.M. I was in the Honda, cruising the streets of Sloan's Ford in search of a man called MacKail.

18

I FOUND HIM astride a telephone pole on Lawrence Road, doing things with wires and singing along with some golden oldie program being blasted from a portable radio that sat on the roof of his panel truck.

Big and burly, late thirties, thick brown hair, thick brown mustache, his voice a surprising tenor. I got out of the car and stood looking up at him.

"A foggy day . . . in London town . . ."

He continued lustily to the end of the sentimental lyric and I applauded. He looked down, saw me, and grinned hugely, showing off magnificent teeth that looked as though they could chew tree bark.

"Thank you, thank you. Stick around, folks, it gets better as it goes along. Now for my next number . . ."

"You're wasting a great talent on that job."

"Ah, lady, if you only knew the half of my talents."

"You're Donald MacKail?"

"Since I was born."

"I'd like to talk to you when you're free."

He made a sorrowful face. "I don't know when that'll be. I've been married awhile now, three kids, nice wife." He grinned again. "But if you're interested in a man parttime . . ."

I laughed. (Laughed! When was the last time?) "This is business," I said.

"Ah, what've I done now? Crossed some wires somewhere?"

"Nothing like that. I work for a newspaper. I want to interview you. The man behind the scenes of cable TV."

He looked amused and scratched his head. "You mean I've been discovered? Going to make a celebrity of me?"

"I'll buy you lunch."

The grin grew wider, if possible. "They can say what they like about female liberation, I'm all for it. The trouble is, I don't keep banker's hours, you see. The schedule says a half hour for lunch and I bring it with me. It's in the truck, all wrapped in plastic Baggies, and a thermos of coffee. The Scots in me won't let me waste it, but it breaks my heart."

"What time do you eat?"

"Twelve thirty. Can you come talk to me then?"

"Will you still be at this address?"

He nodded. "This is a three-hour job. See where that house is, all the way up that hill? Have to make a connection between there and here." The grin hovered. "Not everybody could do it."

"I'll be back."

He burst into song again. "Oh when those saints . . . go marching in."

As I got back into the car a woman came out of a house across the street wearing a blue bathrobe, collected the mail from her mailbox, and squinted across at him with a puzzled look; a demonstration of joy was a strange and possibly dangerous phenomenon.

I found myself smiling at intervals during the next two hours as I wrote letters to the boys and gave George his quota of exercise. Whatever "talents" Donald MacKail had or didn't have, his ability to enjoy life made any other talents superfluous. I realized that the gloom I'd been carrying around like a load of bricks had fallen from my shoulders, and thought what a good thing it would be if MacKail could somehow be bottled and sold over the counter as an antidote to misery: essence of spontaneity, laughter, and freedom from anxiety. So much for the "dour" Scots.

When I got back to Lawrence Road he had opened the back doors of the van and was sitting on the floorboards, legs dangling over the edge, finishing off a fried egg sandwich. He jumped down at sight of me, wiped his hands on his jeans, and spread a piece of Mexican serape on the boards for me to sit on.

"Had that piece of Meh-hee-co for twenty years. Hitched down there when I was a kid, slept in the fields, drank the water, never got sick."

This man was entirely too healthy; there must be *something* wrong with him. Probably got drunk and beat his wife.

"You going to take my picture?" he asked, posing.

I'd brought my camera along as a prop. "Later," I said, "when you go back up the pole." I'd keep the picture, documentary evidence of the phenomenon, and Elliot would say, blandly, "What, you had an affair with a lineman?"

"Tell me about your end of this cable TV business: what does it involve, what problems have you encountered with installations—people being fussy about your coming into their homes—that kind of thing?" I took out my tape recorder and switched it on. I'd erase it later. Maybe.

He assumed an air of stuffy self-importance. "Well now, it's a fact that this is a damn exhausting job. Oh, sorry, not supposed to say 'damn' in the papers." He cleared his throat. "Extremely exhausting job. First of all, you see, it's a matter of making the installations during the day, and you don't get your man of the house at home during the day, it's always the lady. Well, that's a problem for a man of my talents, because these women, you know, have their TV in the bedroom, and first thing you know a half-hour job is taking me two hours and I get behind in my schedule." The green-blue eyes set in a bed of fine lines were laughing at everything: me, himself, the job. "Okay, strike it out, strike it out, I won't joke around anymore."

"Go on."

"All right if I finish my lunch?" He unwrapped another sandwich: two thick slices of rye bread oozing egg and lettuce. "Bite?" I declined. He bit into it with his power-ful white teeth, and spoke through the chewing with amazing articulation, giving me a lot of straight facts liberally laced with technical terminology. Finally he broke off with a rueful look. "Do people really want to read about this?"

"I'll pick and choose. Tell me about odd situations. Times, for instance, when the lady of the house wasn't there and you had to deal with someone who was afraid to let you in. An old grandmother, say, or a cleaning woman. We've had a number of burglaries around here and people are nervous."

"Oh, Lord, yes, we've managed to make off with a good bit of loot. It's a front, you see, this cable busi-ness— sorry, strike it out! Sure, some people are nervous letting a stranger into the house when they're all alone, stands to reason, these days. Most of them have dogs, though. I never saw so many dogs."

I stopped the machine. "This is off the record. Did you by any chance install one of these things last week for the Bryces on Oak Street?"

"I remember the name. Yeah. Bryce. Got it."

"This has nothing to do with the interview, it's just that I think I'm getting a runaround from someone and as long as I've got hold of you—"

"You haven't got hold of me yet, but I'm hoping."

"—you might be able to clear it up for me. Do you happen to remember what day it was?" Surreptitiously I switched on the recorder.

"Last week? Those records are in the office, but I keep my own log—double check, you see—never trust an employer. You did turn that machine off?" I nodded. He unzipped his poplin jacket and brought forth a small memo pad bound in red plastic. "Last week. That would be . . . okay. Bryce. Oak Street. Wednesday, October fifteenth."

"Good. That's the day she was supposed to have been there. A cleaning woman. She was supposed to work for me last Wednesday but she called and said she was ill. Then a friend of mine said she'd seen her working at the Bryces' that day. My friend is vague, so I couldn't be sure it was Wednesday she saw her. Do you remember seeing a cleaning woman in the house? Young, pretty, South American?"

"Would I forget a pretty woman? Let's see"—he chewed ruminatively—"tight pants, big earrings, heels so high she could hardly walk, big eyes looking scared."

The blood jumped around in my arteries. "That's the one. Good thing she was pretty, or you wouldn't have remembered."

"We'll never know the truth of that." The eyes danced. "I've never met a woman who wasn't pretty. I'm famous for remembering women. Where women are concerned I have the world's greatest memory."

"All right, what did my friend look like? The one who told me she'd seen the cleaning woman there?"

"Ah, but I didn't see your friend."

You win some . . . "What time were you there?"

"Late morning. Eleven, a little on either side. She might have been there, but I didn't see her. These people had the TV in the playroom, you see. The girl let me in through the garage. I'd make the carpets dirty, I guess." He poured coffee into the cup top of the thermos and offered it.

I sipped some coffee, handed it back. "What makes you think she might have been there?"

"Well, for one, I could hear people gabbing upstairs. And then, there was a car parked in front. Not in the driveway—there was one there too, and one in the garage—those must be their own cars—but on the street, like a visitor would park."

"What kind of car?"

He gave me a sidelong glance. "Yellow Rolls-Royce."

"Well, never mind, I suppose it's too much to expect cars to stay in your memory the way women do."

"Green Alfa."

I caught my breath. "You get an A for that. Now where were we?" I made a pretense of pressing the lever on the machine. "Are you doing more installations in certain areas than in others?"

I spent another ten minutes asking silly questions and receiving replies garnished with the MacKail brand of irreverent humor, and then he climbed the pole for a picture, grinning down from a height of twenty feet, seeing himself in the papers, the wife and kids and neighbors making a fuss. I felt dishonorable. But I wouldn't mention it to Greenfield.

When I was back in the car, with the address he'd given me written in my notebook so that I could send him a copy of the story, he called down. "I'll be in the neighborhood awhile. Drop around anytime." I drove home smiling. Until I thought of the green Alfa and the woman who should have been driving it that day.

Before we paid our weekly Friday evening visit to Gordon Oliver's study, Greenfield stopped by to listen to the tape. Elliot had wisely arranged his indoor tennis games for Friday nights, and he exchanged a few words with Greenfield in the front hall, his jacket coming off a hanger, Greenfield's going on, before he left. Greenfield sat in the big armchair, George resting his head on one of his shoes, while the tape played itself out.

At the end of it he nodded, not in the least excited that his reconstruction of events had been corroborated: he'd decided that Dina had to have been in Mathilda's vicinity on Wednesday, and so, naturally, it had proved to be so. He had already progressed to the next hurdle.

"I reread your report on the last Village Board meeting." He eased his shoe out from under George's head and George sat up, looking hopeful. (A walk?) "You have indirect quotes from remarks made by several people, Lucas, Moss, and Gardner among them. I assume there were speakers who weren't quoted. What about Mrs.

Bryce?''

"Didn't say a word.''

"Her husband?''

"Smiled a lot. Anyway, if you remember, when I tried, over the phone, wangling an interview with Agnes Bryce on the basis of the school sale, she said she had absolutely no opinion on the matter. Couldn't even get a yes or no. A clam would have been verbose by comparison.''

He rested an ankle on the knee of the other leg. "See if you can think of anyone who might know—and be willing to tell you—how Mrs. Bryce feels about the school sale.''

I got up from the sofa and went to the piano to collect my music. "You know, Charlie, you sit there on Poplar Avenue in your swivel chair, working out your jigsaw puzzle, fitting in all the little pieces, with the finished picture in front of you so you know what you're looking for, and all I do is run around looking for the pieces so you can fit them in. I never see the picture. I don't know if you're working on the Grand Canyon or a scene from *Faust*.''

"Faust?" he mused. "Interesting.''

"Is that it? You're sending me out there to tangle with Mephistopheles?''

"Maggie. It was your idea to begin with.''

I carried the Schubert trio across to his chair. *"Mine?"*

"When Dina Franklin disappeared it was your idea that it might have something to do with her professional life. If you stretch a point, being a member of the Village Board was a professional activity.'' He stood up. "We'd better go.''

I followed him out to the hallway, picking my heavy cardigan off the back of a chair. *"I* see. So you've worked it out that Mathilda was killed because she cleaned for Dina, and Dina was a member of the Village Board. Clever.''

"How many board decisions have you written up?''

"Thousands. Hundreds. A dozen. Why?''

"Then you must know how many votes it takes to pass a zoning change.''

"A simple majority.''

"There are five members of the board, the mayor and four trustees, making three a simple majority. It's rumored that Leonard Gardner and Peter Rush are—for whatever reasons—opposed to the school sale. As long as Dina Franklin was alive there were three members in favor, and it would have passed. If someone had an overpowering reason to keep that sale from going through, removing one of the three board members would do the job, at least temporarily. And if there was a good chance of replacing a trustee in favor with one who was opposed, the goal would be achieved." He got into his jacket and went out, watching George suspiciously for any signs of bolting.

I locked the door and went down the walk to the driveway, trying to take in the concept. Someone who had an overpowering reason. How overpowering could a reason be, in that connection? Well, one man's meat . . . or woman's . . . Naomi had a reason, apparently. And Roberta. And Jessie. And Agnes Bryce wouldn't talk about it—whatever that meant.

We drove through the chilly night to the Olivers' house in the chic-contemporary Dunstan Hill section of Sloan's Ford, Greenfield's cello enthroned on the backseat behind us.

"There are a lot of other people," I said, "opposed to the school sale. Five or six of them spoke up at the meeting, and there were probably some who didn't."

"But only the four we're concerned with had the relevant relationship. And of those four Mrs. Bryce had the best opportunity."

"What about the men?" I said suddenly. "Men these days have taken to complaining about female 'chauvinism,' demanding 'equality.' Fine, let's not keep them out of it. What about Leonard Gardner? You said he was against the sale. And Jordan Moss—If Roberta was against it, he could have been. And Fred Bryce, as well as Agnes."

"I don't think the girl would have opened the door to them. They were at work when she came to clean. She never saw them."

"The girl." I'd thought we were talking about Dina. What could all this possibly have to do with Mathilda? "You still think there's a connection?"

"There has to be."

We snaked up the tortuous driveway to the Olivers' long, woody hilltop house, Greenfield lugged his cello up to the front door, and Shirley Oliver, resplendent in a red jump suit, looking like liquid rubies poured on mocha velvet, opened it.

While we greeted her and shed our respective sweater and jacket, my mind became a battleground for colliding fragments of information that were shooting across it in all directions, like crazed meteors. Dina had been at the Bryce house on Wednesday. Naomi and Jessie and Roberta had a hasty conference that had something to do with Tuesday night. Mathilda had been at the Bryces when Dina . . . Naomi and Jessie and Roberta were evasive about the school sale. Agnes Bryce wouldn't talk about it. Naomi and Jessie and Roberta had all been in some kind of emotional turmoil. Agnes Bryce had been the last one to see Dina.

"Depending on how you use the word," Shirley Oliver was saying, "this town is either coming out of or going into the dark ages. Gordon's just been asked to sit on the Village Board."

We stared at her.

"Well, don't all cheer at once."

"Wonderful!" I said. "Terrific!"

"The mayor," Greenfield said, "not only made that choice, but made it inside a week? Incredible."

We went into Gordon's beautifully ascetic study, where two straight-backed ebony chairs sat behind two music stands next to the Baldwin. Gordon, in dove-gray cashmere pullover and charcoal-gray slacks, was rubbing rosin over his bow with a faintly pleased expression.

"I'll have to congratulate the mayor," Greenfield said, "assuming you're actually going to subject yourself to all that nonsense."

"The board? Oh, I think so. I live here, after all."

Greenfield took his cello out of the case. "Good. That takes care of the high-school orchestra's trip to Vienna. Also, you might be able to find out something I want to know."

"If I can do it ethically, I will." Gordon sat down and

arranged his music.

"A number of people have been against the sale of the school. Give us an A, Maggie. I'd like to know if the Bryces are in that camp."

I sat down at the piano.

"Fred Bryce," Gordon said, "against the sale? I can't see why he would be. He stands to gain a good few dollars by it. He's the agent who interested the Brant Institute in buying the school."

19

THE MAN WITH the burglar alarm system arrived at ten the next morning, carrying his gadgets in a salesman's case, and wearing his shifty smile. I wasn't at all certain that he wasn't a front man for a burglary syndicate that thrived on inside knowledge of where each system had been placed and how to bypass its electronic ear. "There's a room on the side where the window's out of range; you can break the glass there without setting it off." The idea of having to live my life guarded by a mechanical device was abhorrent. In deep gloom I rearranged the bookshelves, while Elliot accompanied the man upstairs and down, making decisions as to where the various sound sensors would be placed.

Removing from the shelf a travel guide now out of date by some ten years, I added it to the growing pile on the living room rug destined for the pending book-sale-in-aid-of-the-library-building-fund. By the time the man departed, hefty check in hand, I had added to the pile by clearing the shelves of a cookbook containing forty-seven French recipes each of which took forty-seven days to prepare, a thick popular-medicine tome outlining a health regime by which one could not fail to live forever, a dictionary so old that one quarter of the words in current use had not been invented at the time of its compilation, a book given to me decades earlier by my mother on what to name the baby, and a dozen science fiction paperbacks picked up by Elliot on his various plane trips; fictions that had already been outdone in monstrousness by science real and live. I bundled them all into a plastic shopping bag bearing the name of a savings bank and unearthed the mailed leaflet telling where the books should be delivered.

Elliot ambled up from the basement looking serene. "All set. Any burglar trying to break into this house will have his eardrums shattered and immediately take to his heels. Now you have nothing to fear while I'm away next week."

"Next week! Where to? For how long?"

"Oregon. Monday morning. Just for a few days."

"Just. And Oregon of all places. They have volcanoes erupting every five minutes." Profound depression descended upon me.

"I wouldn't keep the alarm switched on while you're home during the day. You might set it off by dropping a fork in the sink or causing a vibration of some kind. Just remember to switch it on and bolt the doors before you leave the house. And switch it off when you come in. All right? Now you won't feel so vulnerable?"

"It's a gadget, Elliot, not a person. If it goes off in the middle of the night, I can't ask it if it's a false alarm or a real burglar. Not to mention that if it screams me out of a deep sleep I'll not only have shattered eardrums, but a heart attack! Not vulnerable? Lying in bed waiting for sirens to go off in my ear?"

He patted my shoulder and assured me that no such thing would happen. I was not comforted. Three nights alone in a house that had to be bolted and barred and switched on and off. Gracious living. I picked up the plastic shopping bag. "I'm going to deliver these books before it's too late," I muttered. The address on the leaflet was in Jessie Lucas' neighborhood and I found myself climbing that perpendicular hill once again, this time stopping at a lower altitude, the designated house sitting some thousand yards closer to sea level than Jessie's. There were two cars pulled up at the curb and two more in the driveway.

I lugged the plastic shopping bag to the front door, rang the bell, and a cheerful little woman with cropped fair hair and a child of six or so peering out from behind her denim skirt asked if I would mind lugging it a little farther, specifically to the garage door, which rolled up shortly after I reached it, to reveal a hive of industry. Books in cartons, crates, bushel baskets, and brown paper bags covered the garage floor, and more books covered a trestle table set up at the far end where two more women were busily sorting them into piles. Partly filled cartons along the wall behind them were labeled AD FICT, JUV, AD POP, HIST, NONFICT, and MISC.

"Just find a space and plunk it down," the cheerful woman said. The other two women kept up a constant chatter.

"*Juniper Berries!*" one of the sorters exclaimed. "Where does *that* go? Gardening? It *looks* like fiction."

"Adult or juvenile?"

"Moronic."

I stuffed the plastic shopping bag between a crate and a carton.

"You don't happen to know Lois Beeman?" the cheerful woman asked me. "She offered to sort this morning but she hasn't showed up and there's no answer at her house."

"Afraid I don't know her," I said.

"Oh well. Maybe I can get one of the other volunteers to fill in. We really have to finish this lot today." She smiled at me hopefully, but I had volunteered to transport them once they were sorted and felt no obligation to spend the day in a dusty garage deciding where to put *Juniper Berries*. Recognizing a deadbeat when she saw one, she consulted a cardboard rectangle taped to the wall on which someone had lettered the word VOLUNTEERS at the top, and the days of the week down one side. The week of October thirteenth. Opposite three of the days a name and telephone number were written.

"Maybe I could get Jessie," she chirped. "She's so

close by.''

I looked carefully at the list and saw that "Lucas" came after "Jessie" and they both came after "Wednesday." A flicker of recognition penetrated my depression: Wednesday the fifteenth was significant. "Did Jessie Lucas really spend all that Wednesday sorting books?"

"Oh, no, she was only here from about nine thirty until—oh—after lunch. Two or so in the afternoon. That was our first week, the thirteenth, we weren't really pushing it. I hate to ask her again, but at least she doesn't have kids at home to worry about.''

"Stories of the Operas?" one of the sorters said uncertainly.

"Miscellaneous.''

I drove back down the hill feeling fractionally more lighthearted. If Wednesday was a crucial day, Jessie was in the clear. Now if I could prove the other two equally elsewhere at the time . . . Recent dismal failure at the game told me there was little hope of it. And yet, something teased my memory; something . . . just beyond the edge of recall.

On the principle that ignoring an elusive piece of stored information is the only way to lasso it, I distracted myself with deciding what to wear to dinner at Elliot's brother's house in Connecticut that night. Too cool for the green silk? Too warm for the terra-cotta suit?

It came to me when I saw Elliot's appointment schedule on the chest of drawers in the bedroom. Thirty seconds later I had dumped the contents of a manila envelope onto the dining room table and was poring over dog-eared sheets of my cryptic shorthand notes, generally translatable only within twenty-four hours of having been written. Knowing, however, exactly what I expected to see, I found and deciphered what I was looking for with no trouble. As I stuffed papers and manila envelope back into the briefcase, a folded, printed page caught my eye.

It was the newsletter I'd picked out of the carton in the Bryces' vestibule. I read it through. And then read it again, to be sure it actually said what I thought it did.

From the back door Elliot asked if I felt like going for a walk. I said I had to take care of something and he went off with George. I stared down at the letter with the big black capitals C.M.G. at the top. Citizens for Maternal Guidance. *Mama mia*. I went to the phone and dialed.

"Charlie? Where are you?"

There was a silence, with Telemann faintly in the background, and finally, "At the number you just called."

"I mean upstairs or in the office?"

Telemann suddenly grew in volume, as though Greenfield had held the receiver next to the machine. "Does that answer the question?" Meaning there was no source of music upstairs in the living quarters; needless to say, he had not, anywhere, been able to duplicate his incomparable stolen components.

"I'm coming over," I said.

I started for the front door, then remembered and switched on the alarm, almost hoping Elliot would forget and drop a fork in the sink.

Haydn had replaced Telemann by the time I got there, and Greenfield, ensconced in swivel chair, had created around him his own indoor version of autumn. A drift of discarded and curling sheets of lined yellow paper lay like large fallen leaves on desk and floor, and a few, as though tumbled and lifted by an October gust, had traveled across to nestle in the cracks between the usual printed matter occupying the worn and weathered armchairs. The yellow pad from which they'd come was in his lap, the Parker pen in his hand, and a look of Napoleon anticipating Waterloo on his face.

He ripped yet another sheet from the pad and handed it to me. It was filled with his barely intelligible scrawl. Across the top of the page, underlined, I made out with difficulty the words "Probable Knowledge Girl's Whereabouts Friday," and under that the names Gardner, Bryce, Lucas, Moss.

On the next line, "Whereabouts of Above Relevant Time Friday" and the same list of names, with "not determined" after each one except Bryce after which he'd written "Home. Unconfirmed."

On the next, "Of These, Knowledge Franklin's Whereabouts Wednesday: Bryce, Confirmed."

Followed by, "Whereabouts of All the Above Relevant

Time Wednesday: Bryce, Home, confirmed. Gardner, Lucas, Moss, undetermined.''

And finally, ''Motive: Girl: All of the Above Conceivable. Franklin: Gardner, Lucas, Moss, possible. Bryce, none discovered.''

I handed back the sheet. ''Correction. Whereabouts Relevant Time Wednesday: Gardner, Lucas, Moss, now determined.''

Greenfield turned from his study of maple leaves outside the window and took the earpiece of his horn-rimmed glasses from between his lips. ''You've had a busy morning.''

I made a gesture of modesty. ''It was just a matter of tireless industry brought to fruition by an acute and penetrating mind. And a little dumb luck. Jessie Lucas was busy all of Wednesday sorting books for the Book Fair in the company of a pillar of the Sloan's Ford community. The schedule given me by the lady novelist that didn't tell me where Naomi Gardner was on *Friday*, definitely says that on *Wednesday* she was shepherding the novelist first to an ABC television studio and then to a Fifth Avenue bookstore. And according to the Architectural History guide of Canal Street, it was Wednesday that Roberta Moss took the tour.''

Greenfield looked back at the maple leaves, then heaved a sigh that blew more yellow paper off the desk. ''One with an opportunity and no motive. Three with a motive and no opportunity. Four fish clearly visible in the stream and the hook is missing from the fishing rod.''

''We don't *know* that three of them had a motive.''

''The phrase 'reasonable assumption' was invented to make deduction possible.''

''I'm not sure it's a reasonable assumption. I just can't see any of them working up a homicidal fury over the question of whether or not the school will be . . .'' I broke off. The tape clicked and the music stopped. A bird hopped along the windowsill. I sat there with my hand resting on the reasonable assumption folded inside my bag.

''Will be?'' Greenfield murmured, prompting.

I took the newsletter from my bag and gave it to him.

"A carton of these was standing in the Bryces' entryway last week, obviously a mailing. I found it in the case with my notes. I stuck it in there without reading it at the time."

He read it, his face unimpressed as he waded through the proselytizing prose that demonstrated, beyond a shadow of the authors' doubts, that the rise in crime was directly attributable to the working mother. The home, that rock upon which civilized society was based, had been abandoned by its legendary guardian and keeper of the morals. On her vain and greedy head, as she scurried from her house each morning, taking yet another job away from some deserving male, rested the responsibility for the empty house that invited thieves and turned a formerly safe community into a playground for the underworld. Because of her selfish and unwomanly pursuits, the young were being left to fend for themselves, deprived of the watchful eye that would keep them firmly on the straight and narrow path. The guilt was hers, that children were smoking pot and becoming pregnant in their teens, she alone was putting them on the road to crime and sin and perdition. The Citizens for Maternal Guidance was declaring itself in the vanguard of a movement to create legislation barring a woman who had children under the age of twenty from holding any job but the one ordained for her.

Greenfield read the last sentence and dropped the letter carelessly onto the desk. "Hardly unique," he said; "half the bombast in and out of Washington is based on one warped conviction or another."

"That," I said, pointing to the letter, "is a revised version of *Mein Kampf*."

"It's bilge. How far do you think they'll get with that?"

"One inch is too far. We have to show it to Gordon."

"Gordon?"

"Well, my God, Bryce is the man behind all this, his name is on there, president of the damn thing, and Bryce is the agent for the sale, Gordon *said* he'd make a good bit of money on it! Where do you think that money will go? A Washington lobby, that's where!"

"Do you know what it takes to . . ."

"I don't care! Voting for that sale to go through is as good as funding a terrorist group!"

"Maggie!"

"You might as well start a Fresh Air Fund for the Ku Klux Klan!"

"Maggie!"

"It's like holding a benefit for Idi Amin! It's . . . ."

"When you've run out of hyperbole," he said loudly, and then resumed his normal decibel level, "you might take time to realize that with this letter you've given me grounds for a reasonable assumption."

I sank back against the debris in the armchair. "I know."

"I don't know how Lucas or Gardner or Moss could have gotten their hands on this."

"Mathilda, maybe. She may have picked one up at the Bryces'—or been given a few, to disseminate. The carton I saw needn't have been the first printing."

Greenfield looked surprised at my sudden willingness to draw the net around the three musketeers, and then he realized what was behind it and frowned. "And on the Wednesday in question . . . they were all . . . otherwise engaged."

I smiled. "That's right."

No comment. No movement. He didn't even get up to put on more music. He stared at the newsletter for a while. Then he murmured, "C . . . M . . . G." He went to the file cabinet, rummaged around, and came back with the large, round, orange plastic pin that his new cleaning woman had found under his bed.

"You said this is similar to the pin worn by the Bryce girl?"

"You couldn't tell one from the other. Except for the initials, I suppose."

"You didn't notice the initials on the Bryce pin."

"I was too far away." I looked at the pin with the M.G. initials. Mathilda Gutiérrez. A sad little memento of a pretty girl. "Poor Mathilda. They didn't even do a good job on it." The initials, instead of being evenly spaced, descended vertically from the center of the pin.

"There could have been another initial at the top, that came off."

"You mean her middle initial was also M? Mathilda Marylou Gutiérrez?"

"If it was her pin."

"It was found under your bed. Mrs. Lacey didn't drop it. Unless you've acquired a close friend in the past two weeks . . ."

He gave me one of his heavy-lidded, disdainful glances. "You were told she scavenged. She might have picked it out of someone's wastebasket. At the Bryces', for instance."

"But then the bottom initial would be a B." One cannot be consistently brilliant.

He picked up the newsletter and held it out to me. Citizens for Maternal Guidance. C.M.G.

"Terrific," I breathed scornfully. "They had buttons made up. In plastic. How appropriate."

"People who are trying to achieve an image of sober, responsible citizenship would hardly make an emblem of something you could buy at a carnival. This was the Bryce girl's own idea."

"Could be, I suppose. And when the C fell off it didn't mean anything, so she stopped wearing it, threw it in the wastebasket, and Mathilda scavenged and saw her initials."

"How do you know the Bryce girl stopped wearing it?"

"Really! I saw her one day and she was wearing it, then I saw her a week later when I went to visit her mommy and she *wasn't* wearing it. Charlie, you *are* going to show Gordon that newsletter?"

"What day did you see her wearing it?"

The things he harped on! "*I* don't know, sometime last— Oh, yes, the day Mrs. Lacey resigned. At the shopping center. The girl came barging across the parking lot on a bicycle. She was wearing this big orange pin, and she knocked into Roberta Moss. Groceries flying in all directions. In fact, when I saw the girl without it I thought she'd probably lost it in the scramble to pick up the groceries. Does that constitute a reasonable assumption that the Bryce girl didn't want Dina to vote for the school sale? If the answer's yes, I leave for Tibet in the morning."

He turned and gazed dreamily out the window, as though

he were spending a quiet day planning the spring planting.

"The day Mrs. Lacey resigned," he said, "Tuesday."

"Charlie, if you're not going to show Gordon the newsletter, I'll do it myself. I'll give it to *Shirley. That'll* take care of it."

"Tuesday," he repeated, musingly, to the leaves outside the window.

20

CONNECTICUT IS VERY pretty; at least that part of it through which we drove that Saturday evening to get to Elliot's brother's white colonial house with the black shutters on the green acre surrounded by a white split-rail fence. The grass seems to be a more expensive variety around there and there's a lot more of it around each expensive home. Streams, ponds, and groves of fruit trees abound on private property. Nature, in that part of the state, seems to have been designed by a really classy decorator with an unlimited budget. Admittedly the lavishness dwindles, just short of Michael and Dell's neighborhood, to merely attractive, but it's still nothing to pass up if you're house hunting.

Michael, who designed packages for products, gave us drinks. Dell, an English teacher, fed us beef and broccoli made in a wok, and spinach salad and stewed pears stuck with cloves. The niece and nephew popped in and out, growing, it seemed, even as they said hello. A few recent movies were dissected, and a few absent relatives. I felt restless. I had things to figure out, murders to avenge, Shirley Oliver to see about that newsletter, Elliot's imminent departure with which to make peace. I all but sighed with relief when we left.

But the restlessness remained. I was restless asleep and

restless when I woke, to a gray, raw Sunday morning. Greenfield's obsession with the word "Tuesday" had stirred a buried question, but not sufficiently to bring it to the surface. I opened the Sunday *Times* and read a review of a new play by an old playwright that was either a rave or a pan depending on whether you read the first or last paragraph. I skimmed over the news—it was not something I could afford to read in depth these days—and a word at the bottom of a page triggered my memory.

Jessie. Drinking sherry. My chiding her for leaving her door open. Her reply, "The burglaries have been piling up, haven't they? Three the other week, then Dina Franklin . . ."

How did Jessie know that Dina Franklin's house had been broken into? Dina had discovered it late Tuesday night, told me about it at ten the following morning. Jessie had been sorting books from nine thirty on. Had Jessie and Dina spoken before nine thirty that morning? Where? Why?

The telephone rang. Greenfield.

"Maggie. You mentioned something about"—here we go; he's going to ask me how Jessie knew about the break-in at Dina's house—"Agnes Bryce mailing a parcel. Can you describe it?"

It took me a moment to alter course. Agnes Bryce? What is he— To hell with it. "Certainly," I said, "I'm a trained observer. It was the size and shape of a shoe box."

"First-class mail?"

"Parcel post."

"You didn't by any chance see how it was addressed?"

"I didn't have to. That postal clerk in Gorham is a newscaster manqué. He practices with addresses on parcels, very loud, like a first grader proving he can read. Have you ever walked on the street with a first grader? 'No Parking.' 'Bank of New York.' 'Half-Price Sale.' Every time that clerk put a parcel on the scale the sender's private affairs became public knowledge."

"The address?"

"To somebody called Bryce. In Florida."

"Florida," he said, "is an entire state."

"Oh, the town. Um . . . Seashore, Seabreeze, something like that. One of those retirement communities, I would guess. Sending homemade cookies to Mom and Dad."

"You're certain it was addressed to a Bryce?"

"According to the Walter Cronkite of the post office."

"Seashore. Seabreeze. They probably have one of each every ten miles, the length and breadth of Florida."

"Near Palm Beach, maybe."

"Why there?"

"Cronkite said something about Palm Beach. 'Fancy around there, Palm Beach,' or something of the sort."

"Meaningless," he grunted. "Mention the United States when you're abroad and some European will automatically say Chicago, or New York, or Los Angeles. To some people Florida consists of three cities and Palm Beach is one of them."

"Could be, but I didn't get that impression."

"Well, it's something."

When I realized he'd hung up, I did the same.

An hour later there was a call from upstate. Alan, to say there was something wrong with his car and he didn't want to spend a fortune at the garage, maybe Dad could diagnose it over the phone. Dad listened, asked a lot of questions about piston rings, connecting rods, and crankshafts and finally told him to take it to a garage. I asked Alan about his brother and he said, "He's fine," but vaguely, as though trying to remember when he'd last seen him. I practiced the Schubert for a while, wondering intermittently and without much enthusiasm what significance there could be in Agnes Bryce mailing a parcel of cookies to Florida.

It was afternoon when Greenfield called again. He sounded, for him, tense.

"Could you come over for a few minutes? I'm upstairs."

I had visions of Agnes Bryce trussed to a chair, a bright light shining in her eyes. Or Naomi Gardner, ditto, but having hysterics. The back door was unlocked and I climbed the two flights to find Greenfield in the bedroom, a suitcase, into which he was stuffing shirts and socks, open on the bed.

"Virginia would be tolerable," he said, "even South Carolina. She had to send it to a state that prides itself on alligators and condominiums." He looked up and confronted my startled eyes and open mouth. "I'm going to Palm Beach. I should be back Tuesday—Wednesday at the latest. I'd like you to stay in the office while I'm gone. There's nothing urgent, I've checked most of what's going in this week. Klein has a piece due—look it over, knock out the superlatives. Keep an eye on Dohanis. If you have any questions you'll be able to reach me. I'll call and give you the number when I get there." He looked dubiously at a pale blue pullover, finally folded it, more or less, and dropped it in the suitcase.

I sat down on the bed, my mouth tightly shut to keep the four-letter words from escaping. He saw my expression and deliberately misinterpreted it. "It's a temporary separation. It doesn't call for being stricken."

"You," I said, choking, "would only leave the paper in someone else's hands for something *titanic*. *I* have been running my car to shreds chasing clues, I have demeaned myself. I have suffered trauma and guilt and God knows how many headaches, and now that something *titanic* has happened you're suddenly going to take care of it yourself and leave me here to mind the store?"

"Someone has to mind it, and I can't let you go to Florida. Some of the things that may have to be done there are unlawful."

"Oh, fine. Is that the number where I'll be able to reach you, the county jail?"

He stuffed three Parker pens and a lined yellow pad into the suitcase pocket. "I'm not making this trip for the giddy joy of it. If I could turn it over to Pratt, I would." He took a pair of navy slacks from a hanger in the closet. "But Detective Pratt has the mind of a civil servant; he's not comfortable with the purely theoretical, and he wouldn't act on it. I have to give him hard evidence." He folded the slacks once, lengthwise, put them in the case. They hung over the edge.

"What theory? What evidence?"

He refolded the slacks in thirds. "I paid Howard Franklin a visit last night. He seemed grateful for it; action, as everyone will tell you at the drop of a hat, alleviates grief. We went over the contents of his wife's handbag." He went into the bathroom and emerged with a razor and a toothbrush. "One of the things we found," he shut the suitcase and snapped the locks, "was a black plastic letter C." He took the suitcase into the living room.

I remained sitting on the bed, my mind racing. Black plastic letter. From the Bryce girl's pin. That Mathilda had been wearing when she cleaned Greenfield's bedroom. Found in Dina's bag. And Greenfield was going to Palm Beach. To where Agnes Bryce had sent a box of cookies. . . .

But the puzzle could wait, more urgent matters intruded. Elliot was leaving. I would be home alone with the burglar alarm. It was raw and gray and windy outside. It was balmy and sunny in Palm Beach. If I left George with the Olivers' kids they'd be ecstatic.

I went into the living room where Greenfield was at the phone, dialing, with the Yellow Pages of the phone book open at Airport Limousine Service.

"I refuse," I said. He stopped dialing and looked at me. "I will not stay in the office and take care of the paper. If I can't go down there alone, I'll go with you. You're going to need help. A thousand miles from anyone you can trust, if things don't go according to plan, if you suddenly need another pair of hands, or eyes . . ."

Greenfield put down the receiver and stared at it.

"Leave Stewart in charge," I said.

"Klein! He's barely learned the difference between journalism and Joyce. I'd be on the phone every half hour."

"He's better than no one. Because I'm going. I don't know what we're going after but I'm going."

"Maggie." His voice was low, calm, and not to be trusted. "It's quite possible nothing will come of this. It's an amateur expedition. Instinct and desperation in equal parts. That box could very well contain nothing but carbohydrates. And if it doesn't, it's probably been X-rayed by now and opened by a postal inspector, in which case the trip will have been superfluous. Even assuming it's the relevant Bryce my Florida friend discovered in a place called, by the way, not Seashore or Seabreeze, but Sea*view*.''

Now I knew what we were going after. It still made no sense, but at least I knew. Greenfield was still talking.

"I have no business going after it in any case, much less exposing you to the consequences. Not to mention taking you a thousand miles away from home and husband.''

Good. All this talk was so much face-saving. If he were adamant he would have disposed of the matter with one word.

"Elliot," I said, "is going to be away for the next few days, and I have my own money. If you'd rather take a limousine, go ahead, but I'm driving to the airport and there's plenty of room.''

He went to the window and looked out. "Klein in charge of the paper," he muttered. "Klein. Hearst was timid by comparison." He reached in a pocket and held out a slip of paper. "You'd better call LaGuardia and arrange things. Don't take the car. I'll call the limousine. And I'll get hold of the dauphin.''

I drove home with no illusions about the need for this trip. Instinct be damned, it was sheer desperation. He'd come up against a blank wall with Lucas, Gardner, and Moss, and grabbed at the straw of Agnes Bryce's parcel. Agnes, for whom we couldn't even *fabricate* a motive. Agnes, who didn't even have the nerve to put lipstick on her whole lip! But mine was not to question why. Not when faraway places and no burglar alarms were involved.

Elliot was not pleased. It was one thing for *him* to go flying around in the face of air-control statistics, quite another for me to do the same. But he was cursed with a sense of fairness and the negative visceral response surrendered to it.

In the limousine I casually mentioned that while it was obvious what "hard evidence" we were pursuing, the theory behind it still eluded me. Greenfield glanced at the driver, asked me for my notebook, and wrote one sentence in it. Enough to stagger me, and raise a hundred questions which I knew, from experience, he would answer only when he was good and ready. I watched the driver strug-

gle through the airport traffic congestion, Greenfield beside
me surveying the scene with the sullen mistrust of a New
Guinea plainsman being wheeled into surgery. He had no
faith at all in the principles of aerodynamics as applied to
anything but birds. When we had picked up the tickets
and made our way down the enclosed ramp to the plane
itself, he distinctly hesitated before actually stepping into
the cabin, as though he were standing on a cliff and one
more step would plunge him into the void. He hated the
seats. He hated the seat belts. He hated the smiling flight
attendant with the glazed expression. "She looks like the
outside of a baked ham." He retreated into a thunderous
silence as we taxied and lifted and left the good earth far
below us. I didn't care for the idea much myself.

"Who's the friend in Florida?" I asked finally, when
we'd been airborne for thirty minutes and still hadn't
crashed.

It took a while for him to unlock his larynx, and then
he used it sparingly. "Sam Petrie. A newsman. Retired.
He served a few years at NBC when I was there."

"How did he find these Bryces?"

"Consulted the phone book."

The glazed flight attendant came around with trays of
synthetic food. Greenfield stared at the unidentifiable stew,
handed back the tray and ordered some more bourbon. I
ate it—whatever it was. And then we were descending,
bumping along a runway, stepping out into warm, moist,
sea-smelling air, and a landscape as flat and featureless
as a football field.

I followed Greenfield across to the Rent-A-Car counter
and a maroon Ford compact appeared. Greenfield regarded
it with only slightly less mistrust than he had the plane,
but got staunchly behind the wheel, consulted notes of
his friend's directions, and we drove along streets of
unrelieved dreariness: long, strung-out successions of flimsy
houses, tacky storefronts, dingy coffee shops, garish filling stations, tawdry drugstores.

"Charlie," I said quietly, "I think we got off at the
wrong stop. This is not Palm Beach!"

"They don't usually place airports in areas where the
property values are astronomical." Now that we were on

firm ground his sentences were becoming lengthier.

"I didn't expect the plane to land in a swimming pool surrounded by palm trees," I said loftily, "but this looks like the setting for a fifty-mile roller derby."

No reply. A few minutes later I heard the ocean, and we turned and followed a road that ran parallel to it, a road bordered by high walls dripping with bougainvillea, broken every so often by wrought-iron gates behind which glimmered, in luxurious lamplight, white pebbled drives, velvet lawns, lush, perfumed vegetation, Spanish-tiled roofs, pillared facades, all the trappings of the monumentally rich.

"You're right. It's Palm Beach."

Through the window I breathed in the combined scents of ocean and flowers and oranges, and hoped that Sam Petrie had married a Vanderbilt or one of that ilk, so that I would get to see the inside of one of those pleasure domes. But no, eventually we left Billionaire Boulevard behind and drove on into the area of the merely well-to-do. Mile after mile of Greenfield's detested faceless condominium tower blocks, with here and there a two-story, swimming-pooled, air-conditioned, color-TVed resort motel. A palm tree was stuck in the ground every so often, to keep the franchise, but no lawn, or willow, or chimney, or private, human-sized dwelling existed. And the ocean, the whole point of a beach, though audible and smellable, was totally invisible somewhere behind the works of man.

We pulled in, finally, before an enormous complex of white, balconied buildings that rose like a giant horseshoe around a tropical garden full of dripping ferns and scarlet blossoms and waterfalls. We left the car and stood looking up at it. Greenfield drew his chin up to his lower lip in a gesture of incomprehension.

"If Beethoven had spent his life here," he said, "he would have been John Philip Sousa."

A thin man with a bald, sun-bronzed head, wearing a lot of seersucker, directed us to the correct building; we found the elevator and ascended in a sterile hush. In the blank white wall of the corridor, the blank white door was opened by Sam Petrie, large, trim, debonair, a square, good-looking face under silver hair, an expansive smile. He led us over Nile-green carpet into a white-and-green living room, louvered doors opening onto a balcony, paintings in primary colors, airy, summery, Floridian. His wife Dorothy was equally tan, silvery, and good-looking. Drinks were served, delicacies were handed around. Petrie elicited news of the real world, not so the wife. She listened with the slight, disinterested smile of one who has made a commitment and will not look back.

"Tell me about these Bryces," Greenfield said, finally. "Where is this Seaview?"

"Seaview." Petrie laughed. "They'd have to build a tower to get a view of the sea. It's a small bungalow community, about fifteen minutes' drive. There's a nice fish place we go to down there. Good place to lunch. I've gotten to know the owner pretty well, a New Yorker once, but he's been here twenty years. We play golf. I asked him if he knew these people and evidently this Bryce guy is quite a character. Sell his mother for a nickel if she were alive. Retired and scared to death the money won't last. Gets free bones and meat scraps from the butcher for his dog, only he doesn't own a dog; the wife boils it up with potatoes for dinner. Collects old clothes for some organization and keeps whatever fits. Runs a kind of private taxi service in the community, takes the old ladies to the doctor or the movies and fights with them over the fares. Always has three or four little deals going. And of course all the time he has a fairly decent bank account. What's your interest in him?"

"I'll tell you when it's over."

"I think," Petrie said happily to his wife, "Charlie's on the trail of some laundered money. I think his village mayor's been dealing in Florida contraband."

"More likely," Greenfield said, "I'm on the trail of a wild goose. I'm probably going to do something the law wouldn't smile upon, so the less you know the better. Your friend with the fish restaurant is a man of discretion, I hope?"

"I impressed him with the need for it. And he wouldn't want me to suggest at the Golf Club that he couldn't be trusted."

"Wouldn't want to lose a good customer, either," Dorothy said. "We spend a lot of money there."

"Could you find out what time they get their mail delivery in that area?" Greenfield asked.

"Now?"

Greenfield nodded. Petrie strode across the room to a white telephone, consulted a small green notebook lying beside it, dialed a number.

"Mr. Avenel there? Petrie. Bob? Remember the people we were in with last Friday? The lady says she mailed you that fish recipe, or thought she did, but found she put it in the wrong envelope. What you're going to get is a check for the rent. Well, it happens to the best of us. She wants to come by and pick it up. What time do you get your mail? Right. I'll tell her. Thanks." He came back across the room with a smile as mischievous as urbanity would allow. "Between ten and twelve."

Greenfield nodded his thanks and looked thoughtfully at his empty glass. Dorothy looked perturbed. "What's Freda going to say!"

"Oh, I'll take care of it." Petrie held the decanter over Greenfield's glass but Greenfield waved it away.

"How far is the fish restaurant from the Golf Club?" he asked.

"Not far."

"I could use your help very early tomorrow morning, if it's convenient. You know your way around here and I don't."

Petrie glowed at the prospect of action. Dorothy looked faintly anxious. They made plans, Petrie drew a map of the area in question, and we left, after receiving directions to the resort motel a mile away where Petrie, after a second long-distance call from Greenfield, had booked two rooms.

It was a cheaply built affair disguised with the regulation pool and palms, tennis court and deck chairs. The coffee shop was open and Greenfield, a little flushed with three drinks and no dinner, ordered a chicken sandwich that was superior to the airplane food only in that it was identifiable. I kept him company with a cup of Sanka.

"This is a fool's errand," he said between bites. "If

any part of it is successful I may be forced to believe in miracles. The parcel could have gone astray, parcels do, and that would be the end of it. Parcel post from there to here should take a week to ten days but it could have been delivered this past Saturday, it could be delivered next week. Mrs. Bryce could have a friend visiting her . . ."

"And I could be sitting on the beach—if there is one—doing nothing, because no one told me what I'm supposed to do."

He told me the plan and I had to agree with him: there was hardly a point at which it couldn't go wrong. But grim visage and dire predictions to the contrary, Greenfield was enjoying himself.

Alone in my somewhat clammy room between the tennis court and a kiddie pool, I called upstate New York to tell the boys that if they called home and no one was there it was because Mother was committing an act of folly in the invisible playground of the very rich.

21

GREENFIELD CAME OUT of his room on the opposite side of the kiddie pool looking ridiculous. He had gone, at first light, on a shopping trip, and now wore the results. He had rubbed his face, hands, and neck with some bronze gelstick, sported a straw hat, sunglasses, and shirt of some shiny synthetic fabric with a pattern of dolphins jumping through hoops. I bit my lip and walked around the pool (where three boisterous children were making the early morning delightful with screams and splashing) to join him.

"Gee," I said, "that's real neat."

His expression would have done justice to a scientist infecting himself with a disease for the ultimate good of mankind. "If all that remains for future historians to dig up are tattered remnants of this shirt, and one recording of a country-and-western song, the end of the twentieth century will go down as the watershed that marked the swift and total collapse of civilization."

Petrie drove up in his sky-blue Oldsmobile and stared out the window at Greenfield. "By God, you'll be taking tickets at the Indian Reservation next."

"This pays for the sins I'm about to commit." Greenfield got into the Ford, I got in beside him, and we followed Petrie down the wide boulevard, over a bridge, and out of condominium heaven into what, in that area, passed for countryside: endless flat stretches of scrubby brush and dusty grass dotted at intervals with shopping centers and "communities," all strung, like unmatched beads, on a connecting chain of filling stations.

"What if this doesn't work?" I said to Greenfield as we bowled along.

"When Petrie and I were at NBC, our superior—in title—was fond of saying, 'Let's not shop for a new canary before we know the old one won't sing.' I believe that was his sole contribution to broadcasting."

No alternate plan, in other words. I watched the alleged scenery roll by.

Eventually Petrie turned off onto a side road and pulled up before a rustic shanty on the edge of a lake called, oddly enough, "The Shanty." This was the fish restaurant Petrie had mentioned the night before. Greenfield took the Ford to the far end of the parking lot, parked it, and we got out and got into Petrie's car.

Back briefly to the filling stations, then down another side road that ran through marshy-looking land to a cluster of bungalows in the distance. A peaceful, early-morning quiet descended. Something that looked like a heron flew by. There was a smell of lake water and fish and damp foliage.

The small community was laid out in an orderly fashion: a grid of streets marked by the letters of the alphabet, ten bungalows to a block. The houses were simple, one-story frame structures, all vintage 1940, with the "minimal upkeep" look of summer cottages, and of the four residents we chanced to pass, not one didn't have senior citizen status.

On G Street Petrie slowed to a crawl, and as we passed a faded pink bungalow with a small, sagging front porch, he said, "There it is." Greenfield nodded and we cruised down the rest of the block, out to the marshes, and back to The Shanty.

Greenfield got behind the wheel of Petrie's car and Petrie and I went into the restaurant. Separately. An entrance decorated with shells and a fish tank led to a huge main room with plank tables and a wall of windows overlooking the lake and a family of pelicans. Petrie was greeted by the owner, a small, bespectacled man with a deeply tanned, deeply lined face and shrewd dark eyes. I went to a phone booth in the rear and dialed the number Greenfield had written on a slip of paper.

A prissy female voice said "Hello?" as though the owner had difficulty in opening her mouth.

"I'd like to speak with Mr. Bryce, please."

"Who is this?"

"I need a taxi."

"He's not here right now."

Marvelous. Was the old canary going to die without uttering a note? "When do you expect him back?"

"He should have been back by now. Sometimes he picks up a few extra people and has to drop them off. Where do you want to go?"

"Palm Beach."

"Palm *Beach*? From where?"

"I'm at The Shanty."

"Weeeell . . . I don't know . . . that's a half hour's drive or more."

"I'll pay whatever it costs."

Silence. Except for money talking.

"I'll tell him. You'll probably have to wait ten minutes or so. What's your name?"

On the wall opposite the phone a stuffed fish was mounted on a wooden plaque. "Snapper," I said.

I went out to Petrie's car where Greenfield sat, apparently mesmerized by his watch. He looked up inquiringly from under his eyebrows.

"She's there, he isn't. I left a message. If the canary isn't dead he should be here in ten minutes." I thought that sounded like the proper dialogue for the occasion.

It was closer to fifteen minutes and I was still nursing a glass of tomato juice and watching Petrie talking with the owner, when a figure like an old welterweight boxer gone to seed plodded aggressively into the restaurant, wearing a brown Windbreaker over a shirt of vivid heliotrope, baggy gray trousers, and a black-and-white-plaid cap.

I stood up and he saw me and said, "Snapper?" I went up to him reluctantly.

"You want to go to Palm Beach?" He spoke in the phlegmy voice that makes you want to clear your throat.

"And back," I said.

He lowered his chin and shook his head pessimistically, as though I'd asked him to breach the ozone layer. He had a wide, lipless mouth and a fleshy nose. Whatever his relationship to Fred Bryce, the family resemblance was nonexistent.

"That's not going to be cheap," he said.

"Twenty dollars?"

He raised his small, colorless eyes and sent them quickly around the room as though calculating what he could expect from a patron of this place. "The gas alone. I go to the discount and it still cost a dollar twenty."

I waited. Any offer I made was clearly going to be topped. Finally he said, "I couldn't do it for less than twenty-seven."

I nodded, and as we left the restaurant I saw Petrie heading for Greenfield's maroon Ford and Greenfield starting up Petrie's blue Oldsmobile.

The "taxi" was a dusty, navy blue Chevy, a good ten years old, and the inside hadn't been vacuumed, ever. The wheels tocked as they revolved, a sound like a bicycle with a piece of cardboard caught in the spokes. The windows were all shut. I lowered the one next to me and Bryce's head whipped around. "Oh, boy," he said.

"Fresh air. It's stuffy in here."

"That's how I get a crick in the neck. People open that window, I get a draft and then I have a crick in the neck."

"It's very warm out." Eighty was the *least* it was.

"Warm is how much blood you have. Old people don't have that much blood. On a long drive like this people should show a little consideration for the driver."

He was a darling. I rolled the window up halfway.

"I don't like to complain. I'm not a complainer. But if I get sick I can't drive the car. I don't own a piece of Fort Knox, you know. There's no Greek millionaire left me a bundle in his will. I got to take care of myself."

He went on not complaining, over the bridge, past the condominiums, along the row of plushy, secluded estates, until, happily, we reached the broad, palm-lined avenues of Palm Beach proper.

"Whereabouts you want to go?"

"Worth Street." A name Petrie had given me.

He took me there. Polished, creamy buildings like moneyed dowagers, impeccably powdered, coiffed, and adorned. Acres of diamond-bright plate glass. Pillared, second-story balcony cafés, vine-covered arcades, chic cobbled alleyways lined with boutiques.

"How long you going to be?" His eyes slid around the street with a mixture of greed and disapproval.

I hesitated. There was no way I could pinpoint my departure time and if I told him to pick me up in an hour he'd go tearing off to make another few dollars somewhere. I had to know he was safely far from home for at least that long.

"It depends," I said, "how soon I find what I want. It could be twenty minutes, it could be forty-five."

"I *got* to know when to come back for you. Why don't we say in an hour?"

"I want you to wait."

"*Wait!* If I'd've known! You didn't say I'd have to wait. I can't hang around here waiting. I'm losing money all the time. I could've had two other calls I didn't take because of you. You can't expect me to spend all this time for what you're paying. I thought I was gonna drop you here and come back later—"

I took a five-dollar bill from my bag. "We'll work out the price when I get through," I said coldly. "Just put the car in that parking lot we passed and get yourself some coffee. I'll meet you at the car when I'm ready."

His lipless mouth turned down at the corners. "Lady, you're taking advantage. I got a good mind to give up this business. I get nothing but headaches from it."

I walked away and into the first shop that presented itself: pale pink stone exterior with long-legged, suntanned mannequins in the window dressed in wisps of chiffon, the combined price of which could thoroughly develop an undeveloped country. Inside, pale rose carpet and gleaming chandeliers, a locked glass cabinet edged in gleaming brass that housed assorted five-hundred-dollar baubles of shell pink and vanilla and jungle green. A sleek saleswoman approached and I left hastily.

An hour of Through the Looking Glass while I wondered if Greenfield had gotten lost in the marshes, had been apprehended in the act by an irate senior citizen, had discovered the whole operation to be fruitless, had run into someone's garden hose and had his makeup streaked, revealing him for the sickly, pale Yankee outlaw that he was.

I wandered as I wondered. Something called a "Gallery" which sold a collection of exotica ranging from a six-foot toy lion to a thousand-dollar, scrolled-wicker tea wagon. Tanned ladies in kings' ransoms of pastel slacks and shirts buying bone china at colossal expense. Men's handkerchiefs that cost more than my best blouse. One shoe, one bag, one sweater, one tennis racket, each displayed in single splendor on a swathe of velvet or a spill of brocade as though it were the Koh-i-noor.

On a balcony café I sat drinking iced coffee and pondering all this phenomenal meaningless purchasing. The novelty of acquisition must, by definition, have its limits. And then what? When all the playgrounds had been scavenged and all the walls and wardrobes were bursting with finery, what then? Did all these silken, perfumed people finally, at the end, cry "Rosebud"?

It was time to go back to Bryce and his taxi. From the ridiculous to the repulsive. And where was Greenfield? And what was happening? And what inconceivable passion had cracked the impregnable walls of the Bryce fortress? Agnes, stifled and subjugated. Agnes, with no motive. No motive. . . .

In the parking lot a seething Mr. Bryce, tiny eyes blazing, plodded back and forth near his Chevy with a soft-drink can in his hand. Without a word he flung open the back door and when I got in slammed it after me. I congratulated myself on having effectively silenced him, but too soon. We'd been under way for only minutes when he took up his litany of phlegmy complaints. Now I'd made him late, he had a couple to pick up at the optometrist, regular customers, when he didn't show up on time that would be the end of them, he would lose two good customers, and he'd got a crick in his neck just like he'd said he would, and if he'd known—and so on. It became invidious background noise, like drilling in the street.

With a rush of relief, I saw the facade of The Shanty through the window, battled with him over compensation for loss of revenue, injury to his reputation, and what not, and finally, when he went tocking away, ran across the parking lot to Petrie's Oldsmobile where Greenfield was already starting up the getaway car.

I got in beside him and he pulled away from The Shanty, sending the speedometer up by leaps and bounds: Greenfield, for whom, ordinarily, forty-eight was speeding.

"Well?" I demanded. He looked frazzled. His straw hat was off, sunglasses discarded, hair on end, sleeves of the dolphin shirt pushed up anyhow.

"We can now," he said, "be accused of illegal possession."

"You've *got* it?"

"Under the seat."

"How? What happened?"

"I drove around until I spotted the mailman making deliveries, parked in the street behind the Bryce house, got out, and sauntered around."

"Sauntered!"

"There was no cover. What would you have done, dropped from a helicopter? Why do you think I bothered with the masquerade?"

"Yes, all right. So?"

"Before the mailman started up the Bryces' street he took some mail from the van, including a parcel. I strolled along behind him, slowly, stopping to tie a shoelace, blow my nose, look at flowers—the place offers as much opportunity for sight-seeing as a billiard table—when he started up the path to the Bryce house I stopped, as though I didn't feel well. There was an old crone across the way in a lawn chair watching me. The mailman went up to the porch and I went after him, stumbling, clutching my chest— It's not really *that* amusing!''

''Sorry.''

''Mrs. Bryce opened the door, he handed her the parcel, and I called out, 'Please! Could I have some water to take a pill?' I was searching in my pockets, of course, mouth hanging open— Maggie!''

I wiped the tears from my eyes and pressed my lips together.

''She believed it, naturally. Living down here you can set your clock on the hour by the sound of an ambulance. She dropped the parcel onto a porch chair, went inside, the mailman left, I struggled onto the porch, she came back with the water, I registered desperation, still feeling in the pockets. 'Pills! I left my pills in the car. It's my heart. Around the corner—a white Buick.' . . . Maggie. Don't you have *any* self-restraint?''

I gasped, squealed, shook with laughter. It was partly release of tension but mostly the mental picture of Greenfield competing with Gielgud. Greenfield shut his mouth firmly and drove in silence until I brought myself under control and pleaded for him to go on.

''Mrs. Bryce went off to get the pills, clomping down the street. I grabbed the parcel, went through the house and out the back door, cut across their yard and the yard behind that. Some woman was hanging out a washing but she had her back to me, and I came out on the street where I'd parked the car, and got out of there in a hurry.''

''Good God. It doesn't seem possible.''

''It was always possible. *Probable* is what it wasn't.''

The humor evaporated as I realized what lay on the floor. Very real. Very deadly.

''And it's under the seat. And Agnes Bryce— It's hard to believe. I wouldn't think she had the nerve to *touch* a gun.''

"Oh, she touched it all right. And then was naive enough to believe she could get rid of it without any risk by sending it through the mail to be hidden by relatives. The storm that broke on her head in the bosom of her family when this little maneuver came to light must have been prodigious."

We drove between low stone pillars onto a graveled driveway that snaked past the shaven greens of the Golf Club, left the Oldsmobile in the parking area with the keys behind the sun visor, took the box with its torn wrapping from under the seat, found the Ford with its keys similarly hidden, and drove back to the motel. Any police officer recording a description by a senior citizen in Seaview of a strange blue Oldsmobile, license number whatever, parked on H Street just before a crazy-looking man made off with Mrs. Bryce's parcel, would find that the owner of that Oldsmobile had been innocently playing golf in the company of a couple of bank managers during the entire time in question. There were some things Greenfield hadn't left to chance.

While I ordered omelettes and iced coffee at a table in the coffee shop, Greenfield went to his room to wash and change. He emerged clean, pale-skinned, and soberly dressed, and made an announcement.

"We can't fly back. Or rather, I can't. Not with that hunk of metal in my case. I've taken two bedrooms on the train. It leaves in two hours and gets us in about seven tomorrow night. You can take the plane if you prefer it."

No object in human history ever captured my imagination so completely as The Orient Express. No work of nonfiction ever held me as spellbound as *The Great Railway Bazaar*. What a ship's mast was to Jack London, what India was to Kipling, what the Sirens were to Greek mythology, a train was to me.

"Oh, I don't mind the train," I said.

"Good." He skewered his omelette, looking content; no dubious aerodynamics to think about. Though I couldn't think why he should worry, now that he was forced to believe in miracles.

22

THE TRAIN COMPARTMENT was large, for a Lilliputian. It smelled of steam and sweaty leather and the window was grimy. I loved it. I stowed my bag on the rack, hung my jacket in the upended pencil-box of a locker, let down my tiny metal sink, and washed my hands, and decided that now was the time for all those questions I'd been saving. I made the journey across five or so feet of space to Greenfield's compartment. He wasn't there.

I went down the length of the car, glancing into the rooms on either side where women sat with their shoes off and one man—may his tribe dwindle—smoked a cigar evidently made by Goodyear. At the end of the next car Greenfield sat in a compartment opposite a slender, silver-haired man with a goatee, who, it seemed, had been a violinist with the NBC orchestra when Greenfield worked for that station. They had recognized each other in the corridor and were now embarked on reminiscences. The man, introduced to me as Edwin Buhl, had in his compartment not only a chess set, but a tape recorder and a set of tapes. And that, except for meals, when Mr. Buhl invariably joined us, was the last I saw of Greenfield during the journey.

I went back to my own little space, got the bed pillow out of its hiding place on the wall, settled it in the small of my back, and watched Florida roll by. I'd spent less than twenty-four hours among the alternating concrete and stubble, the carefully cultivated exotic trees and florid displays of horticultural extravagance, but already I was heartsick for real greenery.

I peered out the grimy window for any glimpse of unkempt fields, tangled shrubbery, cow-munched pasture,

a casual kitchen garden, a simple spreading farmyard tree—
anything—any sign of the accidental, untouched beauty
of *real* countryside. I yearned for bulrushes, an unplanned
pond, brambled lane, waist-high grasses, rushes, reeds,
the soft, fuzzy, imprecise contours of clustered elms,
roadside wildflowers. . . .

I saw orange trees growing in sand, as though someone
had transported the beach inland. I saw an army of trucks
piled high with oranges. I saw dead Spanish moss hanging from a dusty roadside tree like the draperies of a
ghoul.

That evening, after dinner in the dining car with Mr.
Buhl ("You really should get a place down here, Charlie,
living is so much easier." "I'd rather live with difficulty
and die of frostbite."), I was distracted from my old copy
of Sylvia Ashton-Warner's *Spinster* by boisterous conversation in the corridor. I drew back the curtain that covered
my doorway. Three women and two men, not one of them
under seventy, were standing in their various doorways
flirting and teasing each other with all the gusto of teen-
agers "hanging out" on a street corner.

"If I was twenty years younger, I'd go around the
world." Hefty woman in a pink pantsuit.

"Oh, the trips I took twenty years ago! Greece, Scan-
dinavia!" A bantamweight dandy of eighty with razor-
sharp crease in his slacks, and white shoes.

"If I could only go there by train—" Another woman,
all bones, sunglasses, and hennaed hair.

"Train is the best way to travel." White shoes. "Look
at all the nice people you meet. Am I right, ladies? Could
you get to know two good-looking guys like us on a
plane?"

Laughter, retorts. I let my curtain fall back. Old people
delighting in the company of those equally aged, like
seeking like for confirmation of their continued viability
as companions, taking comfort in hearing that their own
incapacities were echoed in others. Getting old was no
joke, and you'd better laugh at it while you could. Make
a face at death. Like Jessie.

Jessie, who would be a baby in their company, but was
already dreading the inevitable.

The business of aging, I realized, had been a factor in almost all the events of the past two weeks. Beginning with Mrs. Lacey. And Dina, who'd been a thorn, not because of her accomplishments, but because her opportunities were a result of her youth. And then Jessie's virulent paintings of young women whose bodies, the vessels of youth, were prized while their heads . . . And Naomi's screaming frustration at no longer having the energy for all the jobs required of her; Roberta's fear of not being allowed to enter the world before it was too late; Jessie's acid description of the signs of age in her face.

Was that, I wondered, the bond among those three? Had they found each other because of that common enemy? But what, then, was the reason for that hurried conference at Naomi's? Was there a sort of Aging Anonymous, whose members helped each other at times of crisis? Didn't seem likely. In any case, the three musketeers were no longer our concern, despite their odd behavior and their suspect attitude to the selling of the school. They, obviously, were out of it.

When would I get to ask Greenfield those questions? Possibly in the taxi on the way home.

Brisk, chill air greeted us as we left Pennsylvania Station the next evening. Lovely, exciting smell of chestnuts and dry leaves and bus fumes.

"All in all," I said, "I prefer seasons."

Greenfield verbally manhandled a taxi driver into taking us home to Sloan's Ford.

"What are we going to do," I asked, as we sped up the West Side Highway, "with the—um—hardware? Stop in to see Pratt and hand it over?"

"I've done enough traveling on his behalf. I called before we left that place and told him if he wants the evidence he can come to me." He closed his eyes and took a nap.

So much for my questions. I looked out at the lights of the Palisades across the Hudson, feeling overheated, inadequately washed, and happy.

The taxi stopped at the foot of my driveway and Greenfield opened his eyes. "I thought you said Elliot was out of town."

"So he is."

"There are lights burning."

"He's very tricky with timers and photoelectric contraptions. There's hardly an inch of that house now that isn't activated by clocks, darkness, or the sound of a fork in the sink."

We took both suitcases to the Honda standing in the driveway and stowed them inside. No evidence that we'd been far from home, Greenfield said, in case Pratt was already waiting at the house on Poplar Avenue.

He was. A discreet dark gray sedan was parked in front of the house and the gray eminence himself stood on the long narrow porch, waiting.

"Sorry to keep you waiting," Greenfield said. "We were at the movies."

The twin icicles that were Pratt's eyes bore into us, but he kept his mouth shut. We trudged, single file, around to the back of the house and up the two flights to the living quarters. Greenfield switched on lamps and took his folded raincoat, evidence concealed in it, into the bedroom. Pratt, of course, sat himself down in the chair Greenfield favored, and to punish him, Greenfield made a long business of getting out the decanter, asking me what I'd like to drink, inquiring if Pratt would take anything, alcohol, ginger ale, or plain water if he preferred.

"If you think," Pratt's voice had all the lighthearted insouciance of a tanker plowing through heavy seas, "the police department was organized so you'd have something to play around with . . ."

"I don't think any such thing."

"I *warned* you that I expected you to tell me the minute you found out anything—the minute you *thought* of anything. I've got a good mind to charge you, regardless of who you are in this town."

"Charge me with what? I called you within a half hour of finding the evidence."

Pratt sat forward with his forearms on his knees. "Just get to it, okay?"

Greenfield sat down in the chair opposite Pratt and sipped his bourbon. "If I give you the evidence without giving you the theory behind it, you'll have proof of an illegal act, not murder, and proof of the weapon used on Dina Franklin and the girl, and probably proof of the ownership of the weapon." He swallowed more bourbon. "But you won't necessarily have the murderer."

"*We'll* decide what it proves and what it doesn't prove. Let's have the theory, as long as you've got one."

"Point one. Dina Franklin's car was standing outside the home of Fred and Agnes Bryce between ten and twelve on the morning of the day she was supposed to leave for St. Louis. Fact. Confirmed by a witness." Pratt opened his mouth to interrupt but Greenfield cut him off. "You can ask questions when I'm done. If I can't tell a story coherently I don't tell it. Point two. Dina Franklin's handbag, found beside her, as you know, contained a black plastic letter C, as, no doubt, you also know." Pratt's mouth opened fractionally, but he clamped it shut. "I discovered it accidentally when I paid her husband a sympathy call. Point three. On Tuesday, the day before Dina Franklin was to leave for St. Louis, the Bryces' daughter was wearing a large plastic pin with black initials glued onto it. Fact. Mrs. Rome saw her wearing it. Point four. A week later the girl was not wearing the pin. Same source. Point five. On Tuesday night, the night of the day Mrs. Rome saw the girl wearing the pin, Dina Franklin's home was broken into. As you know. Point six. An identical pin, with only two black initials, was found under my bed by a subsequent cleaning woman, after the girl who was killed had been cleaning my rooms. The catch on the pin was loose. Point seven. The girl who was killed while cleaning my rooms was working at the Bryce home the day that Dina Franklin's car was seen there. Also fact, also confirmed by a witness. Final point. Mrs. Rome, at the post office in Gorham, on the Monday after the girl was killed in this room, saw Mrs. Bryce mail a parcel to someone called Bryce in Seaview, Florida."

Greenfield raised his glass, looked at it, and put it down again without drinking. Pratt leaned back in his chair and slowly crossed his legs. I took a sip of my ginger ale.

"I call what's coming a theory," Greenfield went on, "because it still has to be confirmed, but I'd be surprised if that weren't merely a technicality. I'll give it to you as

I believe it happened, in sequence.''

Pratt laced the fingers of one hand through the fingers of the other and his mouth twitched, but he kept his peace, or whatever it was he was keeping behind that stony face.

"On the Tuesday night before she was to leave for St. Louis, Dina Franklin came home from an errand and found someone had broken into her house. She called the police, but before they got there she found—somewhere—on the carpet, in a corner—a large plastic disc with three black initials glued to the face and a pin arrangement on the back, of which the catch was loose. The initials told her who the intruder must have been—either because she'd seen the Bryces' daughter wearing the pin, or because she recognized the initials as those of an organization headed by Fred Bryce. Mrs. Rome has already told you Dina Franklin didn't want to make any accusations until she'd confirmed her suspicion, but she may have had another reason. At any rate, she concealed the pin from the police.

"The following morning she drove to the Bryce home and confronted Mrs. Bryce with the evidence that her daughter had attempted burglary. Mrs. Bryce is not accustomed to independent action. She called her husband at his office in the village and he drove home to deal with the situation.

"Denial, I imagine, was the response Dina Franklin got from him. 'That pin does not belong to my daughter.' But Mrs. Bryce had probably already given the game away by recognizing it. 'Have you ever seen this pin, Agnes?' 'Oh, yes, that's my daughter's. She told me she'd lost it. Thank you so much for returning it.' So that Fred Bryce's denial was useless. Dina Franklin tells them she hadn't told the police about this yet, but now that she's verified her suspicion she's going to take it to headquarters and let the police deal with it.''

Greenfield got up, wandered to the window, and stood looking out at the night. Pratt watched him like a bull watching a matador.

"I don't know," Greenfield went on, "how well acquainted you are with Fred Bryce. I've had several opportunities of studying him. He got himself appointed to several committees on which I was serving. He's clever, but not highly intelligent. He's full of moral rectitude, but entirely lacking in compassion. He's law-abiding, but feels he alone represents the law. There was a parlor game undergraduates used to play. 'What's the disparaging adjective that would hit so-and-so the hardest?' Napoleon, say, or Thomas Wolfe, or Isadora Duncan. Words like 'short,' or 'mediocre,' or 'ugly.' Typical undergraduate exercise, but occasionally it can explain an otherwise inexplicable action. The word, in the case of Fred Bryce, is 'suspect.'

"He can't afford to be considered suspect. He has built his life around an ostentatious show of virtue. His standing in the community, his embryo political organization, his future career, the things he considers vital to his life, are completely dependent on the image he's built up, of a man so respectable, so blameless, that a saint would seem grubby by comparison."

Greenfield went back to his chair. "Well, it's obvious. The woman was threatening the foundations of his life. She had evidence that his own daughter was one of the scummy band of young criminals about whose existence he himself had publicly been ranting. Even if it couldn't be proved, the news would be abroad in the village in a matter of hours. The embodiment of respectability, the unassailable parent who waged war against negligent parents, had been responsible for rearing a thief. And, of course, the tragedy was"—he took a drink of the bourbon—"that he never doubted the girl's guilt. He believed his daughter was capable of the act. He believed it instantly. No one imitates sainthood unless he lives in mortal fear of his own capacity to sin.

"He asked Dina Franklin not to go to the police until he'd had time to speak with his daughter and find out if there was some other explanation for the presence of that pin in Mrs. Franklin's house. She said she was in a hurry, she was leaving town, the airport limousine was picking her up at two o'clock. He asked for a few minutes to go up to the school and see his daughter. Said he'd report to Mrs. Franklin at her house long before she had to leave.

She agreed and left to go home. He didn't go to see his daughter, of course, convinced that rampant vice had infected her. He was in a rage.

"He waited a half hour or so, went to the Franklin house, told Mrs. Franklin he'd found the guilty party and would prove it to her if she'd come with him for just five minutes. She was persuaded and he drove her to the empty school building on Glenbrook, to which, as he was the realtor involved in the sale, he had a key. They went inside—I don't pretend to know on what pretext—he shot her, took the incriminating pin from her handbag, and in the process one of the initials was detached and remained in the bag. When he got home he dropped the pin in a wastebasket where it was found and appropriated by the cleaning girl because without the initial C the pin held only her own initials."

Greenfield looked at his glass, looked at Pratt, said, "Are you sure you won't have something?"

Pratt looked as though he'd rather accept a piece of silver from Judas Iscariot. Greenfield sighed, rubbed his eyes, and continued.

"Two things subsequently occurred to Fred Bryce. One, that when Dina Franklin was eventually discovered in the school building, the fact that there was no sign of forcible entry would point to anyone with a key, and so, one night, he ripped open the boarding on a back window and smashed the glass. The other, that there had been a witness to the accusation made in his house by Dina Franklin. He decided the cleaning girl was a danger, found out she'd be working for me on Friday—possibly the girl and Dina Franklin mentioned it in his presence—when Mrs. Franklin was leaving the house, for instance. He knew I was bound to be at the County Legislature on Friday, gave me plenty of time to get out of the way—may have called on the phone to make sure she was alone—came to the door through the back where no one would see him, and rang the bell." He raised his head and gave Pratt a level look.

"I told you at the beginning it must have been someone she knew. Ordinarily cleaning women aren't acquainted with the man of the house, but Bryce's office is three minutes from his home, he was probably in and out often enough for her to be comfortable with him. Of course he couldn't shoot her, in my house, with two of my staff in the office on the other side. So he knocked her unconscious with the pistol, then finished the job. He's a muscular man.''

Pratt opened his mouth just wide enough to say, "Where's the evidence?"

Greenfield uncoiled himself from the chair, went to the bedroom, and returned carrying the box with the torn paper wrapping. He stopped a few feet from Pratt. "Short of a warrant, which I doubt could have been issued on the basis of what I've told you, there was no way for you to get possession of this in the time available."

Pratt held out a hand and Greenfield gave him the box. He looked at the wrapping, opened the box, and brought forth the instrument of death.

"Don't handle it!" I cried out.

He turned his bleak eyes on me. "What do you think there is on these surfaces? The butt is crosshatched, the thumb rest is only big enough for a partial; we never yet got any usable prints from one of these things." He looked at Greenfield. "I won't ask you where you got it, but the question's going to be asked and you'd better have an answer ready."

"I found it on my doorstep."

Pratt sniffed and rattled the wrapping paper. "There's nothing on this to indicate who mailed it. Return address gives no name and it isn't even a Sloan's Ford address."

"Mrs. Bryce had her moment," Greenfield said. "Repressed middle-aged woman, a lifetime of being told what she can and can't do, living a straight-laced, hidebound existence in a James Bond–oriented world, a buggy rider in a space-age society."

"I'm not interested in your complicated psychology. I don't want any more 'whys.' You said Bryce was clever. A clever man doesn't give his wife a murder weapon to put in the mail. So if you're right—and that's a big if—she did this on her own. How did she know about it? Knew there was a gun in the house, okay, she'd have to. With all this burglary scare, she'd know where the gun was kept."

"She has a bumper sticker," I said, "that recommends we all start actively protecting our homes."

He pretended I wasn't there. "When she sees the gun is gone, she asks Bryce; he makes some excuse, puts it back, but the next day it's gone again, and she hears about the girl being killed, puts things together—nobody's that dumb. So she gets hysterical and while he's figuring out the best way to get rid of the gun—dump it and report it stolen or whatever—she decides to mail it off to the brother or cousin or whoever this is. Pretty gutsy for a 'repressed, middle-aged' lady. But you definitely saw her mail this parcel?" He turned, recognizing, briefly, my existence.

"I saw her mail it. She didn't see me. The postal clerk in Gorham will remember it."

"There was no letter in here," he asked Greenfield, "a note, or anything?"

"No. She probably thought she was being crafty. Probably called them and told them to expect a parcel and hide it away. She's lucky not to be in the hospital, considering what her husband's reaction must have been when he found out."

Pratt put the revolver back in the box: that steely little object our Constitution says we all have a right to bear. He rose hugely from the chair. "When the lab finds out the bullets didn't come from this automatic, you'll have a few things to account for. I'll be seeing you very soon." He moved to the doorway, stopped, and said with frost on every word, "In case you thought that while you were dreaming up this scenario, the dumb cops were sitting around playing Mah-Jongg, we got the kids who've been breaking into the houses."

"Good." Greenfield was benevolence itself. "Then you've recovered my stereo."

Pratt gave him one last arctic glare and went out and down the stairs.

Greenfield shook his head. "A sore loser," he said.

"Well come on, Charlie, you come up from the audience, play the whole bloody concerto, and after the final cadenza, you hand the violin over to the concertmaster so he can sit there holding it while the orchestra mops up. You can't expect him to like it."

We went down the stairs, he got the Plymouth out of the garage and drove me to the Olivers' to pick up George, and then home. He transferred his suitcase from the Honda to the Plymouth.

"You can sleep tonight," he said. "Now that they've caught the burglars—temporarily."

A thought struck me. "Including the Bryces' daughter."

"I doubt it. She's probably been at a friend's house every night, doing her homework."

"But she must have been at Dina's?"

"It's irrelevant. All that matters is her father believed she was there."

George, crazy with excitement, almost pulled the leash from my hand. I held on with both hands while Greenfield took my suitcase and unlocked the front door. He dropped the suitcase on the floor with a thud. A wild, screaming siren rent the air. I ran and shut it off.

"Even if there *were* any burglars here," he said, "they'd be dead ones. No mortal could survive that sound for more than five seconds." He went out and down to the driveway. I called after him.

"If a rotten mess like this can be said to have anything good about it, I'm glad, at least, about Naomi and Jessie and Roberta. I mean, whatever they were stewing about, they had nothing to do with this."

He turned and looked at me. A few leaves fell slowly in the light of the streetlamp from the oak tree at the corner of the driveway.

"They had everything to do with it," he said. And got into the Plymouth and drove away.

23

ANOTHER WEDNESDAY DAWNED—ominous and blowy, with a charcoal sky. The forecast said rain, but the forecast had been saying it in vain for so long I paid no attention. Greenfield, of course, was incommunicado, effecting an eleventh-hour rescue of the paper from the hands of an underequipped pretender to the throne.

He was due to come for his Wednesday dinner that evening, but there was a problem. I had to transport the books, as I'd promised, from the garage where they'd been collected, to the site of the Book Fair, and the site was no longer the Village Hall, which was in the process of being repainted due to a small but smoky fire in the basement, but an old, disused train station which had to be swept out and set up with tables by another team of volunteers before we could bring in the books. The prognosis was that it would be five thirty or six o'clock before the room was ready, and probably seven thirty before I could start on the vegetables.

I would not, however, withdraw the invitation. I had spent the night in considerable mental turmoil over his unexplained assertion that the three musketeers "had everything to do with it," and I had no intention of spending another. I called the office and told him that dinner would be late, and why. After much growling about trivial distractions while he was trying to organize the Sloan's Ford equivalent of the Book of Ecclesiastes, there was a portentous pause, and then . . .

"Are you carting all those books by yourself?"

"No. There'll be another volunteer."

"Who?"

"Good God, I don't know. Nobody feeble, I'm sure.

You just get here around eight."

An hour later, as I was basting the chicken, he called back. Unheard of on a Wednesday.

"I'll help you with those books."

"It's not necessary, Charlie. We'll manage."

"Three cars carry more than two, and it cuts down the time."

He must be starving. "All right, I'll give you the address."

"I know where it is." He hung up.

Why he'd gone to the trouble, on a Wednesday, of finding out where the books were stored, I couldn't imagine. At any rate, I would get both Greenfield and my explanation that much earlier.

As it turned out, the explanation, though it came earlier, came from another source.

At five forty I drove up the now-familiar steep hill in what seemed to be an incipient gale, trees tossing their heads as though they were having nightmares, leaves whirling through the air and scudding down the street. On the way I passed Jessie Lucas' battered station wagon, descending, and memories and anxieties crowded in on me. The need to know what was behind Greenfield's remark was fast becoming obsessive.

There was no other car at the curb or in the driveway leading to the garage that held the books, and I wondered if the other volunteer had deserted. But no, when I'd staggered as far as the lighted garage, wind tearing at my hair, the cheerful little lady of the house informed me the first load had already gone down, with the key to the station house.

As I lumbered back to the car, my arms around a carton of books, both Greenfield and the rain arrived. He stepped out of the Plymouth and looked up at the sky with an expression that said he expected no less: the elements would naturally wait for him to be engaged in outdoor work before letting loose.

With borrowed slickers and with plastic bags from the cleaners covering the cartons, we loaded up the cars. Rain had turned to storm. We proceeded, in caravan and low gear, down the steep, slick hill and along the road by the banks of the Sloan River. Rolls of thunder, forks of lightning, wipers swinging wildly and inefficiently across the windshields.

The train station was a relic of the first (and long-since dismantled) railway line to connect Sloan's Ford with the city: a nineteenth-century wonder that had chugged peacefully through the valley twice a day at ten miles an hour. The station house, a square stucco building, had eventually been turned over to the Board of Education for storage, and the flat land around it was used as parking space for the school buses. It stood on the far bank of the Sloan, and we inched across the small bridge over the river, wind roaring and rain slashing at the windows. The lights of Greenfield's Plymouth up ahead turned and crept along to the row of yellow buses that took up all but a narrow strip of the paved area to one side of the station house.

Between the paving and the building a quarter acre of weeds bisected by a brick path was fast becoming a sea of mud. An hour earlier we might have driven over the weeds and up to the entrance, but it looked now as though the ground would soon be swampy enough to make getting stuck a probability. Though the other volunteer—and then I realized what I was seeing, through that thick, wavering curtain of rain: parked in the weeds by the entrance was Jessie's station wagon.

The other volunteer. I might have known it wasn't gnawing hunger that prompted Greenfield's offer of assistance. He'd remembered that Jessie had sorted books for the fair, anticipated the possibility, and called someone, somewhere, to find out. Would the sight of me unsettle her? Those three women must have compared notes, decided I was a spy: I had never heard from Naomi about the cleaning woman. Did Jessie suspect that Greenfield knew whatever there was to know?

We parked on the verge left by the buses. When he emerged from his car, I looked pointedly at the station wagon and back to him, but he ignored me, and carrying a carton each, we struggled down the brick path. The door opened as we got to it and Jessie stood framed in the doorway, key in hand, the hood of an old green poncho framing her face.

Her lips parted slightly at sight of us and she quickly averted her eyes from me and gave Greenfield a wary glance. Greenfield looked carefully away and she stood aside for us. I said "Hello, Jessie," and put my carton down alongside Greenfield's.

"Well!" she said. "Here's the key, I'm going back."

"I thought," Greenfield said casually, "we might save some time by setting up a relay system. If you'd be good enough to help."

She could hardly refuse, considering the distance we had to carry the cartons. We stationed ourselves at equidistant points from each other, and Greenfield, looking as though he were crossing the deck of a floundering schooner, removed the cartons from the cars, brought them to me, stationed halfway down the brick path, I passed them to Jessie farther on, and she took them inside.

The rain descended in sheets, in cataracts, in tidal waves. The river just beyond the station house rose steadily between its banks. The brick path on which we stood became a stream. The wheels of our cars stood in an inch of water. Finally, Greenfield came toward me at a slant, rain streaming off his hat and slicker. "This is the last of it," he said, and carried it by me to disappear into the station house. I stumbled in his wake, and Jessie joined me, but stayed in the doorway.

"We'd better get out of here," she said, "while we can. I'll lock up."

"Come in and shut the door, Mrs. Lucas," Greenfield said. "It would be sheer idiocy to drive anywhere in this typhoon."

"It's only rain." She tossed the key onto a table. "*I'm* going, if you aren't." She turned and shut the door behind her and after a moment I heard her starting up the station wagon.

"She'll never get out of that mud." Greenfield took off his slicker and draped it over the end of a table.

Jessie's motor ground and whined and I could imagine the wheels spinning uselessly. After a few minutes the noise stopped, and then the door opened and she came back in.

"I seem to be bogged down," she said with nervous airiness, "but you're on the paving. Why don't we all go and I'll ride with you. It's bound to get worse, you know. You don't want to be stuck here—"

So directly above us that it had the impact of an exploding bomb, there was an apocalyptic crash of thunder, and the torrent that followed made the previous downpour seem like mere mist. Water cascaded down the windows and dinned on the roof. A rivulet of water ran from the crack under the door and wriggled slowly across the floor. We were sitting in the same hollow as the stores on the opposite bank that the rising river had more than once flooded. An image of Fred Bryce exhorting the Public Works men crossed my mind.

"It's not beyond the realm of possibility," Greenfield said, "that we're in the throes of a flash flood. The lot out there is afloat, the roads are bound to be running streams. I suggest we bow to the inevitable."

Jessie was silent but her face was eloquent. "We are marooned. Isolated. Cut off from the world. Two hounds and a fox." Abruptly she discarded her poncho, fished in a pocket, and came up with a cigarette. I looked around the room.

It was a cheerless chamber, bleakly lit by two dim fixtures hanging from opposite sides of the ceiling, rain drumming on the roof, sluicing down the dusty windowpanes, dripping onto the floor from our slickers. The space, except for the narrow aisles between them, was taken up by long trestle tables, with a small square table and a chair near the doorway, presumably for collecting money, and several folding chairs stacked against a wall. The cartons of books had been dropped wherever it was handiest, some on tables, some on the floor. We transferred those on the floor to the tables. Greenfield unfolded one of the stacked chairs and sat down. Jessie stood by a window, smoking. There was a feeling in the room of suspended living, of an imminent and uncertain resolution.

Suddenly, Jessie declaimed, *"If by your art, my dearest father, you have / Put the wild waters in this roar, allay them. / The sky, it seems, would pour down stinking pitch . . ."*

Greenfield had taken a book from one of the cartons and pretended to be glancing through it.

"We should have brought a bottle of wine," Jessie went on, "and a piano. We could have passed the time singing old favorites. 'Down by the Old Mill Stream,' and so on." She was chattering to keep the demons at bay.

Another staggering clap of thunder. I thought of George, a fearless dog except for thunder, cowering in a corner of the house, the world crashing around his ears.

With his eyes still on his book, Greenfield said, "Mrs. Lucas? What do you know about Fred Bryce?"

She looked up sharply, then bent her head, stubbing out her cigarette in a piece of wet cardboard on the windowsill. "Oh, he's a sweetie. I think he's a leftover from the Salem witch trials. Why do you ask?"

"He has come to my attention. I gather you consider him a social threat."

"Don't you?"

"Because of Citizens for Maternal Guidance?" Greenfield asked.

She hesitated again. "If you know about that, how can you consider him anything *but* a threat?"

"The C.M.G. is very small potatoes, Mrs. Lucas."

"Threats always begin with small potatoes. McCarthy didn't start out with a brass band. You do know, of course, that there are two council seats up for grabs on the Town Board, and the Republicans haven't had any luck there for years. They'll nominate anyone who can stand on his feet and provide his own campaign money. Fred Bryce has years of community service behind him. Board of the PTA. The Recreation Committee. President of Little League. A handshaker, a backslapper, an upstanding family man. He's programmed for power, God help us. As soon as he has the money to hire a Madison Avenue PR man to design some hotshot campaign literature, he'll run for the Town Board. And then for State Assembly, and state senator. Oh, yes, he's the goods, Mr. Bryce. If nobody stops him, he'll take his C.M.G. mentality straight to Washington."

"And how far do you think he'd get with it? Given the

armies of determined women marching to work every day?''

"Oh! Really! I weep for your innocence. Even as we speak, there is a bill before Congress designed to protect the sacred institution of the old-fashioned family. How? Simple. We return to the concept that men are made to wander abroad, occasionally bringing back a little dinosaur meat, and women to stay shut up in the cave. They are *considering* it, Mr. Greenfield!''

"It's the function of Congress to have bills introduced. Voting for them is something else.''

"Which is why, you see, we have to be careful about who does the voting.''

"Careful.'' Greenfield studied her through half-shut eyes. "I've met a timid opera diva, a poverty-stricken sheik, and, now, a *careful* militant feminist.''

"Me?" Jessie swept her damp hair back from her forehead. "I'm no tub-thumper. I'm no agitator. I'm just . . .'' She searched the room for inspiration, threw up her hands. "I'm a wounded gazelle''—a self-mocking smile lifted a corner of her mouth—"staggering around the forest trying to keep out the rifle bearers.''

"And Mrs. Gardner and Mrs. Moss? Also members of the antelope family?''

She stood very still, very alert. I could almost hear her heart thumping. Finally, in a low voice, she said, "This has all the earmarks of an interrogation.''

Greenfield shrugged. "I'm a private citizen. My privacy was violated. I set out to find the person responsible, and like an explorer tracking a river to its source, I stumbled on a tributary. Whatever you tell me will only elucidate what I already know.''

They confronted each other, Greenfield relaxed to the point of somnolence, Jessie inwardly spinning through alternating cycles of dismay, speculation, and indecision. She rummaged in her pocket for a cigarette, but forgot to light it and began to pace around the room, through the little puddles of water that had gathered here and there from the rain seeping under the door. "Oh, well,'' she said, rounding a table by a rain-drenched window. "Three cranky, dissatisfied ladies, is that the picture? Three spoiled females who don't know when they're well off? What are they bitching about now, is that it? All right, then. Naomi, Roberta, myself—all three of us belong to an endangered species. We came into the world in the thirties, absorbed the sacrament of wife-and-motherhood with our Pablum, received it like the Eucharist at regular intervals. Believed it without question. Well, it's hardly news these days but unless it happened to you, you can't really understand the weight of it. To marry and keep a man happy took precedence over everything. Not to be married was to be a pariah.

"So Naomi marries this walking Gospel, whose dicta are sacred, and finds, over the years, that running a house is not what she was made to do. She's bright, educated, gregarious, she has mental muscles crying out to be used, she needs to have her opinions valued, which God knows living with the Gospel they aren't. And with much trauma and struggle—because she must simultaneously continue to honor the commitment she's made to home and family, and no one ever told the Gospel he ought to help out—at great cost, she makes a small place for herself in the world. And if you think that was easy, at her age, bear in mind that the business world thinks of average women over forty only as subjects for euthanasia. Nevertheless, Naomi did it. Then along comes Bryce, who says if you're a man who does not thrive on accountancy, you have every right to become a photographer instead, but if you're a woman who doesn't thrive on homemaking, so be it, don't thrive.

"As for Roberta Moss, she's been left behind. Never bothered to develop any resources, because she copped first prize before she was barely out of mental swaddling clothes; she married a doctor. He lives, the children live, and Roberta watches. She only exists to applaud the others. She's an audience in a world where all her peers are performing. She substitutes by latching onto various 'solutions'; yoga, vegetarianism, so on. She would crawl on hands and knees to be allowed to be part of the world outside her little house. And along comes Fred Bryce—et cetera."

She continued to wander about the room, watching the

water lapping over her running shoes.

Greenfield seemed half-asleep, a sign that he was listening to every syllable. "And what's bothering *you*, Mrs. Lucas—purely sympathetic pains?"

Jessie laughed, one short, staccato sound not entirely mirthless. "Oh, the secret life of Jessie Lucas, now known to one and all. When I was twenty-two I won a Tony as best supporting actress. I was a good little actress, might have made a good *big* actress. Not a contribution on a par with Madame Curie's, but still . . .

"However, I had swallowed all those little husband-and-children wafers; they enter the bloodstream, you know, stay a lifetime. We're talking about that kind of world, remember, and Jessie was just as gung ho for marriage as the other girls. Along came Lucas. And I worried about spending all those nights at the theater. I read all those articles about the incompatibility of career and marriage. For the woman, that is. And voilà! The power of the unconscious: I became pregnant. Marvelous excuse to quit the theater. I was a wife and mother, by God, what more could you ask?

"Plunged into it arse over elbows as they say. First a daughter, then a son. No lady on the block was more entranced. Showered man and kids with care and kisses. House full of laughter—and tears, of course. 'They that sow in tears shall reap in joy.' Well, not quite, my dear!

"This Lucas, this foundation of my life, this keeper of my future, had other plans. Doing well, going up the ladder at a great rate, spending less time at home. When the kids reached high-school age I began to long for something to fill the void. Not *some*thing, but the work I'd been good at. I finally made a stab at retrieving my profession. Ha!

"I was hardly a fresh-faced ingenue by then. A little worn around the edges, naturally. And where had I been all these years? 'What have you done lately, darling? So sorry. Why don't you try commercials?'

"And finally, what do you know, Mr. Lucas takes himself off. With an ingenue, of course. One of a series, I might add. Now my darling daughter lives in Sacramento and my darling son in a Gotham tenement, and the sacred wife and mother has the happy home all to herself. And no job—or none that means anything.''

She hoisted herself up on a table and sat, legs dangling. "Lest you misunderstand, I've never for a moment regretted being a wife and mother.'' She gave her short bark of a laugh. "If only I'd died before my time it would have been perfect. It's just this *forced retirement*. With twenty-odd years still to go.'' She looked down at her sodden running shoes. "Cheap workmanship. One flood and they're useless.''

Greenfield opened his eyes. "Which one of you went to Dina Franklin's house that Tuesday night?''

"Oh, which one do you think? The performer, of course. It was Naomi's idea but I was the logical choice. I could run, if I had to. I got a call from Naomi. Roberta had told her the story of her scuffle with Bryce's daughter, how she'd come out of it with a souvenir—some ghastly pin with the letters of Bryce's organization on it; the pin fell off after the girl ran into Roberta and it got scooped up in the groceries. Naomi saw it as a chance to persuade Dina against voting for the school sale, which would put a lot of money in Bryce's pocket.

"Dina knew what he was, but she thought voting for the sale would make her popular and she never concerned herself with anything but her own upward mobility. She never counted the consequences to anyone else.

"Well, there were all these burglaries. We knew she was going to be in the city that night, knew her burglar alarm wasn't connected to headquarters, so the police wouldn't get to see the evidence before Dina did. I went to the house, in my jogging suit, into the backyard, broke the glass of the sliding doors to her dining room with a rock, the alarm went off—what a noise! Wagner would die of envy—reached in, unlocked the doors, threw the pin into the room, and ran like hell.

"Dina, we figured, would be furious at having her house broken into—she was vengeful, too, never let anyone get the better of her. And she'd know where the pin came from.''

Jessie stopped, suddenly, and her shoulders sagged. She saw the unlit cigarette in her hand, put it between her lips, and tore a match from the folder.

Greenfield got up from his chair and looked out at the storm. "The price," he said, "was too high. Muzzling a small-time demagogue was not worth the lives of two women."

Jessie took the cigarette from her mouth and stared at him. The match flame burned her finger, her hand twitched, she dropped the match into a puddle, but her eyes never left his face. Finally she cleared her throat and said, "Bryce? Killed Dina?"

"It's not official, but it will be."

She continued to stare at him, crushing the unlit cigarette in her hand, kneading it, sprinkling tobacco on the table.

"And Mathilda?"

"She was an inadvertent witness."

She slid off the table, went to a window, and stood there with her back to us. "We thought Dina would go to the police. And the Bryce girl would have an alibi, but the incident would be enough to turn Dina against him. We thought . . . ah, God!" She put her forehead against the glass and said nothing for a while, then, huskily, " 'Between two hawks, which flies the higher pitch;/ . . . Between two blades, which bears the better temper;/ . . . I have, perhaps, some shallow spirit of judgment;/ But in these nice sharp quillets of the law,/ Good faith, I am no wiser than a daw.' "

Jessie, going to ground again in quotations.

Greenfield raised his eyebrows and took a tour of the room.

"Yours is the only judgment you'll get," he said. "I don't see any point in telling the police, or anyone else, about this. You should know, however, that you three women swallowed more than one insidious 'wafer.' You grew up expecting life to be accommodating."

As he passed the table on which I was lying prone, I said, not too loudly, "There are times, Charlie, when I think you have just a bit of the male chauvinist in you."

He looked down at me, surprised. "No honest man would claim he hasn't."

24

MOZART, BORODIN, CHAUSSON, Galway playing Debussy's *La Plus Que Lente*. From the most fragile flute note to the most resounding full-orchestra finale, the sound issuing from Greenfield's brand-new, digitalized, encoded, frequency-synthesized, memory-buttoned, selectable-bandwidthed, distortion-free, noninterference-receptioned stereo, freshly enthroned in the armoire in his living room, was quite simply gorgeous.

I was thrilled. Elliot was impressed. Gordon Oliver was transported. Shirley Oliver was hungry.

"I've never heard anything better," Gordon said.

Greenfield was glum. "You didn't hear the one they never found."

About the Author

Lucille Kallen has written for television (including the acclaimed series *Your Show of Shows*) and for the theater, and she is the author of the first feminist comic novel, *Outside There, Somewhere*. She began her mystery-writing career with INTRODUCING C.B. GREENFIELD, which was an American Book Award nominee, and followed with C.B. GREENFIELD: THE TANGLEWOOD MURDER.

C.B. GREENFIELD: NO LADY IN THE HOUSE is the third book in the series, and Lucille Kallen is currently plotting the further adventures of C.B. Greenfield and Maggie Rome.